HELIOPHOBIA

a novel

CHRISTOPHER X. RYAN

MONTAG

A Montag Press Book
www.montagpress.com
Montag Press
777 Morton Street, Unit B
San Francisco CA 94129 USA

Montag Press, the burning book with the hatchet cover, the skewed word mark and the portrayal of the long-suffering fireman mascot are trademarks of Montag Press.

Printed & Digitally Originated in the United States of America
10 9 8 7 6 5 4 3 2 1

For Raisa, who lets my darkness shine through.

"The sentences in Christopher X. Ryan's first novel are things of mystery and beauty. Boiled in Chandler, glazed in Thompson, dunked in Gibson, they go down smooth and sweet but also sharp and hard. I thought of books like *Super Cell Anemia* by Duncan Barlow or movies like *Only Lovers Left Alive* by Jim Jarmusch as I moved through the world they bring into such marvelous, middle-finger-raised focus. I'm excited for the work of this fine, fine writer to be entering the world. Heliophobia is a fabulous debut and its author someone to watch."

—Laird Hunt

"An impressive debut about a pricing gun repairman with a chronic fear of the sun, *Heliophobia* is an odd and hilarious punk album of a novel that manages to be both dark and surreal but also remarkably danceable. A smart, weird joy."

—Matthew Kirkpatrick

I Tell You Where We Meet and Why and then a Jet Lands Beside Me

My heliophobia support group meets in an old schoolhouse whose main doors are welded shut and painted blue. You enter around back, up a Z-shaped wheelchair ramp. I know every hall and stairwell in the place. I even saw the belfry once after shimmying up a secret ladder in the supply closet. There was nothing up there, not even a bell. Just ancient bird shit and some failed eggs. Some sunlight broke through the slats like streaky clown tears but it didn't even scare me. Not then. Because it's not that simple.

"Three minutes," Martin says and clicks his pen once for each minute.

Liza's hand goes up. "Sorry, my pen is dry."

Martin digs for a replacement, finds one. But before pushing himself off his folding chair he takes a gulp of Half Blast! diet soda then sucks in a bunch of air. He rises. The floorboards under the carpet groan. The chalkboard rattles. Some plaster suicides off the wall. The room is dying, just like the sun. Like all of us.

He hands it off, makes a U-turn, heads back.

"Thanks, sweetie."

Liza gets back to scribbling on her map of our solar system. We're supposed to name the celestial bodies after people in our lives. Dad the sun. Jasper the asteroid. That type of thing. It's stupid and easy but tonight a dark mood is gelling in my gut. Plus a window is open and some people are walking by. A voice says, *All you do is sit around and eat asparagus all day.* The other says, *One day you'll wake up to find a brick through your windshield.*

They laugh, turn the corner, fade into the dark.

"I'm sorry," Liza says. "I don't like blue ink."

Martin belches softly and gets ready to repeat the sequence. It takes half a minute for him to get across the room. New pen. U-turn. Half a minute back. His butt slams down, the folding chair's legs threatening to buckle. I'm pretty squishy myself but Martin's huge. We all love him in a weird way and worry he's going to croak right in front of us.

Right after Martin gets settled there's a rap on the hallway door. He mops the sweat-pond from his forehead and gets ready. Leans forward, pushes off again.

It's Annabelle returning from the bathroom. Today she's wearing a lime-green fleece top. Her gangly skeleton floats in some saggy-butt jeans and her feet are trapped in tiny white sneakers. It's the same outfit pretty much every time except that the fleeces change color. She has dozens of them on hangers packed into a closet the size of a healthy poodle. She takes her seat across from me and flashes her smile. It's fake, plastic almost.

Like something you buy on sale after Halloween. Also she is sort of my girlfriend.

Martin jangles his keys and makes a big deal of unlocking the hallway door so we can come and go to pee and poop as we please. But as soon as he returns his butt to the chair there's another knock. This time it's on the ramp door. His face turns white. He's panting like a pregnant cougar, his sweat pipes flowing at max capacity. That's what happens when you weigh over 500 pounds.

Carl Jake saves him though. "Stand down. I'll get it."

All the regular heliophobes are already here. Even Joe Purple. That means this has got to be someone new. Which is a big deal. It happens maybe once a year. Our pens stop. We all levitate slightly in our seats. Our eyes boil in their sockets.

The door swings open. Nothing happens. Maybe it was a branch. The wind. It could be another prank by Stone Cold, the placophobia support group for people who are afraid of tombstones. Maybe it's a bird needing to get out of the cold or a mannequin salesman hoping for an easy sale.

Finally a voice reaches out to tickle us. It's sweet and syrupy but bold. Says, "Oh, hey. I'm Jet." From the dark steps a pixie punk with spiky blond hair and black rectangular eyeglasses. Her skin is creamy but pink like the milk at the bottom of a bowl of Sugar Slams. Her T-shirt has a big red splotch and says *Tampons are for pussies*. In the schoolhouse she stands out like a flaming meteor in a blizzard.

Martin's too out of breath to talk so he motions Jet toward the two open seats in our circle. One is next to Joe Purple. Her eyes land on the shiny gold mask-helmet he's wearing and she winces slightly. Then there is the other chair. Right next to me. She chooses that one.

Now I'm sweating too.

She settles her little fanny onto the folding chair. She puts down her bag and clips her keys to her belt. Then she picks up her bag and digs for gum and something for wiping her glasses. She tosses the bag back onto the floor. Then she changes her mind and unclips her keys and puts them in her bag. She snaps it shut. She doesn't know it but everyone in the room is watching her.

She twists toward me. "Hey, I'm Jet."

I nod.

"Did I already say that? Ha ha, I'm so stupid. What's your name?"

More beads of sweat detonate on my brow. I run my tongue around the inside of my mouth to start working the sounds free from their sticky prison then take a deep breath and push them out like a turd. "*Muh muh muh* Murray."

She gives me a funny look. "Sorry, I didn't catch that."

My hands turn cold and slimy. I loosen my tongue again. Have to make a bigger turd this time. I'm just about to squeeze it off when Channing reaches over and hands Jet a clipboard. Clipped to it is a map of the solar system stamped with the official Heli-Non seal. These are known as Suitable Materials.

"What do I do here?" she asks.

Channing pushes his glasses up his nose and leans in closer. Says, "I'll show you this shit." He's a nerdy dispatcher for a company called Waste-B-Gone. Most of the time I hate him. Such as currently. He gives Jet a big dumb smile and explains what she's supposed to do.

"Cool?" he says.

She shrugs. Like I'm always doing. But she's prettier when she does it. Then she says she doesn't have a pen or anything.

Everyone digs around in their pockets like the world will end if they don't complete this mission. Jet accepts mine though. It's a nice Hollowcore Black Razor. She smiles so big I can almost see the back of her throat. A place I'd like to visit.

"We'll give our new friend a minute to catch up," Carl Jake says from across the circle. As if he's in charge. A smirk cuts open his round face, his eyes brassy like the balls at the top of flagpoles.

Now and then while Jet works she makes whimpering sounds like a baby butterfly or something. When she's done she asks to see my solar system but I haven't written anything. Just filled in all the circles. Because nearly everyone in my life is a black hole. She laughs and says she likes it. She's real exotic. Like a foreign alien.

Martin clicks his pen. "Okay, folks." All the pencils and pens stop scratching. "So what did we learn?"

No one answers. We doodle. We shuffle our feet. We check out the seam in the carpet where a big gray bug is hanging out. Or at the blank spot on the wall where the clock should be. Or at the drawing of a sexy robot I drew on the chalkboard months ago. Everywhere but at Martin.

Finally Marlene raises her hand. She's wearing a flannel top and tropical shorts. She's probably the nicest lady I've ever met. She's Irish or Iranian or something. From a place where people have strong accents and red hair and good luck and ride around on camels. She also has the biggest boobs I've ever seen. On my birthday one year she hugged me and I nearly drowned in them. I liked it. "My moon," she says, "is my dog Choo. Is that wrong?"

"It's entirely up to you," Martin tells her. "The purpose of the exercise is to illustrate which things we can change and which things we can't. Our distance to the sun is fixed but we can always reconsider our relationships with those who surround us."

Annabelle's hand with its little chalk stick fingers rises up and hangs there like a sleepy bat until Martin notices.

"Annabelle, yes."

She sits up straight and says, "I made Murray my Mercury because he's warm and we're close. I put my stepfather on Pluto because he's mean and should be banished to the edge of the universe."

"Actually," Carl Jake says, "that would be the edge of our solar system."

"Whatever," she says.

"Just saying. The Suitable Materials pertain only to our galaxy."

"You always have something to add, don't you?"

He smirks and tries to set an ankle on his knee but the knee says no and the foot slides off. "Well, you know."

FX says, "I'll put you on Saturn, Carl Jake, since you're round and gassy."

We laugh. Jet too, cackling like a coyote. It's super funny and cute and everyone already loves her. Even I want to take her home and feed her warm milk from a bottle.

"Great. Who's next? How about you, Joe Purple?"

Silence falls over the room so thickly you could punch it. Joe doesn't move. We wonder: Is he mad? Is he going to kill us? Is he going to speak this time? We don't know because he wears a mask-helmet every session. For years it's been like this. He walked in one Thursday night with a thing made of duct tape and cardboard covering his face and skull and neck. Also wears gloves so we don't know his race. But over time the masks have evolved. They're always his creation, not some crap from a store. Things with space goggles and hinged jaws and bolts.

Masks so colorful and weird you think you're staring into the sphincter of your own soul. One time it was just three layers of gauze and some aviator eyeglasses. Another time it was a blank white circle with a drawing of a bearded guy wearing a trucker's cap. He's part god, part ghoul. We also don't even know his real name. Laramie Bob the insane hippie saw a business card fall out of his pocket one night. It was for a lawyer named Joseph Q. Purpalia who lives in Upper Southeast Chicowam. Thus we started calling him Joe Purple in secret since he never told us his real name—never told us anything. Then we just started calling him Joe Purple in general. He never got mad or threw chairs like this girl Jane Blue who had a breakdown and didn't come back. Joe has never spoken either, barely even coughs. He only attends sessions on the last Thursday of each month. But he does the assignments and breaks into groups with us and even came to Shine Together, Shine Forever one year. Finally he lifts his paper and shows it to all of us. The inner planets are marked M, JJ, Ma, L, and Walter. The extra planets are X'ed out.

"Those are important people in your life?" Martin asks while exhaling through a waterfall of sweat.

Joe leans back and crosses his arms. But it seems like his mask twitches. We take that for a *Duh, yeah*.

"Excellent. Who else?"

It's hard to follow. No one budges.

"Murray?"

I shake my head.

"Not today? Maybe you could just show us your—?"

I stare at my shoes. Their curled-up Velcro straps like fingers counting off my remaining days.

"Okay then. Maybe next time?"

I'm about to shrug when Jet says, "I'll go."

Everyone turns toward her and drinks her in like fresh grape soda.

Martin gestures. "Go ahead."

She sits up tall as she can. Which isn't very high since she's teensy and huggable. "So I'm Earth," she says, "but I made myself extra big." She shows us her paper. She's redrawn the planet to take up all the white space. People giggle. Everyone wants to marry her. "My two best friends are these twin moons. Not that they revolve around me but they do gravitate toward me." She looks around at all the bright and fearful faces. "That's it."

"Very good work, Jet. Thank you for sharing. And welcome to Heli-Non."

She smiles at me again. My belly turns warm. Across the room Annabelle harumphs and turns pink.

I Clean up then Go Home Which Is Where the Bugle Is and He Howls and I Think About the Time I Rescued a Huge Drowning Guy

Finally someone's watch beeps. "Just one more thing," Martin says. "The Retrieval Seminar is coming up. Do any of you want to be on the planning committee?"

Channing and Marlene fold their papers and head for the door while smacking their cigarette packs like little tam-tams.

"Now wait just a sec everyone," Martin says.

No one waits a sec.

Martin sighs and says, "At least take the new Suitable Materials with you."

No one takes the Suitable Materials except me. I will use them for drawing paper.

Larson the drunk former priest and Laramie Bob push each other out the door. Annabelle gives me an extralong hug and kisses my earlobe six times then says I'm hers and she's mine foreverandever just as a reminder then rushes off to work. Jung waves and smiles and nods his way out the door. Joe Purple simply blends into the air. Then FX and Liza and all the others leave including Jet who is chatty and smiley and asking twelve thousand questions and is already a celebrity. Everyone except me. I'm on cleanup duty.

I get my supplies from the hallway closet. Then I wipe the swears off the chalkboard and dump the coffee sludge out the window. I finish off the bug juice and graham crackers and pick up the paper cups. I fold and stack the chairs. I'm almost done but I have to wait for Martin to finish off his Half Blast!. He tells me he's on a diet. This one is really going to stick. He'll show us. It seems like he's talking to someone in an imaginary bedroom so I just nod. He finally tightens his suspenders and hands me the cup.

"See you next time, Murray."

"Okay, *muh muh* Martin."

I run the stupid little push-sweeper across the rug. I kick it a few times. I call its mother a whore. In conclusion I toss it in the closet. When I step outside Martin's still waddling down the ramp. He zigs, zags, then gives me a wave and crams himself into his cool little Datsun.

Alone. I take a moment to listen to the night. It's so quiet you can almost hear your skin stretching. I wonder if Joe Purple is out there. We don't know if he drives or what. After Heli-Non sessions he marches straight into the cemetery across from the schoolhouse like he was born there. Channing says he followed Joe once but got lost in all the graves and a ghost fondled him so he screamed and ran back.

"That was fun," a voice in the dark says.

My heart does a backflip and I almost throw myself over the railing. It's not Joe Purple though. Sadly it's not Jet either. It's Carl Jake. He steps out of the shadows and comes close enough for me to smell the sharp stink of his cologne. Like taco sauce mixed with mint.

"Didn't mean to scare you, buddy," he says and chuckles long and hard. He leans with his back against the railing and hooks his thumbs into his belt loops, a camouflage belt holding up his baggy jeans. His button-down flannel strains against his gut. "Good session, huh?"

I shrug.

"Yeah… sometimes it seems impossible to find a glimmer of joy in this brilliantly complex existence of ours, doesn't it."

He looks up. So I do too. Above us: stars burning, dead.

"Still," he says with a sigh, "sometimes I think that big ball of gas in the sky might be the smallest problem we've got, you know?"

I shrug, then nod, then both. I don't know. Carl Jake's smart but it's not helpful smart. It's the type of smartness he rubs into your teeth until you can't do anything but swallow it. He merely bugs the others but he gives me the willies from my toes to my nose. He's not like us other heliophobes. He's always charting the sun's path and giving presentations and telling us about possible loopholes he's read in astronomy texts. Such as new reports of distant super-earths thirteen times the size of ours. *Thriving*, he once said, *if only we could reach them.* There are rumors too. That he does things to animals and kids. That he has a lab in his basement. That he's a Republican. That he might be a member of Group 999 which is for people with hexakosioihexekontahexaphobia, fear of the number 666.

"I'm pretty sure there's a geomagnetic storm going on tonight. You feel it?"

Shake.

"I do. Deep down in the groin."

I wince but he doesn't notice. I lean downramp like I'm already halfway home but he continues yammering.

"You like baseball?" he says, his lips pulling back again. It's not really a smile but more like the wind is blowing his face apart. To keep from kicking him I focus on the ring of hair on his shiny skull. "Big game this weekend."

I shrug. I don't like balls. They're just orbs hurtling through space. I prefer lawn darts.

"Nah, you don't seem like the sports type. But you should come over sometime. We can chat."

I'm still looking at him. Through him. Like a superpower. "About *wuh wuh* what?"

"Just—everything! The group, our friends, our affliction, and deeper stuff. The shit that makes us men of madness. Better yet I can show you my 'museum.'"

"*Myew myew—wuh wuh* what's in it?"

"It contains the story of our existence. Life, death, love. The whole picture. From the big bang to our current crisis." He raps out a little drum beat on the railing. "Think about it. Stop by and we'll chat." He smiles and makes a sucking sound with his teeth. "Anyway, *cool*, as the kids say. *Very* cool."

He gives me a salute, then zigs down the ramp and zags toward his red Ford Escort. I hope to have something sporty like that one day. He climbs in, honks twice. *Meep meep.* His tail-lights fade into the dark.

I sigh. Then I too zig, zag. My car is at the far end of the parking area. It's the little white pickup truck that looks like it was used as a soccer ball by a herd of cross-eyed rhinos. It's got two baby spares up front and the right mirror is missing. The left headlight is broken. I want to push it off a cliff but it's all I have.

I usually never lock the truck's doors but tonight I did because inside the cab is a padded case containing guns. They're prototypes, a model so new they don't even have a name. Guns so technologically advanced that robots put them together. Guns so rare you can count on a few fingers how many exist. I climb into the cab and take one out and press the nozzle against my forearm. I give the trigger a gentle squeeze. It's so smooth and whispery I don't even feel it hit my skin.

$9.97.

Mazzie Corp. doesn't just make the best pricing guns in the world—actually that is all they make. But they're thinking about adding a motorized shopping cart and a cash register the size of a toaster. The company headquarters is located near North Gaslin and they loaned me the prototypes so I could test them out. If they like my feedback they'll consider hiring me part-time. "Pricing Gun Consultant." Maybe it's not much of a dream but sometimes dreams are real normal. Like you're walking down a blue sidewalk or washing tarantulas in the sink. Plus there aren't a lot of options for good jobs in North Gaslin. And my uncle Thin Man always says to follow your stupid weird-ass passions you fucking idiot.

I put the guns back in the case and turn the key and feather the pedals and let the engine belch a few times. The spare tires slip and wiggle as I get up to speed. I put them on months ago when I got one flat and then another and just left them there. My brother Tucker said he'd get me some new tires but he forgot and I don't want to ask him since I owe him rent and I don't mow his lawn anymore.

Driving, driving. Almost home.

The Heli-Non bible *Rays of Hope* says every heliophobe needs a Safe Zone. My house isn't safe but it's a zone. It has green plastic siding and a thin metal roof that bows upward in big storms. It contains a bathroom and a couch and other stuff you need for living but not much more. Tucker owns the place. He charges me half rent so he can store chemicals in the basement. I don't know what they're for but when the weather is hot the whole house smells like bacon dipped in paint.

The city's name is North Gaslin. The house is in East North Gaslin. The neighborhood is on the western side of East North Gaslin. It is an unpleasant area filled with empty warehouses and abandoned business parks with some houses jammed into the in-between streets like pickle slices in a box of cookies. It's the type of place where if you get sick of your furniture you just push it into the street and wait for someone to set it on fire. Mostly poor and afraid people live here. People like me, so hard-up we can only afford to put our initials on our mailboxes. *M.S.* Murray Sandman. Miserable Settler. Moneyless Sucker. Even grass hates being here. My front yard contains stray garbage and lawn chairs and wagons and that got stuck in the mud and were abandoned. They're part of the landscape now. Like a shipwreck or rock piles on a trail so you don't lose your way.

I don't lock my front door since you have to rock it back and forth to get it open. No burglar could figure it out. It's not like I have any junk worth stealing anyway. A TV with one knob missing. An old stereo. A peanut butter jar half-full of pennies.

The only thing worth stealing is my dog Bugle. Though I doubt anyone else would want him. I think he's a beagle but he's kind of short and funny looking. Whenever I come home he starts howling so wildly his front paws come off the ground. Which is why I call him Bugle. It's his way of letting me know how pissed he is that I was away or telling me that he's happy I am home. I can't tell. He probably can't either.

He sleeps under the covers on my bed at night. Usually at the bottom. I don't know how he breathes but he never complains. We also watch TV and go places together. When the sun's out I let him out in the yard to do his business and then walk him at night so he can poop on other people's driveways. I had a fish for a while too with the name of Levi. One day the shade fell and the sun boiled him alive in his tank. I buried him in the yard but cats dug him up and dragged off his bones. That's natural, I guess. But it reminded me what the sun does.

I know Bugle will die too someday and that we'll have a funeral in the backyard and that it won't be the sun's fault. I can't say that I'll want to live after that. I know it sounds like an Afternoon Kiddie Special or something but he's part of me. Like an extra heart or something.

Let me give you an example. One time Tucker's friend came over to get some chemicals out of the basement and he left the gate and back door open and Bugle walked away. When I came home the house was silent and I thought I was going to pass out. My vision went black around the edges. I couldn't even see my hands. Or the sun. Or the stop signs. I drove around the neighborhood like my hair was on fire while beeping the horn and asking if anyone had seen a bugle which confused them but I couldn't get the words out right. I blew through an intersection and a cop pulled me over. He thought I was on drugs or crazy and though I might have been he stayed calm and asked what was wrong. When I finally got out *D* followed by *O* and *G* he understood. His police dog had just died and he was upset so he said he'd help. He was only a regular cop but he was a pretty good detective if he needed to be. He said we needed to go back to the scene of the crime. There wasn't much evidence there except some chewy bones and doodies so he started knocking on neighbors' doors. One said she saw Bugle playing with a pony. That didn't make sense until I realized there was a Rottweiler the size of a small horse down the street. We went there and knocked on the door and both the horse-dog and Bugle started barking. I almost peed myself. The cop made some calls and the owner came home. She was pretty and dressed like a cowgirl and I fell in love right there of course. She cried a bit while I squatted on the floor and Bugle howled in my face and the Rottweiler licked my ear. If I were a different me I would have asked the woman on a date as thanks but I was still me. I didn't have the guts. I'm pretty sure she and the cop hooked up and got married and moved to Little Italy or something.

That was a few years ago.

When I rock the door open Bugle comes up and screams at my kneecaps until I pat him on the head a few times.

"Easy, Buges."

He eventually calms down and goes back to the couch but I can tell he's worried I'll leave again in the near future. Which is true. I undo the straps on my shoes and fling off my longcoat and hat.

I sit thinking next to Bugle. Not thinking. Thinking some more. Imagining what I could be if I had a real gun and real guts instead of some plastic pricing guns and a jiggly belly. Then I'd have a real truck or a fancy Escort and could afford a third-floor apartment without a basement so no one could store chemicals anywhere close.

Too bad I'm me.

I haven't always been afraid of stuff. One time I was even a hero. Sort of.

I was walking home from summer school along the river when I heard a dog barking. He sounded really crazy. Like a wolf with rabies. I turned around and ran. But then I got curious and went back. I climbed up a hill and saw a guy drowning in the river below. It was scary so I sat and watched.

Eventually I made my way closer as the guy waved his arms and screamed at me like I'd done a crime just by showing up. Like I'd pushed him myself. He was round and goofy like the yellow statues at Golden China Bell Dragon Tail Pay-'n-Chow Buffet, the only Chinese food restaurant in North Gaslin. I thought about what I should do. I knew Chuck Rollins would help. But I was just a squishy little kid with broken pencils in his pockets and chocolate on his face. Then again the guy could drown and that might get me in trouble.

The dog got wilder as I got closer. His jaws snapped and foam flew off his lips. I picked up a stick and raised it over my head and said, "*Feh* fetch!" That only made him madder. He charged at me like he wanted me to go in the river too. Then I understood. He was trying to drown all the squishy people who came by.

"Well, hello," the drowning guy said as I stepped into the water. "That's my dog Duke. He's friendly but you should put the stick down."

I dropped the stick and the dog stole it.

The guy was in an eddy and seemed stuck. Then he leaned back and lifted a dripping leg stump out of the water. It looked like rotten fruit or a sausage's butt. "Don't be shy. I'm getting waterlogged. Help a brother out?"

The edge of the river was rocky. After a couple of steps I tripped and fell under. I came back up with a splash and a scream. The dog barked. The guy laughed and rolled onto his belly and reached up and offered me his hand. "I'm Paddy."

I stared at him and eventually said, "*Muh muh* Murray."

I tried to pull him out but it was like dragging a melting car up a hill. So he held onto me and we paddled together until I collapsed under the water and he had to pull me out instead. Now it was like we were saving each other. Just two friends drowning together on a sunny day.

When we were close to the shore the dog came at me again. "Duke, shut the fuck up!" the guy yelled.

We lay in the mud. We were both tired and it took us a long time to do anything. Eventually Paddy rolled over and sat up. His belly spilled forward like cookie dough. Duke the dog lay watching us. "I need my leg," Paddy said. He pointed toward the bushes. I crawled in that direction. There I found a cooler and a fake leg. The shoe was still attached. To the leg I mean, not the cooler. I'd never held a fake leg before. It smelled like cat pee and burnt cheese. I brought it to the drowning guy.

"The CIA sent me to Cambodia," he said, "and this was my recompense." He cleaned the dirt and sticks out of the cup where his stump would sit. "Because of my injuries all my missions are close to home now. They have me gathering intel and scouting the borders." He strapped on the leg. Then he requested beer from the cooler and said I could take one.

I shook my head.

"Good choice. This stuff will kill you. Also gives you wings. Wheee!" His hand went through the air and splashed down in the water. "You don't talk much, huh?"

Shake.

"You should work for the CIA. That's why I was always a liability. I like to talk about myself, as you can see. You like girls?"

Shrug.

"You like guys?"

Shake.

"I like the girls myself. I've had them in all corners of the world." His face went red and then he belched so loud I thought he might have broken the sound barrier. He picked up his hand again but it didn't fly this time. He looked at its fat palm. "Truth is, I wasn't a good spy. I wanted to be a soldier. A leg-breaker. Instead I'm stuck in the mud. You a leg-breaker, muh-muh-Murray?"

Shrug.

"Nah. You're as soft as me." He poked me in the gut. "I hope you've got strong bones kid or one day you'll be the goofball sitting in a river calling for help."

He belched. Then he offered me his beer again. I took a sip. It was gross.

"Your nation thanks you, muh-muh-Murray. Duke thanks you. I thank you. Thank you. Thank you. Thank you."

He kept going on like that. After a bit I got up and snuck away. Duke just watched. I waved at them from the top of the hill. It was a warm day. I was dry before I got home.

*   *   *

After a few minutes I've had enough thinking and I stretch out a foot and turn on the TV. It coughs out an infomercial for water balloon launchers. Then one comes on for kitchen knives shaped like medieval swords followed by one for industrial cleansers packaged like candy so it's more fun to do household chores.

Call now and get a gallon of Casket Magic FREE! A whole lifetime of legitimate trickle rasp crystal ruckus beef coward under-taking peach ribbon banter aorta enzyme...

Bugle runs in his sleep. I wonder where he's going. I close my eyes and chase after him.

The Sun Wakes Me and Is Evil and I Have to Go to Shop Now! Where Once Again I Rescue a Person but She Doesn't Know It's a Rescue so It Doesn't Really Count

No matter how much tape I use on the window shades the sun still gets in. At this particular moment an orange dagger of hateful light is stabbing my face. I use a pillow as a shield. I have to poop and pee and but I don't want to get up. So I turn on the radio beside the bed. A voice is going *Next up we'll be discussing recent breakthroughs in deciphering the genetic code. Who are you and where is this transformative kriegspiel slump twaddle manifestation apoplexy...*

I turn it off. Bugle kicks me and rolls over.

Eventually I sit up and blink about five hundred times. Between each one I see gooey bluish blood and in my head I hear the *Rays of Hope* audiobook saying *Nothing makes sense when you're a heliophobe. It's a non-sequitur existence. Two plus two equals aardvark.*

What it means is that we heliophobes do and think and say things that don't make sense. Like the day I lost my floppy hat and ended up handing my wallet to a man who was pointing at a map and asking for directions. He took twenty bucks and got in a cab, leaving the wallet at my feet. Lots of times I put on my shoes before my socks. My hat before my undies. Whole minutes are lost to figuring out how objects got in my hand. Spring or fall. Star or UFO. Coming or going. What is a refrigerator for.

My beeper beeps from somewhere. I get up and go find it under the couch. It's flashing the number for Shop Now!.

They need me.

I poop, pee. Now I need to get dressed. Except I don't have any clean clothes. This reminds me that I need to get my laundry from Honey Mom for my big meeting with Max Codpoodle from Mazzie Corp. tomorrow. For now I turn my favorite gray T-shirt inside-out and switch my socks from one foot to the other. Same old jeans. I rinse my underwear in the sink and put them back on. I need to take a shower but the tub is clogged. Tucker says he's not going to fix it and that I have to hire a plumber myself or stick a snake down the drain which I don't understand. Snakes are not good for pipes and lead to phobias. The rec center isn't open yet either so bathing will have to wait. I settle for tossing some mousse into my hair and sculpt it with my fingers until I almost get the new look I've seen in magazines. I aim the hairdryer at my armpits. In conclusion I take a nip of gel off the toothpaste tube.

After letting Bugle out to sprinkle pee on his favorite tree I'm finally ready to face the day. I feed him then put on my sungoggles and floppy hat. I slide my feet into my shoes and push the Velcro straps down. They flip halfway back up because they are evil pieces of shit. I put on my longcoat last. Sadly the wet underwear makes it feel like I've got boiled clams tucked inside my crotch.

I open the front door. The sun kicks me in the eyeballs and the manballs. Immediately I gasp for air and stagger back inside. Bugle stares at me. I pause, center myself. I take a deep breath like I'm about to jump into a pool of whipped cream then hop outside. I shut the door behind me and sprint to my truck and dive in. I'm already sweating and can barely see out my goggles.

I turn the key. Nothing happens. I've been running on fumes for two days and now even the fumes are gone. I say bad words and get out. I sprint back inside and flop down on the couch.

Bugle's ears perk. He watches me pant and sweat. I get out a spare copy of *Rays of Hope*.

COPING STRATEGY #8: Dream Safely

The word "mediocre" comes from the Latin "mediocris" or "halfway up the stony mountain." In Buddhism such a state of being is called "the middle way." Whatever one calls it, it's a safe place to be.

Not every dream has to be realized because not everyone is destined for greatness. Not every model is a supermodel. Not every athlete is a hero. Most snowflakes are imperfect. Most gorillas can't do sign language. Think about Icarus. He had huge dreams and the sun crushed them.

Focus on daily victories, such as a clean house or successful social interaction, and tangible little accomplishments that you can put on your shelf, such as ceramics, woodworking, or model trains. Try ham radio. Try macramé.

Be comfortable with smallness. You are good enough just as you are. It's okay to fly low. Dream safely.

I peek out the window and see a blue bird hopping down the middle of the street. I pat Bugle on the head and tell him he's beautiful in his own way. Which is what Honey Mom used to tell me when I was little. Then I go.

The bus stop is three blocks away. It takes me ten minutes to get there. Not just because I'm slow but because along the way I hop in and out of shadows and under trees and behind bushes. Once I'm there the other people stand far away from the guy who looks like he's hiding headless cats under his coat. Which is me. I'm basting in sweat like a hippo in a sauna and my sun-goggles are steaming up so badly I can't count to ten. The bus is late. I curse and mutter and kick the shelter wall. When the bus pulls up I realize I don't have enough money but I get on anyway and take a seat. The driver doesn't say anything. He's too afraid. I can't blame him.

I am struggling. The freelance pricing gun repair and consultation industry doesn't pay well. Mostly because it's not really an industry. As a result I owe lots of money to my brother Tucker. To the electric company. To the phone company for a phone I'm too afraid to use. To people like Laramie Bob from Heli-Non. Although he's a mellow old guy with a gray beard and long hair he passes me notes during Heli-Non sessions and it makes me stop breathing. I need the Mazzie thing to go straight so that I can have a solid job and pay rent and not die alone on a sidewalk littered with hubcaps and used toilet paper.

For a while I worked in a bike shop even though I don't even have a bicycle. It didn't matter since no one ever came in. It was just me and this mean old fart who smoked and talked to the handpumps while I rearranged the tools and shined the handlebars. One day I just didn't show up. He probably didn't even notice.

Before that I stocked groceries at night but then I got caught eating on the job. I don't mean having a snack but dining in a nook in the back of the warehouse where the cameras didn't reach. Sometimes I'd go through entire boxes of Snackadoodles and Zip!Zap! cakes. Then one time I fell asleep until the morning manager came in and he saw a bunch of frozen foods melting in the aisle. That was the end of my tenure there. Before that I did stupid stuff like run errands for Tucker or clean up his construction sites at night or mow his lawn in the dark. Then there's the cop gig but that's embarrassing and I don't want to get into it just yet.

I hop off the bus at Malaboose Plaza and speedwalk as best as I can toward Shop Now!. They're my best client. My only client really. It's also the only store left in the plaza. The craft store and dollar store and scissor sharpener are long-gone. Also my best friend Mikey works at Shop Now!.

In the parking lot I have to stop because a mentally retarded girl on a big tricycle is stuck on a pothole. She's pushing real hard but it's not enough to free herself. Her pigtails whip around and her forehead scrunches up with anger. I feel sad for her and decide to be brave.

I tighten my longcoat and wipe my sungoggles and wave to her as I approach. She doesn't say anything. I don't even stutter when

I ask if she needs help. Still she doesn't speak. Maybe her mom told her not to talk to people like me. Sweaty strangers covered with white sun-repellent cream and wearing a longcoat with a thick belt clumsily knotted around the waist. Maybe she's deaf or scared. She just keeps stomping on the pedals while tears make rivers down her plump face. So I give the bike a little shove with my foot and she bumps forward and rides off. It's real funny and makes my day.

The Shop Now! doors open for me with a hiss and cool air washes over my skin. They're piping in a nice song called "Basketball Helmet" by Knock Knock and the Funny Bones. The lyrics are fun, easy to remember, just going *Basketball helmet! I've got a basketball helmet!* over and over. I snap my fingers to the beat and wave to the two huge-haired cashiers up front. They glance at me then go back to eating their stolen candy bars and reading celebrity magazines.

"Murray!" Zeb the manager comes around the corner at top speed. "How are you today?"

I shrug.

He rubs his hands together like he's chilly or plotting something evil. He's a little dark-haired guy, religious. He and his friends leave their footprints in my mud on Sunday afternoons. Bugle barks while I hide until they leave.

"What do you think about the Cinna-Tarts P.O.P.?" he asks and gestures toward a big gaudy display.

Cinna-Tarts are awful. Like stale cookies wrapped in bark and dipped in cardboard.

"Corporate said that if we can get our numbers up we'll be able to integrate a whole new process of product turnover. See, Shop Now! has this whole new thing it's trying to implement where…"

My brain falls asleep and my eyes wander. *Cookies. Chips. Piece of uneaten gum on the floor. Could be peach flavor.*

"Anyway. Meet me in the back?"

I head to the employee room and find Mikey at his cubby. I've caught him at the end of his shift. He's pulling off his blue Shop Now! polo and putting on a tight-fitting T-shirt. He has perfect black hair but his skin is shaved clean and is as brown as Mexico. He and I are so opposite you could make jokes about it and it wouldn't be funny. Something as simple as changing his clothes makes his muscles bulge. He's like a comic book hero come to life. Except the heroes always carry swords on their backs and like girls with big boobs. Mikey likes penises and hair products.

"Heyyyyyyy! What's up?"

I wave and head to the counter. The entire breakroom smells like deodorant and coffee. I pour myself a cup. Of coffee I mean. Brown flakes swirl inside the mug like a polluted snow globe. A North Gaslin globe. It's hot and sour but it's free.

Mikey works his comb like a set of nunchucks, muscles shoving each other out of the way. "Zeb call you in?"

Nod.

"You okay? Things good?"

I shrug. I could tell him that I'm broke and that Tucker wants me to take a housemate named Juggins even though there's only one bedroom. But I don't. I've known Mikey for half of forever if not the whole thing but I don't like to lay my problems on him. Even though we first became friends through such problems. One day I saw him getting beat up and I tried to stop it but I just got beat up too. Then I found out the kids beating us up were his brothers. Turned out his life was as bad as mine. His dad was drunk all the time and in and out of jail and Mikey and his brothers lived with their grandmother who couldn't remember her own name.

I still remember the day in seventh grade when Mikey told me he was gay. I didn't really know what it meant. He said he liked boys but I was a boy and we were good friends. Then I understood it meant he wanted to kiss and hug them and do sex stuff with them. I found it weird at first but I didn't have any other friends so I kept hanging out with him and after a couple of days I didn't care because he was still Mikey. But when he told his family they made his life worse than a game show. They hoped the bruises and scrapes and cuts would turn him straight. When that didn't work they painted his face with makeup and put him in a dress and locked him out of the house to try and humiliate him straight. It was raining, cold. I brought him a towel and took him home but Big Man didn't like Mikey being gay either so I had to hide him in the rotting old barn until he got warm. Because of that he pledged to be my friend forever, through thick and thin, weird and fat. Since then we've done everything together except sleep and go on dates.

Things have been different lately though. A while back we stole some expired soda sitting by the back door of a GasStop and the cops showed up while we were sipping it a mile down the road. Mikey was already on parole for some weightlifter drug thing so he ran into the woods. I took the rap. Mostly because I couldn't run. I didn't go to prison but the cops took an unpleasant photo of me and put me in a pen for a few hours and gave me a warning. We haven't hung out much since then. I mean me and Mikey, not the cops.

The door swings open and Zeb comes in looking like he just ate a hamster. "It's these stupid things again, Murray. Can you do your magic?" He hands over a Montgomery Balance Pro pricing gun. It has a nice shape and poor internals but is overrated, made in China. Then he hands me a vintage Fortran. It's reliable but slow and heavy.

Easy.

I reach into my longcoat and take out my toolkit. From it I remove a spinny screwdriver and poking tool. Then my razor knife and a tiny tube of glue. I set them on the lunch table and sit and sip more coffee.

"Whatcha doing tomorrow?" Zeb asks me while I try to focus. "Got any time to swing by the Hall?"

In the background Mikey snickers and shakes his head.

I remove the Montgomery's body screws and crack open the gun. Next I clear the paper chad from the chamber. I scrape the glue gum off the ejector port. The problem is obvious: the gun's having an issue with A1045 labels which are ejecting at an angle. To solve this I trim some rubber off the rollers and tighten the float screws.

"No?" Zeb says. "So you want to burn in hell for all of eternity?"

I look up at Zeb. Mikey's making goofy faces behind him which makes me laugh and that makes Zeb happy.

"Just kidding Murray." Zeb slaps me on the arm. "But we do have a new pastor. Did I tell you? Paul Poole. He's inventive, a free thinker like you. Our choir sucks so he brought in a brass band called the Holy Blowers. Genius!"

I test the gun on the tabletop. *2@$1.99! 2@$1.99! 2@$1.99!*

Zeb claps his hands. "Fan-fizzly-tastic, my little wunderkind. But will you consider it? Think about the spirit that someone of your, um, skills would add to our congregation."

I open the Fortran. It's like a tank filled with cheap bullets. You can drop it off a cliff or run it over with a lead-filled shopping cart but the parts inside don't do much. The secret is to put little dabs of glue on the wheels and shut the case quick as you can. Tightens the whole thing up.

Special sale! Special sale!

"Sandman the Wonderman. You rock, as my daughter likes to say. Here you go. I hope this makes things decent." Zeb hands me a packet of coupons for Sugar Slams.

I stare at them.

"I know it's not much but things are tight right now with the whole regional restructuring going on and I was hoping that since I put in the word for you with Mazzie that you could do me a goodness this time around and hopefully—okay. You can take a couple of cans of soda too."

I stare at him, trying to make his brain melt.

"And a bag of chips. Say, CornPows? They're on sale."

I gather my tools and coupons.

Mikey and Zeb and I push through the swinging doors where we almost crash into an old lady in a funny yellow sunhat with a babbling toddler in her cart. The kid offers us a slimy half-eaten chocolate bar and Zeb's face stretches into a big public relations smile.

"Cute kid!"

The lady's head snaps around. "He's Jenny Lee's!" she says then picks up some Potato Puffs. She crush-tests them then puts them back and moves on.

Zeb grimaces then turns to us and whispers, "Cunt."

Mikey and I step outside. I shuffle over to the shadows. Mikey doesn't notice and keeps talking. Then he notices I'm absent and slings his gym bag over his shoulder and joins me there without judgment. Says, "I'm off to Grunts."

Grunts is a gym that makes it seem like you're in the Marines. One time Mikey said he was going to help me change my life and so I went there with him. I looked around at all the ropes and ladders and green-and-black weights then left.

"We going to Hell-o-ween this year or what?" he asks. "I hear it's in Knifepoint."

I shrug. Hell-o-ween used to be our tradition until a couple of years back when we woke up in an empty warehouse with our pants tied around our necks. But I like it in general. When I dress up and go out at night I can be anyone. Except for Chuck Rollins. No one can be him. Because everyone wants to fight you to prove you're not Chuck Rollins.

"I hear it's at someone's house, not in some burned-down gymnasium like that time I lost my shoe and earring."

"*Yuh* you don't *wuh wuh* wear earrings."

"I pierced my ear just for that night. It fucking hurt too. I used a paperclip."

I nod. "*Kuh* can you *luh luh* loan me *buh* bus fare?"

"Oh, Murray." He puts his hand on my shoulder. It sits there like a small bag filled with concrete. "When will we get our shit together?"

I shrug.

Mikey gives me a fiver and a hug and takes off jogging. "Call me!" It makes me sweat. Seeing him jog I mean, not the hug. I sigh.

He looks like a sports guy or a muscle actor. I'm not gay but if I were I could never get a guy like Mikey. I probably couldn't get any guy.

I take my fiver to the bus stop. There's a woman and a tiny kid there. The kid's got a Chuck Rollins blanket styled after his hit movie *Chuck Rollins Versus the Z.O.O.* It's awesome. I cram in close to them because the shadow is mightier there but the mother gets weird and slides her son away. I don't blame them.

I hop off the bus in a nice neighborhood down the street from my house. By nice I mean houses with lawns and burglar alarms. I haven't done this in a while but when things are bad a person faces tough choices. I spot a landscaping truck parked at the end of a cul-de-sac and grab a couple of their plastic gas cans and hustle home.

Bugle meets me at the door and doesn't bark, just looks up at me with a question mark on his face. He doesn't like it when I'm mad or sad or scared. Which I usually am. I make him happy by giving him some CornPows. I take the rest to the couch and crack open a soda and wait for *You'll Eat It And You'll Like It!* to come on TV. Instead it's more infomercials. This time they're selling huge lawn chairs with integrated garden hoses and then a bucket that turns into a ladder.

Dynamic folding action rivalry shucking transition performance horsepower variation launch magnitude…

My phone rings. I set down my bowl of CornPows. Bugle stares at me staring at the phone. I wait it out. I always win.

Finally the answering machine comes on with a *cluh-chunk.* The voice on there is not mine but Mikey's. Says, *Heyyyyy, this is Murray's house. He's not gonna answer the phone, so you'd better leave a message. And don't expect him to call you back. But I like you!*

Now there's a pause. Someone chewing something. Then finally words. "Oh, hey, Murray? Cool message. This is Jet. You might remember me. I was at the meeting?"

I nod.

"Cool, yeah. So I was wondering if you wanted to get a beer? I just was, like, hoping you could, you know, tell me more about Heli-Non? That would help me out with the thing I'm working out. So how about tonight at The Memo? It's that weird bar across from the airport?"

I know it. Near my favorite pancake joint, Flipjacks.

"I'll be there at, say, nine? If not, no big deal. I'll just drink my sorrows away and try not to kill myself. Just kidding! I don't shed tears. Anyway, see you then. Or not. Cool."

The machine stops with a *thuh-thunk*. Bugle continues to stare at me. I pull him onto my lap and hold him close. Our hearts beat like crickets that've drunk ten espressos. I think I might pass out.

Honey Is My Mom and I See Thin Man and a Dead Orca

Honey is my mom. Her name is really Lita but she used to tell everyone to call her Honey. Even me and my brother Tucker. My brain always got stuck between the two so I called her Honey Mom. Still do.

Driving, driving. The landscaper guys' gas sounds funny in the truck but I ignore it, keep going. Soon we're bouncing up the long driveway to Honey Mom's house. Our house, I guess. The place where I made the memories that now haunt me like ghosty images on VHS tapes that have been played too many times. The property once looked like a postcard. Now it's the type of place where small dogs disappear. The yard's been overtaken by weeds and weird plants with teeth. The shutters are hanging on by a single claw and the paint is being eaten up by the sun. But you can still see the ruts where Big Man once parked his truck under the huge willow.

I need to build up strength before I go inside. I open *Rays of Hope* and choose a chapter at random.

COPING STRATEGY #2: Sanitize!

If you want to change, you have to reinvent your Inner Self. To do this you must start by clearing out the clutter of your soul to make room for SANITY. That means you must SANITIZE. Clear out the old and the mold and make room for the BOLD new you.

The 3 Tenets of Sanitizing:

1.) The fight does not last forever—nothing does! (Not even the sun.)

2.) Grab hold of life by letting go! The sickness will persist only if you cling to it.

3.) To overcome your phobia, you need Suitable Materials. Get the training necessary so that you know how to wield Proper Knowledge.

Enough of this crazy talk you fill yourself with—it's time to reinvent the very fiber of your life! The moment you sense fear entering into your sense of well-being, remember to SANITIZE. Accept a clean new tomorrow.

I don't feel much better so I take out the Mazzie Prototypes. I try to play with them at least once a day to see how they do in different conditions. Heat. Traffic. Dog hair. Small tornados. Also I keep forgetting to bring them into the house so I can do the official report.

I adjust the knob and make a custom tag then slap one on my mirror.

%wow!

Now I need to go inside and get clean clothes. Currently I'm wearing some pajamas that haven't been washed in six months and my longcoat. I get out and drag Bugle to the door. I knock. No answer. I unlock the door.

"*Huh huh—*"

I flip on the kitchen light. No one's there. I let Bugle go and he starts hunting old smells. I open the fridge. Inside are a couple of onions and some coffee creamer. I take a sip. Of the coffee creamer I mean. Not the onions.

I go to the bottom of the stairs.

"*Huh huh—*"

I go up the stairs.

"*Huh huh—*"

I stop outside Honey Mom's bedroom door with my knuckles high. But I don't knock. For a second I think I can still smell Big Man's cigars. His musty truck-driver's odor.

I lower my knuckles.

Bugle scampers past, stops, scampers the other way.

I go and sit in my old room for a while and stare at the walls. Walls where I once wrote my hopes and dreams with magic markers. *Skydiver. Marching band instructor. Author of a children's book about a blind pigeon named Quimby.* Back when I moved out Honey Mom painted the walls turquoise and rented my room to an alcoholic tree-trimmer named Clever Johnson. Honey Mom drove him nuts so he left. My dreams are probably still there, underneath the paint. But there are none of my toys or familiar lamps or piles of twigs. Just the empty air left behind when you sigh. I look out the window. If I squint hard enough I can almost see my childhood. There are no clouds or stars, just old darkness.

It feels like I'm napping in my own coffin so I go back downstairs. Bugle has his face under the couch, rooting around for a stray crumb.

The door to Big Man's office is open. Honey Mom never cleared it out because she was sure he'd come back and we'd all be happy again. Even though we were never happy when he was here. I take a couple steps inside the room, flip on the light. Binders and newspapers and stacks of papers form columns everywhere. I'm still afraid to walk through them because if you toppled one Big Man would smack you and take away dessert for a week or a year. On top of one column sits a photo of the family. Happy, shoulders close. There's also one of Tucker riding a dirt bike and one of me in a tractor tire. In it I'm bouncy and fat, looking like an idiot. Which I kind of was.

No one ever knew what was wrong with me. If I was dumb and if so how dumb. The truth is that I'm dumb but not a moron. I just always hated talking. I hated being outside and hated math and geography. I only liked drawing. For a long time I was in special classes with kids in helmets, kids wearing glasses so thick their eyes looked like the back of television screens, kids who puked up worms after recess. Years passed before I was able to be with the regular kids but by then the abnormal kids were my friends. I just wanted to go back to the special class.

In one column I find a photo of Big Man with a lady I don't recognize. Her hair is inky black and huge like the whipped sugar stuff you get at the carnival. I take the photo and am about to go looking for Honey Mom when someone sets off the floodlights outside. A dark shape swishes past the window.

It's Thin Man, Big Man's brother. My uncle. I rap on the glass. He looks back. His hand comes up and he flips me off. Then he continues through the weedy field.

I get Bugle and we chase after him.

Thin Man's spine is bending like a branch but he's quick. He's heading toward the Box, the big gray apartment complex where he lives. He doesn't even turn to look at me, just twists sideways so his hands can say, *Fuck off, shit for brains, and take that bag of fleas to the pound before he spreads the plague.*

I laugh. He's the funniest person I've ever met.

Thin Man is mute but not deaf. And I can't speak sign language but I can read it. I learned it when I was in the class with the special kids. I was friends with a deaf boy who ran fast and could jump over anything. When he moved away I broke a window in the lunchroom and locked myself in a toilet stall and that night Big Man spanked me so hard that my poop came out sideways for a few days.

Thin Man takes the concrete steps to his apartment two at a time. Bugle and I pant and wheeze behind him. He slams the door shut in our faces. I open the door and enter and dump my coat and hat in a pile as Bugle starts a new quest.

Thin Man tosses his jacket into the air. It lands on the hook like magic. *What in God's name is that smell?* his fingers ask. *Is it the dog? No, it's you, you blob. Did you eat roadkill or just roll in it?*

I take off my pajamas and kick them aside. I follow him into the kitchen in my T-shirt and undies and wave the photo of Big Man and the lady in his face. "*Hoo hoo* who?"

He glances at it, his eyes like frozen marbles. Then his hands take flight. *I am an old fart but that doesn't mean I'm a fucking dumbass, you idiot.*

I waggle the picture. "*Hoo hoo—*"

His fingers slice up the air. *Shut up, you goddamn owl!* He goes to his fridge and takes out some dark red juice. He pours two glasses. He sets them down. He then gets a bowl of water for Bugle. Thin Man's fingers fly again. *That's your mother, shitforbrains.*

I stick the photo against my nose. I can't believe she ever looked like that. So pretty.

Sit down. He slides a glass across the table. I sit and sip. It's tart, gross. I push it away. Thin Man pushes it back. *My apartment, my rules. You drink my juice.*

I shrug. We drink and look down at the courtyard where some kids are building a mudman. When it's done they attack it with sticks and poles. Most parts of North Gaslin are crappy but the Box is even crappier. There's trash everywhere. The air reeks of rotting turkeys. Everyone's faces are pickled and violent. Thin Man hates it but he lives here because he can't afford anything else. He works for a radio station that has to ask people for money every Christmas.

Bugle laps up water.

Things awful as usual? Thin Man asks.

I shrug-nod.

Drawing?

Shrug.

Do you still go to that stupid group?

Nod.

You dumbshitassholepeckerbreath.

He snorts and finishes his drink and tells me to follow him into the living room. I plop down on the couch, lay a blanket over my legs. Thin Man turns on his TV and VCR. He feeds the machine a tape like it's hungry for a plastic sandwich and pushes *PLAY*.

The sun fills the screen. I wince.

It's basically a horror movie except it's scientific. The topic is the music made by the surface of the sun. It's not something you can dance to though. It's more like someone playing the violin with a chainsaw. The science voice says the sun is singing this screechy murder music to us all the time but we can't hear it. We're not listening properly. It's confusing and the type of thing Carl Jake talks about when you're pinned in a corner and his breath is spackling your face. Even Bugle doesn't like it. He stares at the sun and twists his head from side to side.

Thin Man hits the pause button. *You twat. The sun is beautiful and gives us life. It's also going to be around for millions of years. Do you want a real fear? Try meteorophobia.*

I shrug.

Comets and asteroids hurtling through space at thousands of miles per hour. I won't tell you what'll happen if we get hit. Just kidding. I will tell you. Life on Earth will end. Either immediately. Or slowly. Wars, famine, global catastrophe, cannibalism. He chews on his arm for effect.

"*Meh meh* meteor *fuh fuh*—?"

They're passing by all the time. But don't worry about it.

I'm worrying about it. Then he starts another rant.

Your silly arbitrary fear is simply a manifestation of your inability to cope with the transient nature of human existence, as well as your failures and shortcomings—

I laugh until my stomach hurts. "*Yuh* you're afraid of *kuh* cats."

His hands move like kung fu chops. *That furry fucker bit my ass!* He stands and tugs on the waist of his pants. Luckily he doesn't show me any cheek.

"A *kuh* kitten!" I make a whimpery sound.

He wraps his arm around my neck and rubs his knuckles on my scalp as Bugle barks and hops from side to side. *You idiot. I love you no matter how stupid you are.* Then he picks up Bugle and does the same to his scalp. Bugle licks Thin Man's nose.

We drink more juice. Then I tell Thin Man about the Mazzie job. I thought he'd be proud but instead his fingers say, *Fuck that.*

Huh?

Now his hands move like sonic firecrackers. *Why would you want to repair corporate war machines for these fascist food hoarders? They call them guns for a reason, you monkey. They're killing us with their oppressive demands for what is rightfully ours as residents of this doomed planet!*

I laugh so hard I almost rupture. I barely understand half the words.

You should—he waggles his finger and stands up—*focus on your art.* He leaves. A minute later he comes back with his "Murray Art Box." It's an old silver cardboard box, something I made a long time ago. Inside are drawings I've given him over the years. Big Man didn't want them. Not Honey Mom or Tucker either. Only Thin Man. He hands me the original sketch for Astro Fire Cop. *You have talent*, he says.

I look at my hero in his canvas space pants with his fireman-shaped space helmet and Norbidium© badge.

That thing could make money. It's radical! No, instead you work for Mazzie Corp.

I tell him about how the Mazzie guns make custom tags with funky images and have beveled corners that people remember. But he doesn't care.

You get one chance at life and you're wasting it, you puffball. Now turn on the TV. Our show is on.

Our show is of course *You'll Eat It And You'll Like It!*. The main character is Chef Pierre. He's a supercrappy chef. His catchphrase is "Lard soup! Lard soup!" Pierre's assistant Laurencio fixes all the recipes that Pierre botches but since Laurencio is an escaped convict he keeps it a secret. And since Pierre is goofy and has funny eyebrows and a rubbery face people like him. They don't care how stupid and useless he is. Life goes on episode after episode and no one gets hurt. Only an occasional limb is lost.

In this episode Chef Pierre is in Paris to learn how to make squid pudding. The secret ingredients are mushrooms and maple syrup but he puts in whiskey and chocolate. Turns out he's not really French. It's hilarious. I laugh and Thin Man smacks his knees.

Thin Man heads off to his job at the radio station to fix antennas and such. Bugle and I go back to Honey Mom's.

"*Huh huh*—" I say when I step inside.

Still nothing. Bugle and I go to the basement to collect my laundry. Except it's not near the dryer like normal. Something smells. I stumble toward a dark heap in the far corner. It looks like a dead orca. I grab a mop and dig through it. It's my clothes. My rare Chuck Rollins *Balls Out in Bangkok* shirt is as slimy and stinky as an ogre's ear wax.

"Gahhhhh!"

Blood circulates in my skull like toilet water as my heart thuds in my ears. I grab my knees to keep from passing out. What would Astro Fire Cop do if his favorite shirt was covered in mold and orca slime? He'd go back in time and do his laundry himself. I can't do that yet though. Travel through time I mean, not do laundry. I just prefer not to. What would Chuck Rollins do? He'd break someone's face. That is doable.

I scan the boxes scattered around the basement. "Eggs and Rabbits!" "Turkey Time!" "X-Mas Men!" I slide that one out. It contains stupid nutcrackers in their original boxes. They have big white teeth and are wooden and hollow. Just like the Sandman clan. We haven't celebrated anything in years. Birthdays. Holidays. Deaths. Moon Day. I fling them against the wall. Their arms go one way and their heads the other. I stomp their bodies. I smash their hearts. I am the sun.

Bugle snatches up a wooden head and runs off with it.

There are some other boxes behind these. "TS." Tucker Sandman. One box in the back is marked "MS." Mustard Sandwich. Massive Skunk. Much Suck. I tear it open. It contains my papers from grade school and high school and a birthday card from Honey Mom and Big Man. *You are our son. Enjoy this day.* There's some other stuff like awards for good attendance and a Little League medal I didn't deserve. There's nothing that proves I'm still alive. I spit on it all and go upstairs.

I notice that all the family pictures are missing from the den's walls. Honey Mom must have taken them down recently. Now there are just dark squares where they used to live—negative sunlight. On the shelves are books we never read. A little TV. Lumpy brown sofa. It looks comfy at the moment. I lie down. Soon I'm dreaming about a room where all the candles are hanging from the ceiling.

When I wake up Honey Mom is standing over me. I scratch myself and stretch.

"Why are your eyes so red?" she asks. Bugle stands beside her, panting, watching me too.

I blink.

"Have you been drinking?"

I shrug.

"Oh, Murray."

The kettle sings from the kitchen. She says that she's about to pour tea. We go in there. The radio is on some talk show saying *In communist Russia history was mutable. People were expendable and egghead freightshed cosmic lavatory machine untruth blitzkrieg bacterium muck trigger...*

Honey Mom lays her bones on the same green chair she always sits on and sighs into the steam coming off her mug.

Because Big Man drove trucks he was gone a lot. Then one day he left in his fancy antique truck and never came back. Tucker and I were still in high school, just kids. Honey Mom hired a detective but no one ever found our father. He did however find out that Big Man was involved in shady stuff and had girlfriends on the side. When Honey Mom found out she snapped. Couldn't be fixed. For this reason I don't say anything about the orca in the basement.

"I wasn't expecting company."

I sip the tea. It tastes like the inside of a boot.

"Is that a new outfit?" she asks, nodding her chin at my pajamas.

I choose not to answer this.

"I saw Mikey Priest's father the other day. Are you and Mikey still friends?"

Nod.

"Is he still, you know?" She waggles her hands up and down. "*Guh guh* gay?"

"Lifting weights."

Nod.

"And how about you? Getting any exercise?"

Half-nod.

"Are you taking those vitamins I gave you?"

Half-shrug. I took one or two before gagging. They were huge. Like swallowing a finger.

"You should take them every day. Sometimes little things like that make a difference, you know."

I shrug again and we watch the steam drift off our cups for a while.

"I'm tired of all the drama," Honey Mom says from nowhere. Her eyes are like little ponds lined with fire. Even her hair is angry-looking.

"I need a couple of things from the store. Can you get them?"

She slides over a list. Her handwriting used to look like something from the Craft Lady show on Channel 1. Now it looks like the path worms leave on the sidewalk after the rain. *Soup. Bread. One orange.*

I slide the list back and shake my head.

"No?"

"I *huh* have a *duh duh* date."

"Oh. Don't you have a girlfriend?"

My skin tingles. She's right. But I just shrug. Then I get up before she can ask any more painful questions. Bugle meets me at the door.

Jet's waiting. I wish I had clean underwear.

I Go on a Date that Turns Out not to Be a Date but Beer Loosens Me up and I Put on a Show and Almost Brawl with Some Dinks

Driving, driving. I switch the radio to the college station. The half-asleep stoner DJ says that the next song is called "Thalamocortical Pilferage" by the band Penisbutt and the Pissfarts. It's slow and gloomy and makes me think of decaying black apples and that time I accidentally sliced my ear canal with a razor blade.

Soon the air control tower rises up. The Memo is on the other side of the street but everyone parks at North Gaslin Airport. As I get closer I crane my head and scan the runway. A plane crash would be terrible. But a spectacle I find myself pining for.

I park. The airport lot is nearly empty. So is the airport itself. There's my pancake place inside but that's it. The gift shop went out of business last summer. They used to sell little mascots called

Gassy Gary who is a fuzzy oil machine that just wants to hide under your bed at night and protect your dreams. And now there is talk of knocking down the airport and putting in a cardboard box factory. Sad. No one dreams of making boxes all day. Cardboard planes maybe. Real planes for sure. But not cubes made from tree powder.

I look both ways, cross the street.

The Memo is a bar that's supposed to look like an office. It's got blinky fluorescent lighting. White foam ceiling tiles. Cubicles instead of booths. Old copy machines to lean on while you drink and chat. Junky computers flickering in the corners. It's a gimmick but people like it. Or at least people who don't work in offices do.

When I arrive the jukebox is belting out some scratchy country music by Jimmy Swan and the Daft Ducks. *Doobie doobie doo, yeah! Doobie doobie doo, all right!* A bunch of old guys are sitting around a conference table. They're sailors maybe. Retired firemen possibly. They look up at me and grimace then go back to pushing peanuts around a checkerboard. In a large cubicle in the corner sit a bunch of college dinks in flannels and jeans and white baseball caps turned backward. They're loud. They all look the same. I decide I hate them.

Beverages and food are listed on sticky notes. The bar is a receptionist's desk. There's a kid behind it. No, not a kid. A short dude. He climbs up onto a box of copy machine paper. He's kind of muscular and his hair is in a ponytail. He eyeballs me in my longcoat and filthy clothes and floppy hat and says hello. I stand there dumbly. Not because of the words but because of the voices in my head. Martin's. Mikey's. My brother Tucker's. They're all telling me to be smart and not to choose beer. The thing about beer is that it's like a sword with two edges. One side is magic and the other side is burning hot. Whenever I stick the magic sword down my throat my mouth loosens up and I can talk more freely. But it also makes me real berserk and brings out all my hatred and rage. I usually end up saying the wrong things to the right guy. A couple of times I've gotten punched so hard that some of my hair fell out.

"*Buh buh* beer," I tell the guy on the box of copy paper.

"Tap okay?"

I shrug-nod.

A clear mind is like washed hands, Carl Jake says in my brain. *Drinking to excess is like eating spaghetti with a single chopstick.*

He draws the beer and slides it closer. Drool trickles out the corner of my mouth. "Three bucks."

I check my pockets. A dollar and a couple of dimes left over from the bus fare. Lint. Lots of dirt. "*Tuh tuh* tab."

"What's the name?"

"*Muh muh* Murray."

"Hey, Murray." His little hands drag the beer back. "How about you get a job or rob a gas station and come back here when you have three bucks?"

I cry inside.

"It's okay Dirk," a voice suddenly says. "I got it. And one for me."

Dirk sneers and pushes the beer back. My heart vibrates. I slowly turn to face Jet.

"*Th* thanks," I tell her.

She swings her purse up onto the bar. It lands with a big *thunk*. "No problem. Times are tough, eh?"

The beer tastes like cold hippo pee. I drain half the mug and set it down hard, gasping.

"Nice chug!"

Dirk slides over Jet's beer and hops down from his box. Jet pays and takes a pull, frowns at the taste, says to me, "Your last name is Sandman, right?"

A soft belch emerges from the bottom of my gut. She looks at me for a few seconds then bucks and squints and outbelches me by a thousand decibels.

We laugh.

"*Guh guh* gross!"

We laugh again.

"Hey," she says, "you ever hear of Stutter and Stammer Stoppers? I'm just asking because my friend goes a couple of times a month and they seem to know what they're doing."

I look into the bottom of my beer. I hate talking about my speech stuff. I wish people just wouldn't comment on my stutter. But how could they not? It's like a dump truck with one wheel missing. Everyone notices.

"He said most stutters are the result of some sort of abuse. Did your father beat on you? Or other people? Maybe bullies at school?"

I shrug. Then nod.

"When I was a teenager I was always twisting my finger in my hair. I'd do it without thinking until all of a sudden there was a bloody bald patch." She demonstrates. I shudder. "I realized that I was acting out because I was being forced into multiple societal conventions that simply didn't suit my psychological makeup. Know what I mean?"

I have no idea but I nod anyway. She realizes she's talking fancy and giggles and pokes me, either playing around or testing my squishiness. We laugh but it's a shy laugh.

"Enough serious stuff. You want to get your ass kicked by Devil Donkey or what?"

"*Wuh wuh* what?"

"Devil Donkey!"

She's talking about one of the video games in the Breakroom at the back of the bar. I nod and continue to nod myself all the way over to Devil Donkey. The whole time I'm watching Jet's butt dance in her jeans. She inserts a quarter and slides on the boxing glove and starts punching the screen. Her shirt flips up and shows off her little belly and a studded belt. She also has a couple of blurry tattoos of stepped-on flowers. Or maybe they're deflated planets. Hard to say. Her jeans are rolled up and she's got on the kind of big black boots you wear when you want to kick in someone's teeth.

"Fuck you!" she says when Devil Donkey gets hit by an airplane.

More beer appears from the sky. I open my mouth and it flows down my throat like raw sewage. I can already feel the crazies settling in. Jet's saying something about her job and such but I'm too busy drowning out the voices in my head to listen so I just nod.

Jet dies again when Devil Donkey falls into an earthquake pit. "Sonofabitch!"

It's my turn. I slide my hand into the sweaty glove. Punch. Punch. Panting. Every time I go to jump over an aircraft carrier Jet tickles me with her tiny fingers. It feels like spider tongues and makes me want to sneeze. It's real funny.

"So what's your story, Murray?"

Devil Donkey falls off a freight train and splatters on the ground.

"How long have you been attending this Heli-Non group?"

"*Luh luh* long time."

"Do you mind if I ask how you first heard about it?"

I think hard. The beer's like smog in my brain. In the end I just shrug. "*Huh* how did *yuh* you?"

"I, uh, found the guidebook in the free bin at the library. So I did some investigation and found out about the meetings at the school."

I die again.

"I'm intrigued. I mean it's *really* interesting."

"*Wuh wuh* what is?"

"I don't know. The book itself is kind of fear-mongering, you know? But then it puts out all these amazing facts like how there are three *sextillion* suns in the universe. I mean, holy fuck! That's a three followed by twenty-three zeros. How can someone wrap their brain around that and be terrified of the little itty-bitty sun that gives us life? Except our sun's not that itty-bitty because you can fit almost a hundred million Earths inside it. And then it said how the sun is middle-aged. I noticed that most of the people in the group are close to middle age too. So it's weird, you know?"

I can't see straight. There are sunspots on my brain.

"What can you tell me about the people who go there? In general."

I shrug.

"'Suitable Materials.' I mean, what the fuck is that? What are 'unsuitable' materials?"

Unsuitable Materials would be religious stuff and psychology texts. But I keep that to myself.

Jet taps me on the forehead and makes me look at her. I think she's about to give me more advice. Which I need about as much as a hippopotomonstrosesquipedaliophobic needs to join a spelling bee. But she's full of questions tonight and says, "The group leader, for example. What's he like?"

I don't have to close my eyes to see his shiny sneakers with double-knotted laces. His baggy blue jeans and goofball face. But then I realize that she's talking about Martin. Not Carl Jake.

"Does he ever make you do anything against your will?"

I shrug. Then shake my head. It's hard to answer. Or maybe I don't want to.

"Okay, so how about the musician guy. I know him from around town. What's his story?"

His story is his to tell. I scowl and punch-jab-punch so hard my fist almost comes loose.

She bites her lip like a kiddie. "Alright. Let's go for the obvious one. Mr. Mask. You *have* to tell me what's up with that."

Joe Purple, she means. I could tell her how one time he came to Heli-Non without a mask which shocked us all until we realized it was an illusion. He'd made a skin-thin and lifelike mask from rubber and he looked like a common white guy with a cop-style mustache. But I just shrug. "*Duh duh* dunno anything. *Nuh* name. Age. *Kuh* color."

"Okay… um, hey, I'll get us some more beer and then we can continue the interview, alright?"

I nod. But I'm not sure what interview she's talking about. When she returns with the beer we move to Qua-Babliconicus. It's the hardest arcade game ever invented. You have to build a planet while fighting off alien overlords. Jet and I guzzle and bang into one another.

"Tell me about yourself then. What are you into?"

"*Arr* art."

"Oh yeah? What kind?"

"Cool stuff. *Kuh* comics. *Ch* Chuck Rollins. Astro *fuh* Fire Cop."

"Astro Fire Cop? What the fuck is that?"

I laugh-snort and hand over the Qua-Babliconicus controls.

I've only been on a couple of dates. And though this probably isn't even one I am smart enough to know I should be asking her stuff too. Favorite movies. Favorite tree. Favorite soda and such. I'm technically dating Annabelle but maybe not tonight.

And as usual the beer is kicking in. Words are starting to make sense but my mind is like a fishing reel hooked on a speedboat in a hurricane.

When a new song starts up real loud Jet yells, "I love this song! It's 'Blow Me Up, Blow Me Down' by Ahab and the Sperms. You know them?"

No. But I nod so hard my head falls off and rolls across the floor.

"Sing with me!"

Jet snaps her fingers and dances and belts out the lyrics which are about whale pirates and drunken mermaids and seaweed. Dirk the bartender bobs his head while wiping off cubicles and desks. Even the old grumps at their conference table tap their feet. I mumble some words and clap my hands. I'm sweating and I need to fart. But right when the song ends Jet puts in another quarter and plays "Love Is A Rocket Ship with A Broken Tail Fin Sailing Over the Moon" by Big Blam and the Kickbacks. It goes

You are my sunshine, my ray of light. I want to boogie with you every night! Now we have to jump around. It's really fun. Probably the best night ever.

"Let's go fuck!"

My face burns red. "*Wuh* what?"

"I said I'm so fucked up! But tell me more about the other heliofreaks."

I'm nodding like a bobblehead when the college dinks in the corner notice Jet jiggling her butt. One of them stumbles over and asks if she wants to dance.

"I think I'll pass," she says and spins in a circle.

"Wanna make out then?" the guy asks. He's tall and wide and has a joker face. His shirt buttons are off by one hole.

"Nah," Jet says. "I'm cool." She bounces and I snap my fingers and bob up and down.

"You're cool. But look at this guy."

"Oh yeah?" Jet says. "What are you going to do about it?"

"More like what's Mr. Cool going to do about it?"

There's no more snapping or bobbing. Rage hurtles through my arms and shins. The beer makes it easy. I loosen my tongue and tilt my head back and say, "*Shh shh* she's with *muh* me!"

The dink looks at me like I just pooped in my hand and showed it to him. "And who the fuck are you?"

"*Muh* Murray *suh* Sandman!"

"All right," he says and steps back. "Good luck, retard moron Murray."

Jet laughs then growls like a panda and nudges me. The room tilts. I think I am going to puke. I point at the back of The Memo because that's where the bathroom is. Jet laughs again. Just to be safe I laugh too. Then I stumble away.

I find a door in the corner. I push until I realize it slides. It's the worst door ever. I go down a hall. A single light bulb floats overhead with snot dripping out its nose. No, just a light. I find the bathroom and try to slide the door open but it doesn't slide. It's like an accordion. Something you'd find in Japan maybe. Even worse than the worst door ever. But it was closed for a reason. It looks like someone died on the toilet then exploded. I retreat and stumble toward the fire exit at the end of the hall. This door opens normally. I step out onto the side street. I lay my head against the cold bricks and open my zipper.

I pee. I pee.

I zip up. But now the back door is locked. I zigzag from wall to wall and eventually circle the building and make it to the front. But I don't go inside. I take a moment to press my face against the window. It's cool, pleasant. I feel okay. But then I see Jet swinging her hips by the jukebox. The dink is standing beside her. A single fat finger of his sits on her shoulder. She doesn't tell him to fuck off and die or anything like that. He slides his hand lower. She keeps dancing. Then leans into him.

I open my mouth and scream into the glass. Except the scream travels backward down my throat like cold sunlight. It swirls through my chest and explodes in my stomach. I am a falling star.

I Shake off a Brief Death and Head to Flipjacks for a Late-night Snack and Meet a Guy Who Might Be a Serial Killer and then the Universe Flips Upside Down

When I return to Earth Jet is gone. The dinks are gone. Dirk is gone and so are the sailors and Qua-Babliconicus. Because The Memo is closed. I'm lying in a heap of trash. It's comfy. I could stay. But I prefer my own bed. Bugle always keeps it warm. I wonder if Annabelle is still awake.

To test whether I'm sober enough to drive I take my keys out of my pocket and hold them in the air. Good enough.

I zigzag across the street to the airport. My truck comes closer. Then it gets farther away. To solve this problem I go in a big circle then divide it in half a few times and eventually am within spitting distance of my vehicle. But then I blink and the keys vanish from my fingers like it's a magic trick. I drop to my hands and knees and molest the grimy pavement. Four years later my pinky catches them. Maybe I am not as sober as I thought. I sit there long enough for my stomach to stop gurgling and for the sound of Jet's cackling to fade. Eventually I hear only my lungs wheezing and soon the good ol' self-hatred in my chest is replaced with something else.

Hunger.

Food doesn't grow without sunlight! the audio version of *Rays of Hope* says. *And neither can you!*

Yes. Food will straighten me out. I'll sober up, calm down, get the feeling back in my fingers. Good thing Flipjacks is open until three in the morning. I stand up with a grunt.

I unlock the truck and dig around in the console and between the seats. I find four bucks and seventy-five cents. Enough for a short stack. I lock the truck.

Zigging, zagging.

The airport's sliding doors get stuck halfway and I have to squeeze through. Or maybe they don't slide. I curse, kick.

It's cool inside. My feetslaps echo across the empty terminal. At the far end is my destination, Flipjacks. It's lit up with pink and blue neon lights on the outside. The insides are plain though. Brown tables. Beige chairs. Yellow placemats. Their pancakes taste like silicone and the maple syrup is fake but I have no scruples. As long as they're cooked all the way through and don't have olives.

Only one other customer is there, a goofy salesman-type who keeps calling the waitress "Mrs. Love."

"Mm?" the waitress says when it's my turn to order. She's new, a nice lady. Her words make my head hurt though. I wish people would talk without speaking. I point to the menu. Short stack. Coffee.

"Coupla minutes," she says so loudly I shiver.

In the terminal a door opens and a golf cart zips past then disappears behind another door. The radio at Flipjacks is belting out scratchy country music by Jess E. Jameson and the Banditos. *You polished my saddle and then you said skedaddle. Baby, love don't have to be such a battle.* The waitress walks past, dropping off my coffee along the way. Her butt is shaped like a lemon that's been stepped on but her legs make sense.

My trembly hands lift my mug. I sip, trying not to slurp, and close my eyes and think about that time two floor polishers got into a fistfight. No one saw it but me. They were evenly matched but at the end one lay slumped against the wall making squeaky noises and the other guy went on polishing.

Soon the waitress arrives with my short stack. Turns out her name really is Mrs. Love. Says *K. Love* on her shirt. I leave the pile of filthy coins for her and apologize in my head.

I take a little bite. Then a bigger one. My rage fades chew by chew.

Mrs. Love refills my coffee. "Enjoying your cakes, hon'?" she asks.

I would like to hold her hand for a minute and tell her about my problems. About how I am broke and sleep above toxic chemicals and how Jet tricked me and how Bugle needs his walk soon. But I just nod and she leaves.

I'm usually happy at Flipjacks. I like watching the planes bouncing on the tarmac. Occasionally groups of people passing through as quickly as possible. No one can find me here and I'm halfway toward being somewhere else. I also like to draw on the napkins. I have ideas for things. Creatures, fighters, worlds, pricing gun features. Scenes for Astro Fire Cop. I continue digging into the short stack and try not to moan with joy as syrup dribbles down my chin. This goes on for a while until a phlegmy shadow says "Ahem" as it overtakes my table.

I look up to see the sales-type who was sitting at the counter. He's got a plateful of pancakes and a cup of Blast! cola with flaky ice floating around in it. "Didn't mean to scare you, buddy," he says, rocking on his heels. His suit is baggy and his tie is looped over his shoulder. His face looks kicked-in from birth. His fingertips are dirty. I'm not the sharpest corncob-holder in the junk drawer but I know when a guy is putting on a front. "Mind if I join?"

I have a decision to make. Awkward chatter or awkward distance. Before I can even shrug though he sits down. The stench of musky cologne and hard liquor immediately overtakes the pleasantness of my woodsy fake maple syrup.

"The name's Alphonse Polish," he says but pronounces the last part like the shoe stuff and not a type of sausage. "Pleased to greet you." He offers a hand.

I nod and ignore the sticky digits. In the background Mrs. Love leans against the counter and does those games where you circle real words in a jumble of fake words. *ILLICIT. BOOTY. DIGEST.* The cook leaves his pancake station with a pack of cigarettes and heads outside. I should follow him.

"And you? Got a name?" this guy asks me.

I nod and continue my work but very slowly. I like it when the pancakes reach the edge of staleness but don't fully commit.

"I see. The quiet type. A lone wolf, like me."

I look around, study the cafe. The faded old airline posters. Mrs. Love's scrunched-up face as she erases a circle. *PROBOSCIS. WARPER.* I know I'll never come back here. It's ruined for me now. I'll find somewhere else. A bowling alley maybe. A train station perhaps. Another place where people arrive and do something and then leave.

"I get it, believe me," the guy with the concave face says. "You can't find places like this anymore where some blathering idiot doesn't corner you and ask what you do for a living. So what do you do for a living, Mr. Silent?"

I set down my fork. It's not a rude enough sound though. It just sounds like I'm finished with the pancakes. Which I'm not. A yellow quarter moon remains to be consumed. I run a napkin around my mouth then take a sip of coffee and loosen up my tongue. "*Fuh fuh* fuck *aw aw* off."

This guy Alphonse Polish stares at me for ten seconds then pitches forward and lets out a hiccuppy laugh that goes on forever. When Mrs. Love looks over I start sweating. I don't like looks. I don't like hiccups. To calm myself I use my right foot to push down the Velcro straps on my left shoe, then the other one.

"Is that Chinese?" Alphonse says, slapping the table. "Hello, I Fukoo. Who you? I Fukoo." His face is so red it looks like it might explode and tomato the whole place.

I get back to work on the sliver of pancake. Alphonse eventually calms down, saying, "Good stuff, good stuff." He doesn't get it. Just sits there like we were in the War together. Soon he's vacuuming the bottom of his cup and Mrs. Love swings by to replenish it.

He leans back and continues.

"I like to sit here and think, you know? You ever do that? It's like, imagine something, anything. A cow. A refrigerator. Or better yet a Swiss Army knife. Who was the guy who decided to cram all those gadgets and junk in there? So now every time you need to stab someone, first you have to uncork a champagne bottle or pick your teeth or saw off some poor schmuck's limb, right?"

He laughs then starts draining his new soda but the fizziness gets to him and he coughs up another thought.

"Or think about language, you know? Our stupid words. You of all people can relate to this, I'm sure of it. Me, I'm Polish, dumb as a rock, so I'm a Pole named Polish. But why aren't people from Holland called Holes? Ha ha. What crock. Language. *Thppt. Thppt.* Hello, I Fukoo." He snorts. "Man, I wish they had something stronger to drink here. That reminds me, why do my feet smell and my nose runs?" He sets off another epic giggle jag.

I scratch at some dried syrup on the table. The cook slips back in behind the counter and cracks open a beer.

"So who died?" Alphonse says. "Or is this your standard state of mind?"

I clench my eyes shut.

"Look, if it's about the *spee—spee—speeth impedimenth*, don't worry about it. I have ugly feet. My girlfriend has scurvy. We've all got issues, you know?"

Sometimes when I'm almost asleep I can hear Big Man humming a stupid country song he always liked, a tune about lonely miners. Or was it pretty minors? I think I hear it now.

"I'm all ears if you want to lay it on me. I'm a blabberbutt with a healthy smile but to you I'm just one big wax-filled ear. Tell me what's up. Give me the rundown."

I look at Alphonse now. His bleary eyes. The pale circle of skin on his finger where a ring used to sit. Finally someone wants to hear my woes, to look inside my pale soul. Perhaps this is the man I've been waiting for.

I shrug.

"Alrighty then. An easy one. What do you love?"

This inquiry I ponder. The answers would be Bugle. Comic books. Pricing guns. Okay maybe not pricing guns but the idea of getting paid to fix them. And a girl named Elinor who had a locker three doors down from mine in high school and once let me borrow a pen with tassels. She said I could keep it. Probably because I'd chewed on it. I guess I love Annabelle too. At least on weekends and when she's asleep. "*Puh puh* pancakes," is my answer.

He smiles so wide I can see his gums. "Keep going. Now what do you hate?"

I think about that while studying his expectant face. Like he's Jesus and I'm a fish. "*Yuh yuh* you."

His face turns as blank as a movie screen when you show up too early and his shoulders rise like he's going to sneeze or hurl. But then the guffawing erupts again. It goes on for so long that his face puffs out like a medicine ball. "That's a good one, friendo."

The cook shakes his head and sips his beer and Mrs. Love turns up the music. Now we're listening to Gangrene Lunchmeat. There are no words, just guitars going *bwwwwong bwwwwong* like we're surfing on an island or playing lawn darts on a summer afternoon.

Alphonse's throat makes a dry sucking sound and he wipes away laugh-tears. Then he leans in, haunting me like a math teacher. "Look, I see you here in the wee hours and I assume you're just like me. A freak. A creature of the night. You probably, what, steal cash machines to get by? No? Break into old people's homes and suck up all their oxygen? I can tell, Mr. Fukoo, you're a devious motherfucker like me. Why don't we get to know one another, discuss our portfolios?" He sets a battered brown briefcase on the table and smacks the leather like it's a sexy butt.

"I—*wuh wuh* what's in *th thh* there?"

He smiles and sits back and sucks at his ice. "My tools of the trade. Like nothing you've ever seen before. I'll show you once you tell me what your game is. The long and the short."

I dab my chin and take my last sip. "*Nuh* no *thh th* thanks." I put on my floppy hat and longcoat and get ready to go.

"Whoa, whoa, whoa," Alphonse says, buffeting the air between us. His eyes turn into bloody moons and the smile oozes into a grimace. "Just like that you say no?"

I shrug.

"Hey, hey. Look, you can insult me. You can insult my girlfriend—hell, I do it just breathing—but you can't insult the briefcase."

I toss my crumpled-up napkin onto my plate.

"Come on, pal. You don't gotta be like that."

As I pass the counter I nod to the cook. He salutes me with his spatula. He doesn't know I'll never see him again. He also doesn't know that one time I saw him fondle a cockroach.

"Bye, hon'," Mrs. Love says as I sweep past. I almost cry.

I cut through the silent airport and step out into the night air.

"Hey, you big jerk," Alphonse calls out while slapfooting toward me across the parking lot, his briefcase swinging beside him like it has its own gravity. "Listen, I'm a nice guy. People like me. But that—that was something else, embarrassing me like that in front of a lady and—and—and rejecting my life's work."

I make a plan. I will unlock the door and grab one of the Mazzies and point it at Alphonse's forehead. He'll think it's a real gun or maybe a laser device such as a Berserker Pistol, the preferred weaponry of Chuck Rollins. He'll be so freaked out he'll hand over his briefcase.

"If you'd given me a chance you'd see that I have thoughts. I have feelings. I like connecting with people. Hell, I got money too. I would have bought your pancakes and coffee, maybe a refill. All I ask is that you open yourself up to a potential partnership. You show me yours, I show you mine."

I stop short. It seems that my eyes are still screwy. I take out my keys and hold them up. Steady. But something looks weird. Near my truck are shiny bits. They're all over the ground. I hope they are jewels but that is dreamtalk and I'm pretty sure I'm awake. I shuffle closer.

It is glass. Some hooligans have smashed a hole in the rear window of my truck.

Behind me Alphonse's cheap office shoes slow down. "Wait, is that your sled?" he asks with a snort.

I unlock the door and pull it open. Where the box of Mazzie pricing guns should be is a pile of crap. As if a wormhole opened up above my truck and left shit behind. I step back and make a fist and look up at the sky. Except that the sun isn't there. Just a section of the moon. "*Fuh* fuck! Fuckity fuck fuck!"

"Damn. What happened to you, Fukoo?"

I search the truck. There is nothing but glass and poop and junk and garbage. But then I find a scrap of paper that reads *hi murry   fuk u!*

I sit on the ground and weep.

"Wow, pal. And I thought I was a sad sack. Well, fine sir, may your days be fruitful and your evenings merry. I'll leave you to it."

Suddenly I don't want to be alone. But it's too late. Alphonse slapfoots away, leaving me in dark peace.

My life is over. My dream is as dead as meteor dust.

One time at Heli-Non we were arguing. I mean we're always arguing but this time it was different. Laramie Bob was saying to FX, *We may be afraid of the sun but the truth is that we think the sun revolves around us.* And Carl Jake said, *The sun doesn't but the moon does.* We all thought about that. I still wonder about it actually. But what does it mean?

Eventually I get myself into the truck. A piece of poop clings to the stick shift. I flick it off. There's broken glass all over the seat but I don't care. I sit right on it.

When I'm up to speed I roll down the window. With the smashed-out rear window the truck turns into half a cyclone but I need the air. Occasionally I swerve a little in my lane. It could be the beer in my veins or it could be the bad tires. I don't care. Don't care if I die. I just hope someone walks Bugle.

I turn up the radio. It's playing a song called "Pedophilia is a Touchy Subject" by Blaze and the Retardants. It's punk, the lyrics like *Fuck you! Fuck you! Blah blah blah. Fuck you!* I feel dirty, mean, rotten. And slightly better.

Some thoughts arrive and some courage too. I consider organizing a special Heli-Non session to discuss my problem or maybe a search party and Personal Crime Task Force. But that would require speaking. I wonder if I should go buy a fingerprint kit and test the glass myself. It must have been the dinks from the bar who did me wrong. They were mean. They stole Jet and the Mazzies.

Yes.

I shake my fist in the wind and howl and head to my brother Tucker's house. It's time for revenge.

I Try to Rob Tucker Which Goes Over Poorly and I Tell You About Our Relationship Which Has Also Gone Over Poorly

Tucker and I are like two peas in a pod. Except he's a weird black-eyed one and I'm green. The only thing we have in common is the pod. Okay we have similar noses but after that nothing's alike.

When our father left a lot changed in our house. Tucker had to be the man since all I did was sit in my room and draw or cry with happiness or hang out with Mikey. Honey Mom lost it both because of the news about Big Man's other life and because she missed him. She didn't go pull-your-hair-out crazy, just slow inside-crazy. When she quit working we sold Big Man's semi-trailer to pay for stuff even though Tucker said he was going to drive it and take over Big Man's route. But no one could figure out what Big Man did or where he went so Tucker said fuck it okay you assholes and called up a truck dealer.

After that Honey Mom stopped cleaning parts of the house but other parts she cleaned over and over. She stopped making real food too. She used to be a good cook but over time everything turned into puketastic microwave glop. Even dessert. After a while Tucker had to take over dinners. Usually it was Sugar Slams or toaster waffles.

Tucker took over my punishment too. Even though he's only a couple of years older he spanked me a lot if I was lazy or sassy. I was lazy a lot. I was sassy for a while but then I just got quiet and mad and scared. I never told Tucker about my phobia but it was always there so he could probably see that something big wasn't right with me in addition to all the other smaller not-right things. Mostly he kept his distance. In the halls of our high school he would give me a glance or a nod but that was it. Most people didn't know we were related. He never took the bus to school but would somehow show up on time every day. Meanwhile I had to walk to the end of the street and stand in the wind rain sunshine snow hurricanes until the bus clanked its way toward me. Then I'd have to get down the bus aisle safely to Mikey or the deaf kid. Most mornings I got a train of punches to the thigh and could barely walk by the time homeroom started.

The truth is that Tucker and I don't like each other that much. For a while I went over to his house and hung out with him and his wife Roxanne. We would set up trays and eat lots of chips and CornPows and watch *Marriage On The Rocks* on their TV which is so big I could drown inside it. I love Roxanne. She's pretty in a cigarette model type of way. She's bitchy and mean and swears but she's not afraid to fart in front of me or tell me the truth. Like how I have gum in my hair or that my pants are on inside out. When it came time to leave I wouldn't want to.

A few times Bugle and I slept on the couch. But it was obvious that they didn't want me to. So I stopped. Eventually I stopped coming over to watch TV too. We'd already seen every episode twice anyway and they don't like *You'll Eat It And You'll Like It!*.

Their house is big. White and brown. Tucker built it himself. He's real successful with stuff like that. He used to pay me to mow the lawn. I had to do it at night with a flashlight strapped to my forehead but I ran over a sprinkler and destroyed the lawnmower so I got fired.

I park and get out. I try to shut my door quietly but I'm angry and pancake-filled and still a little beery and it slips from my greasy fingers and bangs loudly. A yard wolf howls in the distance. I scamper across the lawn and hide behind Tucker's truck. I could almost park mine inside the back of his if it wasn't filled with construction machines and tools and gear. Then I crouch down and hustle over to the bushes. Next I circle the house to the back of the garage. The key is under a fake rock that shines in the dark like a slice of dirty gold.

I unlock the door and crawl inside and turn on the light and hustle over to the other side and switch it off. Darkness. I lay my hand on the doorknob and twist it so slowly you could cook and eat a burrito while I'm standing there. The door goes *weeee* as it opens.

A nightlight shines in the hall. I hear no noises except my breathing which is like *Hzzzt hzzzzt*. I slide past the nightlight. At the end of the hall I turn toward Tucker's office. I pray the door's unlocked. Pray to who? To anyone. Everyone.

I open his office door and cool air rushes out. There's a lamp on the desk. I close the door and molest the lamp from top to bottom until I realize the switch is on the cord. The light's about five thousand times as bright as the sun though. I grab the cord to flick the switch again but I pull too hard and the lamp topples over. Papers and pens and chunks of wood and golf tees and magazines spill onto the floor. My heart gets stuck in my throat and sweat pours down my crotch.

I cover the lamp with my longcoat. It gives me enough light and creates a nice ambiance. I open the cabinet door which isn't locked. Inside is a thick glass case. This is locked but I know where the key is. It's under a small statue of a golfer humping a sheep. *I love ewe!*

The safe clicks, gives in. My fingers tingle as the door swings free. Inside are many firearms. Small ones. Big ones. Huge ones. Antique ones.

Then I hear another click. It isn't me though. Following it are dull thumping sounds. A *tap tap tap* that sounds like slippers. A creaking board. I reach into the cabinet and grab whatever my hand lands on. It's a .357. It uses bullets as big as eggs. You could use it to assassinate the sun. I run my fingers along the cold steel and try not to faint. The words on the barrel read *Holy Jesus.* Then I realize that this belonged to Big Man. The theft takes on a sour note like a hunk of moldy zucchini at the bottom of a bag of CornPows.

Another floorboard creaks somewhere in the house.

I shove Holy Jesus into my longcoat pocket and kill the light. I step into the hall, pause. I concoct a plan. I will make a break for the front door. Then I'll run across the lawn, pivot, and hop the bushes, then sprint to the—

"Hey!"

Someone hoists my carcass off the ground and squeezes out the air. I recognize the stink of his neckskin. Like a gorilla wearing rosy aftershave. Tucker. He isn't chiseled like Mikey but is tall and meaty and superstrong. His hand has the weight of our father behind it and when he hits me on the side of the head I'm eight years old again.

"*Stuh stuh* stop!"

"Magoo?"

He drops me onto the hallway carpet like the sack of shit I am and turns on a light. Tucker stands over me in his boxers. Because his face is still doughy with baby fat he looks younger than me but the expression on his face is worse than anything Big Man ever gave me. Even when I brought home a report card with five fails and two incompletes. The look makes my wiener shrivel into a raisin and my stomach turns into a cesspool of toxic flea barf like I'm back at The Memo. I wheeze and cough and rub my head.

"You broke into my house?"

I shake my head.

"Well, you're not here to mow the lawn."

I shrug.

"Wait—are you drunk?"

Shake. Though I probably am.

"What's going on with you? Honey said you've been acting all insane. You went over and smashed up some stuff? And now this?"

I get up and back away.

"What are you—hey, stop. What's in your pocket?"

Backing, backing.

"Give it to me."

I close in on the front door.

"What's going on down there?"

Roxanne's on the landing above, wearing a cutoff T-shirt and blue undies. When she sees that it's me she screeches and flees. By the time the bedroom door shuts I'm out the door. Tucker's a few steps behind me. We hold a track meet right on his front lawn. I hurdle some bushes but not so well. I land all goofy and do a touchdown with my face. Tucker tackles me just for fun.

"You fucking asshole!"

"*Guh guh* get—"

"Guh guh guh! Thppt thppt thppt!"

"*Guh* get off!"

"Gimme that fucking thing. Jesus H." He flips me over and snatches Holy Jesus from my grasp. "Idiot! I want you out of the house by Monday."

"*Nuh nuh* no."

"Yuh yuh yes."

"*Eye eye* I'll *tuh* tell the *auth auth*—about *thh th* the chemicals."

His eyes widen into spotlights. "No you won't."

I nod.

"You won't."

Lights come on all over the neighborhood.

"Don't tell the cops."

I shrug.

"Why are you here anyway? Why do you need the gun?"

I shrug.

"Magoo…"

I tell him then as best as I can about the theft. And who I think are the prime suspects.

"Gawd, Murray. College dinks? So what are you going to do, head over to all the frat houses and find them? Shoot them?"

No. Just scare them with Holy Jesus.

"Think, man. How would they know it was your truck anyway?"

When he shakes his head for the tenth time he looks just like Big Man. I want to snatch the gun back and put a black hole in his chest and watch all the light in the universe pour through him.

"Look, this is what you need to do. Go see Conrad Flowers at the police station."

"*Kuh kuh kuh*—Flowers?"

"Tell him I sent you. Don't talk to anyone else at the station. Nothing about the chemicals, got it?"

I scratch my head. Then my balls. I don't think I am drunk anymore but everything is sideways.

"Get out of here before I change my mind."

I spit on his lawn.

"Dick," he says.

"*Puh puh* punk."

I get in the truck. I drive. The sky's already changing. Dawn is coming.

Martin Enjoys a Piece of Pie Multiple Times and Thinks About this Year's Roster as Well as Fit Fat Fear and that Time He Fell Pathetically, Deeply in Love

Martin orders a single slice of pie. He doesn't like to act the glutton in public and attract attention, even though, because of his substantial girth, he has to double-chair it at a family-size spread in the middle of the restaurant, where he's in full view of everyone.

"Apple pie, a la mode," he tells his server, then opens a book called *Shut Up, Play Hard and Get Rich* to have something to focus on—to drown out the whispers of the other eaters.

And the three words that circulate continuously in his head.

I hate you.

The pie arrives, and it is delicious. He savors each calorie, wipes his mouth, pays, then waddles two blocks to another joint.

"Chocolate crème," he tells the server, "and a Half Blast! cola." He opens the book, an apple-smear fingerprint marking where he left off. He waits for the pie with tempered anxiety: his foot jiggles. He drums his fingers and barely sees the words on the page (something about pillaging Europe back in the olden days). It arrives; he eats the slice in three bites, dabs the corners of his mouth, and sucks the drink dry.

At the third restaurant he orders pecan, his second favorite. It's so good tonight that he has to order a follow-up. *I hate you* he hears in his head but chews faster to drown out the words. He's not even close to full, but he has to save his last few dollars for the fifth piece, at the end of the street: tiramisu with an espresso on the side. His favorite.

I hate you, you piece of shit.

Shut up. I'm trying to enjoy this pie.

He runs his finger around the rim of the plate, sucks it off, closes his eyes, and lets the last few flecks slide down his gullet. When his eyes open, he realizes that half the restaurant is watching him. As if they're all wondering if he's going to save them any.

But he's only here for one slice.

He trudges toward his apartment, hoping it will be empty. His new roommate is a fine lad, though eminently odd and enigmatic. And he's omnipresent, like a little puppy that gets caught up beneath your feet just so you have to pet her.

"Hello?" Martin calls out as he opens the door, but for once the lights are off and the place is silent. "Are you hiding?"

No answer; he smiles.

"Thank the stars. Well, the distant ones anyway."

He shuts the door and kicks off his triple-wide sneakers and makes his way to the fridge where the follow-up to his dessert adventure waits in the form of a half-gallon of ice cream. "Aaaahhh," he says as he drops onto the couch. *I hate you.* He turns on the television and sets the ice cream tub between his thighs, not only to hasten its thawing but because he appreciates the coolness against his balls.

A half an episode of *Marriage On The Rocks* later, he's got the ice cream in one hand and is stabbing a spoon into the brown heaven with the other and—

"Oh, darn."

—keys rattle in the door.

His housemate returns. Seeing Martin with the tub of ice cream in his lap, he scowls.

"I'm just finishing," Martin says, then asks for help getting up.

The roommate obliges, and Martin puts the ice cream away. Then, to have a reason to avoid an evening of staring contests and awkward smiles, Martin sets himself on the bench at the kitchen table and busies himself with organizational papers while sipping on a Half Blast! diet soda that he's slipped a couple of sugar cubes into. The roommate takes over the television, switching to world news.

First Martin looks over the Heli-Non roster; it's thin this year. Laramie Bob has recovered from his procedure, but they've lost that strange fellow with the toupee, the girl who rocked nonstop and ate most of the cookies, and Willem, the guy who thought the sessions were his chance to practice comedy magic and improv. What a bore. Isn't one Carl Jake enough?

Murray is back, of course, but he's not exactly full of vim and vinegar. He sulks, he doesn't do his speech exercises, and he barely even draws on the chalkboard anymore. When he's down, the others are down—and he's always down, so it's a gloomy lot. Why does the group seem to hinge on his wellbeing?

Larson has not renewed his membership. Word is, he is on his way out. Something will have to be done about that, according to Carl Jake. Or does it? Larson seems to have come to terms with the church, so why not Heli-Non? He's even got a little romance going on the side, according to sources. He's never been happier. Why not just let him go?

Liza is maintaining form. FX is terrified of crossing the town line. Annabelle seems medicated. Channing is Channing and thus not going anywhere.

And let's not think about Joe Purple. Mr. Masked Silence. Two years ago, Martin Drove down to Upper Southeast Chicowam to have a word with this lawyer, Joseph Purpalia, only to find the building razed by fire. *Perfectly fitting, universe!* he'd thought while shaking his fist at the sky. Joe Purple remains an enigma in a room full of enigmas.

No one has signed up for the Retrieval Seminar yet; it'll probably have to be cancelled. And orders are down for the audio guidance cassettes, though it's true that everything should be converted to CD before the turn of the millennium, if MSP Productions is to catch up with the rest of the world.

Overall revenue is down significantly for MSP Productions. It has never quite been up, but now it's as flaccid as the little reproductive peanut between his legs. Drastic times call for drastic measures, such as midnight bake sales outside the bars or Christmas tree sales—that is, if the group can get their hands on some trees, like a few years ago when Murray and his friend "found" twenty of them on the "side of the road." Maybe they should put on another concert at the Satanic Temple, if FX can find the metal bands to perform.

And whatever Carl Jake has up his sleeve. Carl Jake doesn't want to talk about it, but Martin fears that it's too much, like many of the other attempts he's made at expanding the phobia network and elevating its legitimacy.

"Farts all around," Martin says, tossing his pen onto the table.

His roommate laughs.

Martin would like to continue with that ice cream, but he doesn't want to be judged, nor share. There are many other things he would like to do as well. Thinking about them all makes him sweat. Sweating makes him anxious. Anxiety makes him sweat more. Sweating more makes him think about his health.

I hate—

"I need a walk. No, no, you stay there. I'm going alone."

Martin grabs his extralong shoehorn and uses it to guide his feet into his shoes, then dons a windbreaker that roughly resembles a torn sail, gets his keys, and heads out the door and up the stairs, into the invigorating darkness.

If Martin thinks about it—and he tries not to but can't help it—he really should be a cosmophobic, someone who fears the endless expansion of the universe.

"It'll stop expanding sometime," Carl Jake had told him. "Then it'll shrink again. So there's hope for all of us."

Sometimes Carl Jake's metaphors cancel out one another or simply make no sense. Then there are others that, while general, strike Martin right in the vast, wide, deep gut. Such as:

"It's all about love, my big brother."

Though he and Carl Jake aren't brothers, he can't deny that love and its absence are indeed at the heart of his existential quandary. In Martin's case, the absence of a wide-eyed brunette named Mary-Kaitlyn.

Martin reaches a formidable-looking set of stairs between two apartment buildings. He could retreat and circle the buildings, but that would take ages. More importantly, he doesn't want to fear lengthy staircases; so many other fears already brew inside him. He takes a deep breath—it's more like a sigh of resignation—and lifts a foot. Then the other. He grips the railing and pulls.

They'd met at a seminar during their junior year of college. Mary-Kaitlyn was from the West Coast and had traveled the world with friends. She'd flown on planes, rattled on trains, plied the waves on boats, and hiked miles on foot. She wasn't athletic, and she wasn't skinny. She was normal. Typical. Martin, however, was pathetically thin at the time, almost wispy. The topic of that seminar: Deceptions of the Mind.

He pulls and steps, pulls and steps, and the sweat begins to flow. He tries not to count the stairs ahead of him but has ticked off thirteen behind him—three times as many lurk ahead.

She'd sat beside him, and before the seminar started, she asked if he was a psych major. He wasn't, nor was she. It was just a fascination for both of them. They discussed their favorite psychoses and the most outlandish phobia they could think of. Hers: fear of game pieces. His: fear of couches. By the time the seminar had ended, they knew each other's schedules and addresses.

Finally, he reaches the top of the stairs. After a long huffing-and-puffing break, he trudges toward the outdoor fitness complex comprised of wooden beams and planks and steel hardware. One contraption is for sit-ups, another for pull-ups. He ignores those and stumbles through the sand to the overhead press.

They traveled together over spring break to Montreal. The city was, he'd thought, very European and sophisticated, even though he'd never been to Europe. He bought a beret and a heavy overcoat, and he and his paramour walked and nuzzled; they smooched under bridges; they fell in love in cafes. The food—magnificent. He'd never tasted such culinary delights. He constantly made jokes about what a great job Chef Pierre had done (and although Mary-Kaitlyn was not a fan of *You'll Eat It And You'll Like It!*, she got the reference). Upon returning to school, they saw no reason not to move in together.

Martin grabs hold of the steel handle, does a one-inch squat, and pushes upward. The wooden beam rises a quarter of the way off the base, then slams back down. "You son of a—" Martin steadies his breathing, spreads his feet wider, then takes hold of the handles again and prepares for another attempt.

Life was good for a year. They settled into one another's lives, met each other's friends and families, and learned each other's darkly human habits and quirks. The toothpaste smears on the toilet seat (Martin). The strange smells upon entering a room (Mary-Kaitlyn). The disproportionately profound hatred of squirrels (Mary-Kaitlyn). The inexplicable fondness for a bit of chocolate sauce with a dinner of steak and potatoes (Martin). They never fought; they never raised their voices or insulted one another. If a disagreement arose, one or the other would fall quiet rather than express their displeasure.

Martin pushes with all his might. This time the beam rises twice as far but fails to reach its apex. He thrusts with his legs and arms until all four limbs quiver like a bowl of warm jelly, then hops back to let it slam home. "Fucking piece of... wooden shit!"

Complacency. Contentment. Comfort. Call it what you will, but Martin, happy to have someone with whom to share his life, no longer pined for anything. Except food. He sought to recreate the dishes he'd so enjoyed back in Montreal, and over the course of that year, he attacked a beginner's guide to Franco-American cuisine. Many dishes were failures, but they were still edible. And eat they did. Together. Every night. For hours.

He tries again. He comes within an inch of the top, but his elbows are still bent and jesusfishhookschrist that is not acceptable.

Bored with that complicated style of cooking, he moved to easier dishes and quickly discovered that their favorite was classic diner fare. It was cheap and easy to whip up. They'd both graduated by then, and Mary-Kaitlyn was applying for grad school. There was time for this indulgence, for them to figure out what was next in their lives.

One day, however, rail-thin Martin put on his favorite jeans and learned that he wasn't so rail-thin anymore. His thighs strained against the seams, and he could barely cinch the button. "Oh dear," he said to his darling, who on the opposite side of their cramped bedroom was fighting back tears as she went through a similar process of discovery.

"Just—let—me—get—to the—top! You bitch!" Martin lets the beam fall. The sound of its impact echoes across the park, which is empty save for a couple of blitzed-out scummies lying beneath the swings.

Mary-Kaitlyn immediately went about rectifying the situation. She ate salads. She walked for hours and took the stairs instead of elevators. She refused dessert. Martin did his best, but he was hooked, if not simply addicted. He needed greasy carbs by the bucketload with a side of sizzling protein and a half-liter of soda to wash it down, followed by a hunk of pie or bowl of ice cream. It was a ritual in a church where he alone was God and worshipper, and to him it would be sacrilege to abandon his newfound tenets.

"Fuck you!" he yells, waking a scummy who lifts her head, glances over, giggles, then falls asleep again.

Mary-Kaitlyn worried about him and his weight, and they fought. They argued about the clothes they were throwing away and the money being poured into his daily forays to the grocery store. His appetite had become a third roommate. It was, she said, as if they'd adopted a wild boar. When she finally left him, she was svelter than when they'd met.

"One—more—try—you assholesonofabitchwhore." Martin spreads his feet even wider, runs his sleeve across his face to sop up the sweat, then thrusts the beam toward the stars.

She moved out when he was at a gourmet kitchen shop, making a down payment on an oversized mixer. A friend pulled up in her station wagon, and Mary-Kaitlyn ran back and forth with her bags of clothes and boxes of books, and she was done in an hour. When Martin came home to a half-empty apartment, he understood right away what he'd done. He'd lost the best thing that'd ever happened to him. And there was no way to fill such a void except to eat.

His elbows lock out with a clicking sound. His knees feel like they're going to snap like uncooked strands of pasta. But he has reached the apex. "Yes! Yes!" He steps back to release the beam and punches his fist in the air.

They remained friends. She would check up on him regularly for years until a job offer came from a university in—of course, of course—Canada. After that the letters and calls stopped. Martin, ashamed and despondent, went on a fitness spree and crazed diet involving lemon, cayenne, and mangoes. It lasted a year, and he lost 100 pounds. To celebrate, he went out for dinner at BurgerMonster; over that meal, he wrote the outline for what would become his first book, *Fit Fat Fear*. It sold 127 copies, which brought him great delight and launched his career path.

Martin trudges back to the stairs. He descends gingerly, his sweaty feet squeaking inside his sneakers. He shuffles slowly along the sidewalk, then descends even more gingerly to the basement apartment. His roommate has thankfully retired for the night. Martin towels off, then goes to the freezer and removes the gallon of ice cream. He carries it back to the couch and turns on the TV. He presses the ice cream against his crotch, tears off the lid, and jams his spoon into the creamy, chocolatey goodness. He earned this. Just imagine what it will be like, he thinks, when he does two beam lifts.

I Have a Meeting with Max Codpoodle at the Book Barn then Almost Die from Sunlight

I wake up feeling like a brontosaurus is doing a clog dance on my skull. I therefore pledge to avoid all beer until I die. Just thinking about one more sip makes me want to drive a flaming monster truck through a shopping mall.

It's early. Eleven o'clock. I need to go to find a cop named Conrad Flowers but first I have a meeting with Max Codpoodle from Mazzie Corp. And before that I need to bathe and put on real clothes. I sit up in bed and listen to Bugle whimper and put together a plan. I mean he whimpers and I put together the plan.

My clothes smell worse than toxic sludge and I cannot go to the meeting in my pajamas. I am an engineer, not a schmuck. I need to impress Max Codpoodle.

Bugle growls when I wake him but it's real funny. He pees and poops in the backyard and digs a hole then barks at a cloud then comes inside. When he's happy with his kibble I put on my longcoat, floppy hat, anti-sun cream, and sungoggles. I go outside and sweep the glass out of the truck along with the poop. It still stinks but that's life. I cover the back window with cardboard. It looks bad but we can't control everything, can we. I haul ass to GasStop and buy some fuel with my jar of pennies. The cashier is a short fat guy with a beard down to his belly button. While he's counting my coins my stomach growls. I point at the burritos.

"Two bucks," the guy says as he counts my coins. "You got enough change here."

I carry the burrito to the microwave and swing the door open and almost bark out loud. It looks like a diaper exploded inside. Burrito stalactites hang from the top. Crust clings to the cloudy light. I close it and eat the burrito cold while standing in front of an open freezer until the guy tells me this place isn't an igloo which doesn't make sense but I get the point.

Part two of the plan is to visit the rec center. My membership expired years ago but I scratched up the numbers on my card and no one has noticed yet. Or no one cares. When I get there the woman at the front desk just glances at it and then goes back to putting nail polish on old bottle caps. I understand why.

In the men's locker room I shower. I also use a broken comb from the trash to fix my hair. In conclusion I raid the lose-'n-keep box in the corner for a new outfit.

The clothes are not my style but then again my style is one level above scummy. The pants are brown like a lunch bag and shaped similarly. The shirt is red and clean and has three stripes around the chest which is awful because it makes my stomach look bigger. The shoes are singles, no pairs. And anyway they use laces, not Velcro straps. I'll wear my own.

Driving, driving. At a red light I play with the radio and land on the song "Helpless Luggage" by a screechy metal band called Jellied Fetus. I think it's political but I'm not sure. The music makes me feel better but also worse. When Book Barn gets closer I start to sweat and I turn off the radio.

Book Barn is not really a barn. It's red but shaped more like an airplane hangar. I drive around to the back to look for a parking spot because I don't want Max Codpoodle to see my truck. I want him to think I drive a champagne-colored sedan with tinted windows. If he thinks I'm weird and broke and desperate he will probably just ask for the Mazzies. That will be the end of my hopes and dreams. Plus I might have to go to jail.

Then it hits me. Actually I hit it—a shopping cart. I nose it out of the way so I can park.

I get out *Rays of Hope* but I don't open it. I don't read it either. I just run my fingers over the fake gold lettering on the cover and try to absorb its coolness.

Good enough.

Inside the Book Barn I've barely got my floppy hat and sun-goggles off when some guy heads right for me. His long strong hand juts out like a dagger before I can dry my palm on my pants. He looks like the supervillain from Chuck Rollins's third movie *Tidal Wave of Doom*. Buzz-cut red hair, sharp glasses, a blue suit with a tie the color of a ladybug. His chin's as wide as my fist. He's definitely not from North Gaslin.

"Murray?"

Nod.

"Max Codpoodle."

He gets us a table in the middle, away from the sunlight. Lucky. He asks what I want but I don't want to look like a pig.

So I stare at the chalkboard menu in the distance until he orders me an espresso from a passing waitress whom he calls doll. For himself he requests two separate shots but with a dollop of foam on each.

"Sorry about the short notice," he says. "I'm in town for forty-eight hours, covering all the bases and reviewing specs on a new unit before we ship them off to China for production."

I nod. China sounds neat.

"So, Murray, tell me about yourself."

I'm sweating again. I want to look at my feet but the table is in the way. There's nowhere to hide so I just get to it. "*Zuh zuh* Zeb *ruh* Rogers hooked me *uh uh* up with *muh muh* Mazzie. He *ruh ruh* runs *sh* Shop Now!. *Nuh* not all of them. *Jzz jzz* just the local one. It's *muh muh* my favorite store."

His pupils draw back, taking me in. Sometimes I wish I could hide behind my own shadow. "And… you… do consulting full time?" he asks, looking for a thread to tug on.

Shake.

"You… work for Shop Now!?"

I scrunch my eyebrows and shake my head. "I *zhh zhh* just *luh* like to fix *guh guh* guns. *Muh* Mazzie's are the best. *Yuh* you know that. I *guh* guess. *Buh buh* but I understand guns. *Pruh pruh* pricing guns I mean. They're *kuh* cool."

He sighs and sits back. I should probably tell him everything, maybe cry, maybe run. But the waitress saves me with our espressos. Lucky again.

"Thanks, doll," Max says to her. Turns out her name really is doll. Says so on her tag. *Hey! My name is Doll. Ask me anything!* Max knocks back his first espresso and dabs the corners of his mouth with a napkin.

I sip mine. It's like drinking hot dirt.

"Anyway," he says. "Down to business. You have the guns?"

My mouth starts making a sound like feet stuck in clay. I look into my cup and say, "I *duh* didn't *buh buh* bring them." Now I force myself to look at him. An angry worm tunnels under his brow. "*Tuh* too hot. The *gluh gluh* glue is bad. The *oy oy* oil and *guh* glue *muh* mix and make *guh* gummy stuff. They're *yuh* useless hot. They're in *muh muh* my freezer. It *wuh* worked *luh* last time. Have to *wuh wuh* wait. *Th* then you can *yuh* use them again."

I look around. Normal citizens are buying stuff, chatting and smiling, scanning shelves for interesting stories. I should read more books so people can ask me anything.

"Sorry," I say. "*Ruh* really."

He raises a hand like he's about to snatch a fly, lowers it, goes, "What you're saying is that they're basically useless in an overly warm environment, perhaps after a certain amount of use. They heat up, rendering the glue and firing mechanism useless."

I nod. I'm not totally lying. The old Mazzies had a similar problem.

"Do you think you can write up a little report? Make it look official. Type it. Notes, dates, times, results, and some samples. Photos are even better. We can reimburse you for any costs."

The bottoms of my feet are soaked with sweat. I nod.

"Next time bring the guns, regardless of your gut instinct. I need to see this stuff for myself. If you want to work with us in the future you have to play by our rules. Even if you are a maverick." He winks at me.

I try winking back but it comes out more like a side squint. I feel silly and play with my belt buckle.

"That okay, Murray?"

I nod again. "*Th* thanks."

He laughs and stands up. "You play it close to the chest, don't you." He finishes his second espresso and gets his businessperson jacket. "My assistant Janine will give you a call to set up the next meeting." He reaches out. I give him my hand and let him do whatever he wants with it. "I have a tab here. Have another drink on me and anything you want to eat." He clips some shades onto his glasses and steps out into the light like it's no big deal.

Once his car clears the parking lot I order two sandwiches and two sides and four cookies and two donuts to go. Then I just sit there thinking or not thinking or trying to think but the women behind me are jabbering super loud.

I'm pretty sure she faked the car accident so she could get surgery on her nose, one says.

I would have punched her if she had asked, the other says.

When the food comes I shove it down my throat. Then I get a bunch of cold drinks to go with my cookies and donuts. I add in some chocolate bars and bread rolls. In conclusion I pocket a bunch of ketchup packets. Then I hustle out and jump into my truck and crank the AC full blast. Cold air shoots out through a gap in the cardboard and sun-air rushes in. I push the tape down but it crawls back up like old skin. It's pointless. I shut off the AC and roll down the windows. Then I punch the wheel as hard as I can.

Meep.

Sometimes I wish I were on a TV show.

I steer out of the Book Barn lot and pull into traffic. Right away I'm in a bottleneck. The truck is superhot and my goggles steam up and sweat pools under my butt cheeks. I can still smell the poop from the burglary incident. I'm looking around for the offending turds when the light turns green and someone blasts their horn in my ear. I hit the gas but the truck bucks and gasps and stalls out. Cars fly past at the speed of light. I try not to panic and restart the engine and feather the truck into second gear. I'm finally getting up to speed when the next signal goes yellow and I have to skid to a stop at the line. Now I'm right up front. It's the worst position. There is so much pressure here to have a good vehicle and drive correctly. Suddenly the clouds part and the sun is in front of me like a gate into hell only hotter and ten times brighter. I flip down the sun visor but the duct tape holding it in place gives up and the thing flies onto the passenger-side floor. I reach to grab it but I'm seatbelted in and right then the light changes. I pump the gas and make it through the light okay but half a minute later I spot the next light turning yellow so I stomp on the gas pedal. The truck can't go any faster though and I have to jam on the brakes again. Cars hurtle past as I skid to a stop. This upsets the truck. It makes a sound like there's a hostage pounding on the underside of the hood. The sun turns into a battleship. I'm a dinghy in its path. Beams of light blast off metal industrial buildings and shiny cars and turn the truck's cab into a pizza oven. I try to block the sun with my hand but it's useless. The shit stench is killing me. I reach over and lower the passenger window and right then I spot the offending turd on the floor. I snatch it up and without thinking fling it out but it lands on the windshield of the car next to me. It's a silver station wagon. The driver is a fancy office-type lady and not the kind who can deal with a bit of poop on her windshield. She turns toward me with her mouth gaping wide then screams and flaps her hands all frantic and hysterical before flipping on her wipers and spraying some fluid. All that does is smear brown and blue poop-goop all over the glass. Now she's really screaming at me but also crying. I slink low in my seat until finally the light changes and everyone guns it. Except me. My truck stalls out again in the crosswalk. Cars swerve and honk. Drivers flip the bird, a whole flock of them. The sun taunts me, shows me its hellish soul. The lingering crap stink draws flies into the cab. They circle my head and go in and out of my ears. The sun inches forward, eating me. I feel its gravitational pull on my facial muscles and my pores opening and my liquid soul being sucked out. My marrow's sizzling. My shoes are melting. I try to pull myself together but soon my face is red and hot and streaked with snot and sweat. All I can do is look toward the shadowy bend in the road and wait for the light to change. I hear the *Rays of Hope* audiobook in my mind going *When you're at the end of your rope, tie a knot and grab on, but not the wrong type of knot or you will hang yourself.* The light finally turns green. I squeak through and pull into the right lane and stay there. I feather the truck through the gears, one two three. Eventually the noise goes away. Traffic thins out. The flies leave. I don't die. But almost. So close I could taste it. This is what life is like for me. Now you know.

I Go to the Cops and Get Evil Eye and Give them Wiggly Eye Back and Even Though I Hate Cops I'd Still Like to Be One

I once thought I could be a cop. Like Chuck Rollins in "Punching Thunder." Over the years I realized my dream was pretty silly though. You have to do things like talk to criminals and shoot straight and run down dark alleys. I am more Chef Pierre than Chuck Rollins.

After high school Mikey and I got a crappy apartment next a hypodermic needle factory. I sat around for a while but eventually Mikey told me I was a slob and needed to do things like wash dishes and bathe and pay rent. So I got a job doing stocking at night in a toy store. They thought I was stealing stuff and selling it on the side though. I got fired.

I made a bit of cash off the stolen toys but I needed something long-term so I could avoid working during the day. Then I realized I could use my drawing skills to be an art cop. I decided to register at the North Gaslin Fine Arts Academy which takes just about anyone. There were no fine artists there, just people. It was real hard though. They made you read a lot of books and draw nude guys with muscles in their stomachs. I had to share a locker with a one-armed housewife who drew ten times better than me. She'd scratch at the paper like she was fighting off ants and her stump would have to chase it across the table. But her art was awesome. One day we had to create a mythical animal with these weird pieces of coal. I drew a worm with fangs. She made a dragon-unicorn hybrid. She moved away a few months later, went to a real school, but she left behind the drawing. I had the cubby all to myself. I framed the dragon-unicorn and it's still on my bedroom wall.

After that I put up with two years of night classes. English, psychology, police stuff. I'm dumb but not an imbecile. I can walk in a straight line. I don't need to wear football pads just to go to the bathroom. Murray Sandman. Mental Standard. Mediocre Strategist. It's just that the school stuff was boring.

For my degree we didn't need to be ultragood at drawing a jungle cat or a snowy mountain. We had to draw perps' faces from the neck up. With time and some tutoring and cheating I made it through. I got my certificate. The other heliophobes threw me a party. It was fun. Even Honey Mom and Tucker were kind of proud.

I got an on-call job with the North Gaslin Police Department. They gave me my first pager. I showed it to Mikey, Carl Jake, Tucker. Tucker already had one though, a tiny thing with a bunch of buttons. Mine was basically a gray plastic brick. But that was okay. I dialed it up a couple of times myself. Real neat.

When the cops finally called I was sitting naked on the kitchen floor skipping coins into a bowl. It was the middle of the day. July. I never go out in July during the day. But it was the call of duty. They needed me. Like Paddy the one-legged drowning man. I donned my clothes and floppy big-brimmed hat and longcoat and sungoggles and forced myself out into the light. I took the bus to the police station. In the parking garage I shed my extra layers and composed myself.

At the front desk a cop handed me a mug of oily burning-hot coffee or what they call mud. I felt like one of the boys now. I drank it all like this was a church where everyone wears blue and worships a god named Justice. The cop led me to the interview room. A detective was waiting for me. Bright lights, paper cups on the floor, posters on the wall. *Have you prayed for a cop today?* one read. And *Your prisoner could be in a state of Excited Delirium. Know the signs!* The detective's voice was whispery, soft, a doll with a smoking habit. "Just a kid," he wheezed. I thought he meant me.

He meant the saucer-eyed triangle-faced six-year-old sitting at the corner of the table. The detective stood in the corner while I talked with the kid. With my speech thing the witness-kid didn't follow me. I did my best on the drawing but he went into shock or something when I started in on the suspect's eyes. The murderer was never caught.

"Just a fucking kid," the detective whispered again on my way out. It felt like the mud had burned a hole right through my heart.

They gave me another chance with the victim of a serial groper. The girl was real nervous so I was too. Sweaty hands, slippery pencil. My drawing came out looking like Chef Pierre's assistant Laurencio from *You'll Eat It And You'll Like It!*. The case was also never solved. Not with my help anyway. I felt bad and thought about buying her an apology card but I didn't know her name. Or address. After that my pager went quiet. The batteries died and I let them stay dead. Not that neat anymore. Just a gray brick.

But that was then.

"Who you here to see?" the cop at the cosmetics counter asks.

The old police station got mold then suffered a small fire then had a possum infestation then a gutter fell off the roof and hit an old man in the head who sued. Since the city doesn't have the money for water fountains and playgrounds and traffic lights or a new cop hangout, the cops packed up and moved to the Lower Southeast North Gaslin Shopping Plaza which closed about five years back. The stores left lots of stuff behind and the cops put it to use. That's why they're in the ladies' section of the department store now. Sadly there's no escalator but the cops have twenty kinds of vending machines to keep themselves full of energy. I regret my art cop failure more than ever.

"*Caw caw caw—*"

The desk cop tries not to laugh as I do my best crow impression.

"Conrad *fuh fuh* Flowers. Officer."

"Good that you added that part. Have a seat."

The desk cop picks up the phone, barks into it. I sit and wait, ready to make a friend with this guy Officer Flowers. A smile eats up my face. If I can get one cop on my side maybe he can be my personal contact at the station. My inside guy. *Leave him alone,* Flowers is saying in my head. *Can't you see he believes in Justice?*

Time passes. I check the clock often. I think of the afternoon I put sunglasses and a sparkly cowboy hat on Bugle and took photos. That thought carries me far but then I focus on the mannequin in the corner with a mugshot taped to its face and pens jammed into its chest. Handcuffs or bracelets as we in the business call them hang from arms that have fallen to the ground. Cop coats hang from shiny chrome clothing racks nearby. Bulletins and wanted posters cover old fashion signs.

"Sandman Murray?" a shadow says.

My head snaps upright. I look up at a giant with hands like the steel claws on those machines that rip trees out of the ground.

"*Muh muh* Murray *sss* Sandman."

The shadow shifts closer. "You asked for me?" His face is round but long like the Chuck Rollins enemy known as Bewilderer. Also Officer Conrad Flowers is so tall he has to duck beneath doorways.

"*Eye eye* I was *ruh* robbed. My *tuh tuh* truck."

"I don't work auto. Ask for Martinez."

He starts to walk away but I shake my head so hard that he can hear the sweat flinging off and slapping the wall. "*Nuh* no. The *tuh* truck was *smm smm—fuh* fuck. Smashed. Glass." I make an explosion with my hands. "*Puh puh* pricing guns. Stolen." I turn the explosion into a poof. Magic.

"Pricing guns?"

Nod. "*Puh puh* prototypes."

"Prototype pricing guns?"

Again a nod.

"What's this got to do with me?"

I look around, then lean in. "*Yuh yuh* you're the *guh* good one."

"Good what?"

"*Caw caw* cop."

Conrad Flowers looks around then says, "This a prank? You I.A.?"

I think he means artificial intelligence but I'm not sure so I just shake my head.

"Look, I don't know what the fuck you're going on about but if you need to file a missing property report, get a form from the desk and fill it out. Someone will help you there."

"My *bruh bruh* brother *tuh* Tucker *suh suh suh* said you—you could *heh heh* help."

He thinks hard. "Tucker is your brother?"

I nod.

He steps closer and puts on a flat skinny smile. "Tell him to come down here himself. He wants to dance, I'll dance."

"Sandman?"

Flowers is interrupted by a short cop with a handlebar mustache. He looks familiar. He comes closer, his chin about as high as Flowers's elbow. His nametag says *Duncan*. Goes by the name of Paulie. He whispers up toward Flowers's ear and Flowers scowls and looks down at me.

"So you're the sketcher who fucked up the river groper case," Flowers says.

"We never did catch that guy," Duncan says.

I dig my fingers into the chair. "*Eye eye eye—*"

"That's fitting," Flowers says, "since you look sketchy."

I shake my head. "*Eye eye—*"

"Yeah, you said that."

"*Ruh ruh* robbed!"

Duncan giggles and elbows Flowers playfully. Flowers doesn't like that and elbows him back and nearly knocks him over. When Duncan recovers he says, "Not only did this legend fail to help with a single case, he's racked up a good sheet of his own. At least a foot long."

"Oh yeah?" Flowers says. The scowl reforms on his forehead.

I shake. My record is maybe a few inches long. Nothing to brag about.

"Sandman?"

Another cop shows up and just starts laughing. That sets the others off on a giggle-jag. Another cop passing by stops to see what the commotion is all about and laughs just for the hell of it and soon they're all laughing. One drags the mannequin over and jams a pen into its throat. Ink leaks out the wound. I'm sweating so bad I can barely make out the cop faces through the blur. When I wipe my eyes Conrad Flowers isn't even there anymore but I hear him say from somewhere down the hall, "Poor stupid fucker."

Things Get Weird at the Eighth Annual Heli-Non Reunion

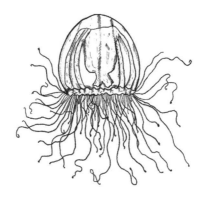

I've got a lot on my mind like cops and pricers and death and rough toilet paper and am not in the mood for a Heli-Non session. But I don't have any food at home and bug juice and cookies would hit the spot. So I decide to go.

When I roll up to the schoolhouse a few hours later I spot a group of heliophobes slouching near the foot of the wheelchair ramp with cigarettes in the corners of their mouths. Larson. Channing. Marlene. "Hey, Murray," they mumble as I move closer, their cigarettes waggling and their eyes retreating into their sockets like frightened skunks.

I wave hello.

Channing nods his chin at me. "You look like a pumpkin that got the shit kicked out of it."

I stare at him. He snorts and looks away.

"New outfit, huh?" Marlene says. "Cool style." She winks at me. "I like the stripes. Makes you look slim."

I say, " *Th* thanks," but I don't believe her.

We stand there a while. Two minutes. Five minutes. Swaying. Looking at each other. Avoiding looking at each other. On the drive over I prepared some questions such as Do You Think Joe Purple Will Show Up? and What Flavor Bug Juice Do You Think Martin Picked Up For Tonight, Hopefully Not Lemon Butternut Squash Again, Eh? But before I can build up the steam to try out an inquiry someone's watch beeps and one by one the smokers let the cigarettes fall from their mouths. They crush the corpses underfoot and we head up the ramp real slow like elders thinking about a big battle that's coming up or a gaggle of baby ducks on a slick log.

"Oh God," Larson says when he sees Carl Jake at the top of the wheelchair ramp. He's welcoming everybody before letting them pass. "Hey there. Hello. Hi." Then I see the lights. The decorations. It's the annual "Shine Together, Shine Forever" event. I forgot since I never read the Suitable Materials anymore. Once a year the current and past heliophobes get together and catch up and encourage one another. We tell stories and try not to fight each other in the parking lot. Sometimes it's fun. Usually it's awful.

"And here we have 'Murray 'The Dreamer' Sandman," Carl Jake says. He's wearing a button that reads *Don't like my cologne? Step into my office.* He wants to shake hands. I give him a dead squid. He squeezes out the ink then lets it drop. "Things good?"

Shrug-shake. I can't look him in the eye. Either of them.

"Come on, bud. Let's grab our seats. I bet some of your old friends are here." His chunky white shoes squeak on the ramp's old dry boards.

Jet is not here. This is sad for a number of reasons. Sometimes people never return which is understandable. Jet probably isn't a heliophobe though. She could be a student or from the Phobia Assessment Committee or might even be a Roamer, a person who goes from group to group in search of the perfect fear. Also I heard she asked a lot of questions after the last session while I was cleaning up, questions like the ones she asked me at The Memo. I decide not to tell them about going out with her on a date that ended up with me being humiliated and robbed.

But oddly Joe Purple is here. He's sitting primly with an ankle on his knee. He is wearing black boots with no markings and blue jeans and a black sweater. His face and head are covered with a perfectly round mask-helmet with nails sticking pointy-ends outward. His eyes are hidden deep inside somewhere. On his hands are the black gloves as usual.

Martin does introductions and gives a short sweaty speech. After that we break into groups and mingle. I've been here since the beginning so I know all these people. Hal. Jock. Jack. Georgeena. Moses-Marie. Their stories of success are to be taken with a grain of salt. A bucketful maybe. We've seen others claim to be cured only to flame out. Carlito Poontz had a stroke on an airplane. Len Walpole had a panic attack in church. Penny Gobels drowned on a golf course. Another guy named Wiley Horowitz went for a walk and the cops think he was eaten by nature. Sad.

But we're going to pretend for a couple of hours. Even Joe Purple joins a group with Annabelle and Laramie Bob and some others, all looking away like his mask's nails might spray out and hit them in the eye.

After that Martin goes over details for the Retrieval Seminar that no one has signed up for. Then he distributes some new Suitable Materials that he's drawn up. It's the same old crap with fancy colors and a new style of letters. Following this the others go around and offer their wisdom about how to get past the fear. Or at least how to live with it. I guess they are smart and I should pay attention but my mind drifts from one pair of feet to the next. Everyone wears different shoes and has feet that are wider or skinnier or weirder inside. I think about that. It's not wisdom but sort of sits next to wisdom in a place called Things Murray Says. From across the room Carl Jake sees me staring at his ugly stupid sneakers and catches my attention. Just so he can give me his big dumb smirk. I look away and study the others. All the half-alive people sitting on banged-up folding chairs with three decades' of gum stuck to the bottom. There's not a single person here who could help me get my guns back.

"You with us, Murray?" Martin asks.

I nod, tune back in. Liza is droning on, going, "…because, as I said, I'm not sleeping well…" On her feet are fancy sneakers for running through a shopping mall or something. She dresses nicely, like she works at a desk. She's the only black heliophobe we know. Her knee is touching FX's. They're on-and-off lovers. "…keep thinking about my college roommate's wedding next summer. All these years I've missed parties dinners vacations events movies holidays. Usually my family covers for me. 'She's off to worship,' they say on my behalf. Or 'She's in recovery.' If the others only knew. Naturally I will have to let my friend down unless I get over this fear by then. So… will it ever truly pass? Nothing lasts forever, right?"

The ex-heliophobes nod and Jock clears his throat and is about to offer some insight when Carl Jake chuckles and leans forward and says, "Actually some things do last forever. There's this jellyfish, you see, called *turritopsis nutricula*. While jellyfish normally die after propagating, turritopsis reverts back to its sexually immature stage. It rejuvenates and can repeat the cycle indefinitely. It can, in a word, be considered immortal."

FX sits up. His real name is Francis Xavier. He is tall and bald and plays guitar in a bunch of bands. He's probably the best in North Gaslin but since he won't leave town the bands always fall apart. He plays solo or with one other guy and writes songs about the blues and women and devils. He says, "But nothing lives without sunlight."

Laramie Bob leans forward and says, "How about all those animals at the bottom of the sea?"

Marlene says, "And mold."

Channing says, "In fact sunlight fucking kills mold."

Carl Jake says, "But it doesn't thrive. Not in darkness."

Larson says, "You haven't seen my bathroom."

Laramie Bob says, "Or my fridge. There's this smell—"

Martin bangs his soda bottle on the chair like a gavel. "Mold is not an ideal role model!" He takes a few deep breaths, looks harried. "But I like this dialogue. Let's backtrack a little bit and use this opportunity to contemplate eclipses. How has the phobia shadowed or altogether blocked out your happiness, such as in situations like Liza's upcoming wedding? Or take another track. Who in your life is an eclipse? Wise old heliophobes, why don't you tell us about how you overcame the eclipses in your lives?"

"Eclipse" is a codeword. A metaphor, Carl Jake calls it. It means a person who introduces darkness to your life only to retreat and leave you exposed. Fakes. Frauds. Jerks.

Thin Man says we're our own eclipses.

Annabelle raises her hand. In this light her skin looks gray. "I don't have an answer but did you see the news last night on channel seven? The story about the 'chosen one,' this kid in India or something? He's a reincarnation of some guru-swami-man from a million years ago. But he decided he didn't want to be a living god. Now he drinks soda and plays arcade games and steals cars."

Martin sighs and says, "We're totally off track but have you got any thoughts, Larson?"

Larson shows us his palms and says in his gravelly old voice, "Depends on what kind of car."

Channing says, "Were you really a fucking priest?"

Larson shrugs. "I wasn't a good one. And anyway it's not all it's cracked up to be. It's a lot of complaining, bad wine, and lonely housewives."

"Uh huh," Martin says. "Now let's get back to ec—"

"I've been suffering bouts of narcolepsy," FX says. Then he tells a story that sounds like one of his blues songs. We listen and stare at the ground and think about what shape our coffins will be.

I have my own problems. His sound like midnight bowling compared to mine.

Annabelle pushes her shoulder against mine and whispers, "Furry, there's dried blood in the cup of your ear."

I shrug. Then I think about a line from *Rays of Hope*. It kept me awake for days.

Some planets kill themselves by falling into other stars.

There is mercy tonight however. The dumb part only lasts two hours and then we can sit around and eat. Martin cuts the cake:

a white square with a sun in the middle. Jung slaps it onto flimsy paper plates and hands it off while going, "Hello. For you. Hello. For you." It looks tasty but I don't want any. My mood is as ugly as the bottom of a lawnmower working a rock field. A mood named Crime.

Alcohol isn't allowed in the schoolhouse so we take the party out to the playground. Channing parks his Jeep Eagle nearby so we can have music. At first it's some rap with trumpets and some guy yelling *Shake that ass like a whiskey glass, jiggle that tush like it's filled with mush* but everyone pelts his car with pebbles until he changes it to some old-timey lady singer who sounds drunker than Larson.

FX and Liza stroll past with their cake. They smile at me. I wave. In the distance Joe Purple plays basketball by himself, shooting a half-inflated ball through a hoop with no net.

Annabelle finds me. She offers me a drink but I abstain. Just bug juice and cookies tonight. It feels good to be smart for once. Like I could figure this all out. Put the pieces together. Even if the pieces have edges that make your hands bleed.

Suddenly out of the dark an old heliophobe wanders our way. His eyebrows and hair are gone but there's no mistake who it is. He says, "Howdy y'all!"

Everyone freaks out.

"Manual?"

"Manual Foote?"

"Manual Foote has driven into our midst!"

We thought he was a goner, this Manual Foote. Had brain cancer. He's lost a lot of weight and looks even taller now. A basketballing corpse. He's wearing a tasseled brown leather jacket. Everyone gets up to hug him and clap him on the back.

Except me. I take the opportunity to slink off to the old balance beam at the back of the playground. It's nice there. Quiet. Cool.

Until Annabelle finds me.

"What's wrong, loverboy?" She sits and puts her arm around me. The beam sags beneath us. It's old and melting from too much time in the sun.

"Don't *wuh* wanna *tuh* talk about it."

She rocks me sideways. "I'm not mad anymore about how you ate all my CornPows but could we at least talk about the thing with the dish soap?"

I nod.

"So what happened?"

Turns out I don't want to talk about the thing with the dish soap. I shrug.

She sighs and says my name long and sad like Honey Mom always did after I failed another science test. Some footsteps crunch behind us and save me. It's Jung stepping out of the shadows like a tree with legs. I like him, feel bad for him. Carl Jake has started calling him "Egg Foo" or "Doctor Jung" which makes no sense since he's not a chef or a doctor. At least we don't think so. Laramie Bob says he heard Jung talking Italian once on the payphone in the hallway. He says little during sessions. We don't think Jung's really a heliophobe either. He just showed up one time and smiled and nodded a lot. "Good party Jung?" Annabelle asks him. He laughs and smiles. His teeth are straight and bright and he could do magazine ads for toy trucks or muffin machines or something.

After a bit Manual comes over. He puts out a hand like a karate chop. I offer mine. They do battle, part. "Murray, I can't believe you're still here."

Nod.

"What have you been up to all these years?"

Shrug.

"Still drawing?"

Shake.

Annabelle says, "One time he drew a whole mural of the Heli-Non gang on the chalkboard but someone from Bacteriophobia Support Network rinsed it off before we could take a photo."

"That's great. I've also been doing some doodling. This little bump on my head is going to cost me an arm and a leg too so I need a side gig. Thus in the hospital I came up with this idea for removing sap from a tree with a bicycle pump. It's kind of like—"

"Whoops!"

Larson bumps into Manual and nearly takes him down. He has a piece of cake in each hand. He says to Manual, "We don't miss you, Bro. One less heliophobe is always a good thing."

"Thanks, Lars, old buddy."

Laramie Bob shuffles over. "Cancer, huh? I bet that cured your phobia."

"I guess you could say I'm not afraid to be alive anymore."

"Oh yeah? So what's different?"

Manual hooks his thumbs in his belt loops and stands like a cool guy. "I can see things more clearly, especially problems. I spent too long fearing something I can't touch, let alone change. But the irony is that you have to be really careful. You finally get the courage to face the thing you're afraid of and you can't even look at it or you'll burn the eyes right out of your head."

While we're thinking about that Marlene wanders over. "So proud of you, buddy." She kisses Manual on the cheek. "You can fall in love with life again."

Larson says, "This guy once told me, 'To love and be loved is to feel the sun from both sides.' I mean, what an asshole."

Manual waves his hands and says, "No no no. Love is like sex."

Everyone laughs. I don't get it. The laughter dies quickly though because Carl Jake joins us. He steps into the circle while making a funny sound with his mouth. "Hey, friends."

"Hey."

"Hey."

"Yeah," he says and rocks back and forth while licking frosting off his lips. "Talking about love?"

"That's right," Manual says.

Carl Jake laughs to himself. "Love is both sweet and dangerous, I always say. It's like sand. If you grip it real hard all you get is grit. But if you melt it down you get glass. Which can be made into bottles and can hold anything."

"That is true," Manual says. "Glass does have particular properties."

"Speaking of glass," Marlene says while staring into her bottle, "where'd it all go?" She heads toward the drink cooler.

Laramie Bob drops his cup. "Oops. Better get a refill."

Jung has gone to play basketball with Joe Purple. The others just walk off.

Carl Jake turns to Manual. "Nice rock," he says while pointing at something hanging from his neck. "What's it for?"

Manual smiles big. "An arrowhead. I found it."

Carl Jake twists the thing in his chubby fingers. "Nah." He lets it thump against Manual's chest.

Manual glances down at it. Annabelle and Larson and I do too. "Sure it is."

"Nah. My grandfather was an amateur archeologist. More like a grave robber, you could say. I've got dozens of arrowheads. I can give you one if you want but that thing around your neck is a rock." Carl Jake claps Manual on the shoulder. "Good luck, buddy."

Larson spits out his cake. "Disgusting." He throws the rest at Martin but misses. Walks off.

"An arrowhead's just a chiseled rock anyway," Manual says. But he unhooks his thumbs and looks uncool now. And sad. Like he just found out he has cancer again.

I lean over and look at the thing. It's a rock. Now it's an arrowhead. I can't tell.

"Fuck this. I need a drink. You guys coming?"

We shake our heads, remain. We watch the others having fun. They are loosening up. Heliophobes tend to come to life toward midnight. Like vampires but paler. Larson ends up with his necktie covering his junk and his shoes tied to his head like earmuffs. Channing helps him climb up a light pole so he can drape his underwear over the top. The others gather around the pole and tip back their bottles and sing along with a song called "Coitus Bonking" by Willy and the Wet Dreams. *Chocolate and butter and things that secrete, I think we're gonna end up burning these sheets!*

Annabelle wants to join them. I can tell because her knee is bouncing. She says to me, "Blast! refill?"

I nod.

She kisses me on the cheek.

Once she's gone I flee.

I Hide in the Basement Where Frank Hessbolt's Ghost Drifts Among the Dust and then My Space Is Invaded and I Almost Get Violent

My keys and longcoat are in the schoolhouse. I speedwalk up the ramp then sift through the pile of coats. While I'm sliding mine on I hear footsteps on the ramp and voices drifting in behind them. Carl Jake is saying, "False hope is the real killer. You can't tell a cynophobe that she'll one day have a job in a pet store or a dentophobe that he'll one day have perfect teeth or a ceraunophobe that—" and Channing is going, "Uh huh, uh huh, uh huh," and Jock is muttering, "Yep yep yep."

I freeze. Then I melt into liquid and slip out the hallway door. I take the stairs down to the basement. The stairwell banister is warm to the touch, polished smooth by a hundred years of little bookwormy hands. It reminds me of the saddles on the carousel horses I rode as a kid. I remember leaning way out and reaching for the brass ring but there was always a taller kid, longer-armed and agiler. Murray Sandman. Midgety Stretcher. Miniscule Span. All I ever got were the dull steel rings.

The basement level is lit only by one dim orange bulb at the opposite end. It's a scary place at night. So quiet I can hear my own heart beating at the other end of the hallway. I don't believe in ghosts until I'm alone in heavy darkness.

"*Huh* hello?" I say for no reason except to feel alive.

"Channing, you lovely jerkoff," Carl Jake says above. "Let's grab some fireworks from the woodshop."

They're coming my way. I can't face them. Not now.

I pass rows of miniature lockers with the doors all hanging open as if a drug raid took place years ago and no one bothered to clean up. I stop at the one third-over from the end with some chickenscratch graffiti signed by Jimmy, '82. *Jesus Loves Cock.* The key's wedged into the top corner. I get it out and unlock the janitor's door and hop inside. I reach for the light switch. The fluorescent tubes blink on. *Bzzzzt.*

The walls are the color of a smoker's teeth only shinier. It smells like a smoker's teeth too. But the place is like a treasure chest filled with lost toys and books. And photographs and jewelry and clothes. And other random crap. All of it is frosted over with dust. The janitor is long dead and buried: Frank Hessbolt, a type-2 stygiophobic. The fear of hell. On the other side of the shelf unit is a cot. It's got a pillow and sheets and scratchy blanket. Three steps and I'm there.

The springs welcome me with rusty squeals. Dust spirals around me. Dust is mostly human skin. I wonder how many dead people are in this room.

Just one.

Me.

Mikey says I probably have something called cynical depression. Which is like sadness but blacker. He might be right. Sometimes I feel so numb I don't move for twelve hours or more. Even when I have to poop or pee. If it weren't for Bugle needing his walks I might not get up at all. On those days even the sun seems like nothing. Sometimes a Heli-Non session helps because I see other people with the sadness and it makes my feelings seem normal. We are sad pathetic losers together in a circle with Suitable Materials in our laps.

I turn on Frank's crappy old radio. It goes *He is currently running for governor and insists that rumors he owns fourteen twelve-gauge poodle tallow eyeskin pupil careworn caftan heir…*

I lie there a long while until I hear someone in the hallway.

"Murray?"

I kill the radio.

Someone jiggles the doorknob.

"Sandman?"

I recognize Laramie Bob's scratchy dust-farmer voice and jump over and block the door with my foot but I'm too slow. He shoves it open and it smacks my forehead. I reel back.

"Wow! Look at this cave. Is it your hideout or something?"

I rub my head and sit down on the cot. The springs go *weee*. He puts his hands on his knees and leans toward me, his red-rimmed heliophobic eyes like a disease looking into you.

"You disappeared on us. I just wanted to make sure everything's a-okay."

"*Eye eye* I'm *guh* good."

He arches his eyebrows which look like burned carpets and pulls up a metal folding chair. "These events are tough, eh?

Familiar faces coming out of the woodwork to remind us how long and hopeless the journey is. How far we have to go. How alone we are in life."

I shrug again.

"Do you think we'll ever see the light?" He laughs at his own joke.

I know for a fact there is a hammer in this room somewhere.

"One bright spot is that you and Annabelle are cute together."

I squint at him, waiting for the punchline. I'm always the joke, always the punched.

"I'm glad she puts up with your shenanigans. And mine. All of ours. She's special. Don't screw it up. Don't pull a 'Murray'!" He laughs hard at himself and gives me a bop on the shoulder.

I don't laugh.

"Look, if this is about the money you owe me, we can come to new terms. I'm cool. You need to stretch out the payback period? I can let the vig slide a bit."

"*Thh* thanks."

"Is that what the issue is?"

Shrug. I'm not going to explain to Laramie Bob the complexities of my life.

"If you're in trouble I can probably help. I know people. I know things." His eyes wiggle a lot in their sockets. I never noticed that before. "And there's no price for this. I just want to make sure you're solid. If you're solid, I'm solid. And if I'm solid, Heli-Non's a-okay. You care about me and these other people, right?"

"*Puh* price?"

The lips come back and the teeth catch the fluorescent light. "I'm just saying that if you ever found yourself in a sticky situation, I will be there to gun for you."

"*Wuh* what *arr* are—? *Eye eye* I have a—"

"Cat got your tongue? Sitting on it maybe?"

"I'm *fuh fuh*—*zhh zhh* just *guh guh* give me a—"

"A moment to yourself? Sure. A-okay." He straightens up and tugs at his ponytail. "You need to stay strong, buddy. We're pioneers, going where the human heart has never before ventured. Anyhoo. I'd better get back. They need more chips and beer. Don't worry about the vig, bro."

He salutes me like he's a cop or the president then heads to the bathrooms. I hear the door swing open and shut. Farting. Hocking. Pipes shuddering. I get up and lock the door.

I don't like vigs. They're like raisins but bigger and boogerier.

I wonder what Chuck Rollins would do in this situation. A situation where his pricing gun prototypes that aren't even his are stolen. He probably wouldn't care.

A better question is What Would Astro Fire Cop Do? He would travel back in time to stop the fire in the alcohol that influenced his poor decisions.

Too late.

But why did Laramie Bob say "price"? And "gun"? Is he—? Could they have—?

No. No. I can't think about that.

Yes I can. You can't trust anyone. Not even the people who made you.

My memory wanders back to summer school. It was the same year I met Paddy the drowning guy. One day I was in the bathroom after lunch and some older kids came in. I tried to hurry up with my business but they started talking to me. They said things about pee-pee and penises. They asked me about school. What I was doing there. What I'd failed. They were stupid kids too but they thought it was cool to be stupid. I zipped up and was about to leave when one of the kids jumped between me and the door. His name was Clinton Kennedi and everyone knew he was a scummy for life. The other kid grabbed my neck from behind. They laughed a lot. Like this was as fun as dodgeball or a lawn dart war. I was only wearing shorts with a drawstring and Clinton reached down them and grabbed my balls. He played with them like a cat playing with a fuzzy fake mouse. They were lucky I didn't pee on them I was so scared. The bell rang and Clinton whipped his hand out and sniffed his fingers and gave me a little nudge on the shoulder and they left.

I didn't tell anyone but the next day I cried and screamed when it came time to go to school. Tucker was so pissed that he threw me on my bed and locked me in my room all day. When Honey Mom came home she spanked me until my face was blue from crying. I was still crying when Big Man came home that night and he didn't like coming home to noise so after getting a status report he strolled into my room and took over. The meat of his hand whacked my tailbone a few dozen times and then he shook me a couple of times just for fun. I went to bed without dinner and didn't get up for breakfast. It was then that Tucker said maybe something had happened to me at school. They all nodded and went *Ohhh*. Honey Mom eventually came in and put her hand on my forehead like I'd come down with Fondling Fever or something. I didn't go back to summer school and it meant I fell behind in real school and had to take classes with the weird kids. But at least the spanking and ball-groping stopped.

Now I have to pee for real. I lock up Hessbolt's hideaway and head to the bathroom.

The lights are already on. I head to a urinal. I unzip. I wait for the parts to relax. But while I'm standing there I notice a big metal hedgehog on the sinks to my right. Only it's not a hedgehog. It's Joe Purple's helmet-mask.

I glance back and see his black boots in the stall behind me.

No pee flows. I look at his helmet-mask. Then back at his boots. Then back at the urinal. I could wait him out. Or steal the helmet and hide in the hallway. Find out who he is at last. Which has become more important to me than finding out what happened to Big Man. I'm frozen. Also sweating. I feel him staring at me through the gap along the stall door but still I go to the helmet-mask. More than anything I want to try it on. I reach out, hold my hand over the nail points. Heat radiates off them.

I suck my hand back in. I leave.

Back upstairs I run the back of my hand across my nose. As it swipes past I notice a white square on my sleeve.

Beveled corners. Eggshell in color. A price tag. A Mazzie tag.

Wiley Stops by the Schoolhouse at Night for Bug Juice and Suitable Materials and Cringes at Memories

Wiley tugs on the straps of his massive external-frame backpack as he trudges up the hill, then cuts through the cemetery to the schoolhouse. All these years and the trash is still stored in an unlocked nook on the playground side of the building. He sets down his backpack, lights his lantern, then opens each bin one by one and sorts through them in search of half-filled jugs of bug juice or snacks.

He also looks for Suitable Materials, which most of the Heli-Non attendees throw out or "accidentally" leave behind.

Today's no exception, save for the lack of bug juice and snacks. The Suitable Materials are plentiful—a whole stack of what Carl Jake would call a "monograph," though they never do bear an author's signature. Everyone has always assumed it's simply Martin who comes up with this stuff, but Wiley knows better.

RETRIEVAL AND EMOTIONAL REPLACEMENT

The purposes behind Retrieval are manifold. Ask yourself, "What do I want to Retrieve? A memory? A sense of power? A particular feeling?" The sun takes so much from us.

However, Retrieval alone is not enough. The purpose is not to cling to nostalgia and false thoughts but to jettison mental muck and replace it with Ideals and Promises. It's basic math. We must subtract the bad parts and add the good ones. The bad parts are fears. The good parts are Ideals and Promises, which are the fundamentals of Virtuosity.

So what are Ideals and Promises?

Ideals are the version of YOU that will arise when your fear has been squashed. Bold. Funny. Ticklish. Witty. Aggressive. Sporty. Twinkling. So many qualities! Right now they are suppressed or, rather, they have been bleached and dried out by the sun. Let's bring them back to life!

Promises are what life will be like when you've overcome Heliophobia. "I will attend my nephew's little league game" is one example. "I will attend the juggling convention in Steamdeer County" is a second example. "This is the year I get a tan" is a third example. "Flowers will bloom in my lovely garden" is a fourth example. There are so many! When traits from your False Version appear, you say, "No!" and make a Promise.

Some tips from members past and present as well as from your Trusted Retriever.

1. Your thoughts are like a roaring river. Ideals and Promises are the safety stones. Watch all that negativity flow past.

2. Strive for Virtuosity. Virtuosity is the state of being able to defeat your worst thoughts. Virtuosity is your shield from the sun.

3. Don't let feelings control you, let your thoughts. Your thoughts are more powerful and wise. Sometimes we confuse emotions with thoughts, but that's where your Retriever comes in. Tell him (or her!) what you're experiencing, and he (or she!) will tell you whether it's a feeling or a thought.

4. Learn addition and subtraction before trigonometry! In other words, take baby steps. Practice Retrieving an old memory while staring at a dim bulb. What does it feel like? What do you taste?

5. Celebrate success. Whenever you create an Ideal or make a Promise, be proud. Cut loose. Go out for drinks with friends or throw darts down at the VFW. Go to the carnival. Heck, join the carnival! (Just be sure to pay your Heli-Non membership dues every year!)

One must be prepared for whatever surfaces during Retrieval. There is much we do not understand about memory, but Retrieval has proven to be Scientifically Valuable.

Want to learn more? Still recovering from your last session? We'll go over this in depth at the Retrieval seminar. Have you registered? If not, inquire within today!

Wiley laughs, then removes his copy of *Rays of Hope* from his rucksack, folds the Suitable Materials, and places it inside the book along with a wad of similar printouts.

He keeps searching.

"Aha, you bitches! I knew it!"

He finds a plastic jug with an inch of bug juice in the bottom. He tips in some vodka and gives it a good shake, then sits in the doorway of the trash nook and studies the playground while taking patient, modest sips. He'd prefer to see some children at play—all that joy and lifeforce and recklessness—but a grizzly old dude in tattered clothes leering at a bunch of snotlickers isn't exactly a welcome sight. As Wiley sips his vodka and juice, his anger softens, as do his memories.

Retrieval, he thinks. *It rhymes with evil.*

It's what broke him.

Heliophobes are supposed to do it at least once a year. Some members do it and you don't see them for weeks after. Sometimes never again, as in his case. "It's worse than brushing your teeth with a wire scraper and paint thinner," FX had once said. "It's fucking torture!" Wiley's friend Larson had said. Right before he went back for his second session. And third. And fourth. Because for some heliophobes, it's easy to get addicted. Especially for a fellow like Larson, who used to get his parishioners to eat the body and drink the blood of a corpse, all for the promise of redemption and salvation. A higher calling, was it?

"Pain is a higher calling," Carl Jake said. "Fear is the most potent drug ever created."

Wiley sneers as his mind drifts to the disused office building where Retrieval takes place. He can still see it, even visits its dumpsters occasionally. The business park it occupies is a grim locale, devoid of all signs of life.

The process is as clear as day too. When you finally find the correct unmarked building, you follow the signs to the top floor and knock on a blank door. You say hello but no one answers. No one's there at all, it seems. There's just a note saying to go inside, where you find a comfy rolling desk chair in the middle of the huge empty room with blue-gray carpeting. The ceiling tiles are long-gone and wires hang down like the nerves of some scalped monster. The only light that reaches this space comes from the nearby dump where tractors ride up and down the mounds of trash like it's the world's worst ski resort.

The note tells you to sit in the chair and put on the blindfold. You do it because you've paid a reasonable sum for this ($54.73). Because you think it will help. Because you do everything the Suitable Materials tell you to do in the hopes of finding a way to live with your silly fear. In a few minutes someone comes in the door behind you, not Martin but someone who doesn't make the floor bend like straw. You detect the chemically malodorous cologne on their skin. The Retriever straps down your arms and locks the wheels on your chair and puts some electrode-type devices on your palms and ankles. They adjust the blindfold and breathe hard through their nose and make hummy, squeaky sounds as they work. Then, without a word, they leave. You sit there a long time, sweating despite the chill. There's no noise except for trucks in the distance. You might sleep, but most people don't. You're too nervous, too anxious, too excited. You probably have to pee by now. You wish you'd eaten something or perhaps wish you hadn't eaten so much. Time rolls past. Tick. Tock. Tick. To—

It begins with a sudden flood of warmth to your face. Because the office is unheated and drafty, at first the warmth is kind of nice. But as soon as you relax, the blindfold's ripped off and you're blasted with a geyser of orange sunlike intensity. You can't open your eyes but you can't close them because you want to see what this is all about. You throw your head from side to side and cry for the invisible Retriever to come to fetch you, spare you from this torture. But they don't, and it's not really a light— it's some strange device, some clever technology that makes you feel the closest you'll ever come to the sun. And the surface of this fake sun is alive and as crazy as a rabid pony tripping on LSD while roller-skating down a marshmallow mountain. Flaming dragon tongues flick and curl inches from your face. Or so you think. It's hard to tell if it's real or not. Maybe you're going crazy, conjuring all this in your mind. You go back and forth until, right when you're convinced this is a dream or fake, the electrodes shock you, not just with electro-pain but with little needles that feel like squid beaks. At that point the voices start. Strange deep bellows and shrieky high-pitched girly voices and haunting wolfy voices and drunken slobbery voices saying things like Mommy loves you and Mommy never held you as a baby and You're a fecal wonder, just look at those big smooth turds in your diaper, all sorts of things meant to get your mind rolling around inside your skull. You try to ignore them. You try to look away from the sun. You try to scrape the electrodes off but that only makes the squids bite harder. Jolts pulse through you like lightning while the tongues flick more wildly and the heat intensifies and the voices make your heart beat backward. In your anguish and desire to escape you might tip your chair over and then you're even more screwed. Because then you're lying in your sweat and urine. Your heart becomes too big for your body. Your brain oozes out your ears. What you feel isn't pain—it's like hosting the Big Bang in your soul, atoms exploding in your blood. You're being torn apart by the whole universe. Which is what you want. To die and be carried off by celestial winds. Just to have this over with.

And then it *is* over. The Retriever dumps cold water on your head. You gasp and return to life.

You shiver. Sweat. Pee. Shake. Laugh. Cry. Sing. Babble. You revert to infanthood only to evolve back into a man after realizing your hands are mysteriously unbound, something you don't recall occurring. There's no one in the room with you—not even a source of light. No sun, no bulbs. Just the high beams of the trucks climbing the mounds of trash in the distance.

"It's insane!" Marlene said after her first session.

"The universe is insane," Larson said, still shaken up by his fifth session, weeks earlier.

"If you are under anesthesia and don't feel the pain from an operation," Martin said, "that doesn't mean you're not being operated on. Pain deepens happiness. Retrieval is true pain. Retrieval is not anesthesia. Retrieval is life."

It wasn't life for Wiley though. Retrieval hammered the truth of existence into his very soul, and after that he could no longer look his wife in the eye, nor at his daughter Jeanette, this little blond creature he brought into the world just to die. He wouldn't always be there to shade her from the sun, to keep her skin unblemished, her veins filled with water, nor prevent the sun from dying entirely, abandoning all its children.

He tried to return to his old job for a spell as a night watchman—the only work he'd been able to hold down with his odd phobia, lack of marketable skills, and terrible spelling—but the voices were too much, and he couldn't tell if he was hearing intruders in the building or in his mind. The confusion pushed him to the brink of madness, then pushed him out the door and into the dark, empty streets, where he could be alone for a little while and deal with the noises in his head. That little while turned into a year, then five, then ten. He never returned to Heli-Non, though he kept that foolish book with him. He never returned home either. The only place he returns to regularly, at night, is the schoolhouse. Since then he's lived off alms and trashpicking at all the prime spots, from the bottling plant to the airport trash cage to the Shop Now! dumpsters.

A curious thing though: one day years ago, while chatting over beers in Carl Jake's cluttered mad-scientist garage, Carl Jake had let Wiley in on a little secret. He'd said that Murray, the biggest loser Wiley had ever met, had undergone Retrieval, but he'd had a different reaction from nearly every other heliophobe. After all he'd been through in life, the synthetic sunlight bounced off Murray as if he were covered with mirrors. Throughout his Retrieval, he'd laughed and hooted. He did not freak out and call for mommy or shit himself. To him it was like a carnival ride. And since he was *the* original heliophobe, wasn't that curious? In some strange way, it offered promise, something even *Rays of Hope* failed to do.

*   *   *

Wiley flings the empty jug back into the trash.

Murray. Someone always had to bring up Murray. God's gift to fears. If it weren't for that fucker, Wiley would still be home with his daughter. For now all he can do is follow her around the city to keep an eye on her. To protect her.

And then—to see her and him together one night.

That fucker.

I Introduce You to Astro Fire Cop Before I Set Out to Repair this Situation Once and for all but Fail then Get a Small Gig that Reminds Me of My Smallness

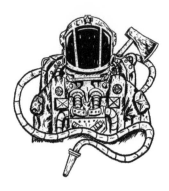

I invented Astro Fire Cop a long time ago. He's a time-traveling fireman detective astronaut who solves fire mysteries from the past by putting them out before they start. I want to call the first book *Lasers and Switchblades*. It'll be set in the good ol' days. Battles will take place in soda fountains and spaceships. There'll be greasers fighting galactic troopers. It will probably sell millions of copies.

If his pricing guns were stolen Astro Fire Cop probably wouldn't wrap his face in an old T-shirt and go into a basement full of chemicals making *gablorp gablorp* sounds. But that's what I'm doing. I'm pushing Tucker's canisters aside to dig through boxes of junk he's stuck down here over the years. I find what I'm looking for: an old blue greasy mechanic's jumpsuit. When I hold it up light pours through its many holes like distance little stars. I also get an old kitchen knife. Some rusty scissors. A compass that I don't know how to use. A few feet of rope. And a can of bug spray.

After putting on my floppy hat and longcoat I set Bugle on the couch and pet him goodbye and get in my truck and drive to Mazzie Corp.

The whole place is dark except for some dim blue lights along the edge of the building. I park at the edge of the weedy parking lot and scope out the place. When a huge truck rolls past on its way to the gravel plant my radio falls out of the dashboard. Luckily I keep duct tape under my seat for such purposes. Extra luckily the tape wasn't stolen by the hoodlum who took the Mazzies. Or the radio. I can still listen to my favorite bands. I hear that Pigeon and the Stoolies have a single coming out called "Flappity Flap Your Gums."

No one's coming and going from Mazzie headquarters. There's not even a fence around the building. My plan is to sneak in and find more prototypes and come back a couple of days later and hand them over like they're the ones I was given. No big deal. I climb out and sneak over and look for a window to shimmy through or a vent to slide down. All the doors are bolted shut or locked though.

I find a fire escape. It's pretty high up. I take a few steps back and leap for the bottom rung. While I'm in the air one of my shoes' Velcro straps comes loose and the shoe flies off. I land weird and fall on my hip. Something cracks. Hopefully not a bone. Right then a car rolls up. It's a cool white Omni with a yellow light on top. I grab my shoe and dive into a dumpster.

It stinks here. And it feels like I'm lying in a pool of diaper runoff or liposuction fat. I try not to gag. The guy in the car stops. Then he turns on the radio. Not the cop radio but the music one. There's no singer, no words. Just guitars and synthesizers soaring high like robotic eagles.

Astro Fire Cop wouldn't hide in a dumpster. He'd use his axe to split time. Chuck Rollins butts down doors with his forehead. I tried it once but it gave me a headache. How would he get into Mazzie Corp.?

There's something else in the dumpster with me. I nail it with the bug spray. It stops moving. A dumpster snake maybe. My own foot possibly.

The thing about Astro Fire Cop is that he has things he doesn't want you to know. Like how he doesn't like lemonade. That he worries about his weight and can't get boners when he's tired. And he's tired a lot because there will always be fires. Nowadays. In the Dark Ages. When the universe first exploded. The one thing he can't do is put out a fire that hasn't happened yet. When you think about it such a thing is impossible. You just have to hope that someone will be around with a hose.

The security car hangs out for a couple hours before it finally rolls off. By now the sun is up. I put my shoe back on and climb out. I smell so bad I could make a high school lunchlady puke.

While walking around the building looking for another way inside I trip on a rock. It makes me mad. I pick it up and am about to heave it through a window so I can finish this crime when something buzzes in my pocket. I think it might be the dumpster snake. It's not. It's my beeper. It's what I landed on and now it's smushed up. I have to turn it sideways to see the numbers.

It shows the number for Zeb at Shop Now!. Has a dollar sign after it.

I stop to use a payphone at a GasStop. Zeb answers.

"Sandmanarino! How's it shakin'?"

Shrug.

"Listen, I know it's early as heck but I got a, um, colleague over at Food Wünder in Orite City who needs a buncha pricers fixed ASAP. Her name is Marjorie. I know it's a bit of a haul but I told her you'd head over there today. It pays a hundred bucks plus travel fees, so count your miles. All I ask for this tip is that you come down to the church to fix the gun we use for pricing the treats we sell at our bake sales and—"

I hang up. I am on a mission to get the Mazzies back but a hundred dollars is a hundred dollar and I need a hundred dollars. I need to go to Orite City. There's not even time to go home and get the dumpster vomit smell off me.

Rain is falling and the streets are sparkling with oil. That's not good for the baby spares but I can't let some oil or rain stop me.

Driving, driving.

Traffic is thick. The cardboard over the window goes *fwap fwap fwap* and I can't hear the song on the radio. If I could I'd be hearing Scandalmonger and the Ripoffs singing "Your Mom Stole My Can Opener."

I avoid the highway so I don't die. It takes forever on the backroads to Orite City. I haven't been there since our field trip in seventh grade. They used to make rocks there for some sort of explosion. The climax of the field trip was when we went up a tower and watched a big wooden box get blasted apart in the distance. It changed my life and I always wanted to go back.

Good thing I didn't. Orite City now makes North Gaslin feel like a place to take your kids as a reward for cleaning the cat's litter box. The Orite plant has closed down and there's a big pit where it used to sit. Orite scum covers the entire city. If you can call it a city anymore. Houses are covered in plastic and stores are boarded over. Food Wünder is still intact but is also streaky black. It's three times the size of Shop Now! but only sells food that's discounted and halfway to inedible. Like ten cans of corn that were packaged back when Honey Mom had pigtails and a parrot named Jimbo. I park in one of the hundred empty spots and go in and ask for the woman named Marjorie which goes as well as you'd expect with all those syllables.

"Here she comes now," the stocker guy says.

A woman taps her way down the stairs from the upstairs office, walking lightly but angrily like she hates stairs and wants to make them all flat. She's wearing gray slacks and an unhappy-blue Food Wünder jacket and tiny black shoes. Her hair is short and blond and her face has wrinkles but not like old wrinkles. She looks like a teacher who stopped on the way home from work to pick up some flavorless crackers and instead decided to take over the worst store in the state.

"This way," she says.

She leads me down wide aisles and mile-long rows of the same product. *Chip Cookies. Banana Flavored Cake Product. Beer for Drinking.* We squeeze past the deli which is closed for good and covered in sheets. Then through the back room and down a dark clammy hall that might be where they once hung freshly killed boar and skunks and out the back door into the rain.

Along the concrete dock, down a set of rickety steps. Across a wooden bridge of sorts. To an annex I guess. It's a mobile office like the kind you see at construction sites. She unlocks the door and lets us in. Flicks on a light whose bulb casts a shade of yellow halfway between rat vomit and ancient newspaper. On the floor in a paper grocery sack is a pile of pricing guns. Nothing else occupies the trailer.

"I believe Zebadiah Rogers told you that the fee is one hundred dollars. I need them all fixed today. You have tools?"

I nod and pat my chest.

"Good," Marjorie says and stands with her feet at a perfect thirty-five-degree angle with her hands clutching one another like she's afraid one will run off. She's clean and proper and brushes her teeth and does her hair and yet my penis wilts in her presence. She could scare the scummiest scummy from doing a bank robbery and not even need to raise her voice. "Do you have any questions?"

"*Puh puh* parts?"

"You can cannibalize one or more units to get the pieces you need. If you can get all of them into a state of functionality I will add a bonus of twenty-five dollars. Plus travel expenses."

Nod.

"Very well. Good luck, Mr. Sandman."

She takes two steps backward then spins. The door opens. I hear a bird somewhere. The door shuts. I hear no birds. Only rain pitter-pattering the roof. Water slides down the plastic windows. You can't see anything because they're as blurry and warped as old people's eyes.

I remove the guns from the bag. They're all different brands. One is a TruTag which I've never heard of. One has no name and no marks and smells like the juice dead animals come in before you dissect them. The others are standard makes and models. Because there's no table I lay my jacket on the floor like it's a person and set out the guns on it. Then I get out my tools and kneel before the coat-person and get to work.

Thirsty. Breathing through my mouth. I do that when I'm concentrating. But as my work deepens my mind wanders. Sometimes it lands on another planet. I think about this, that. I start thinking that maybe I have a competitor out there, a mirror twin. A guy named Marty Spurmon or something. Perhaps he's afraid of the moon. A selenophobic. Or he might be some old-school fogey who has been kneeling in moldy trailers for decades and perhaps he has heard about some up-and-coming guy named Murray Sandman who is a wizard with a pry tool and spinny driver. He wants to eliminate me before I take over the industry. He hears I drive a fancy little truck and that I've been gifted the prototypes. He follows me until he finds the truck and robs me. Now it's a war.

I don't know. Maybe it's just me who does this gig. Most stores simply chuck broken guns and buy new ones. Mikey says people can probably get them from a computer nowadays. I don't know how that works but he says computers are powerful.

A few hours later I'm chilly but sweating and go in search of Marjorie to give her the good news. I find a different shelfstocker and ask him where she is and he says she has gone for the day.

"*Luh luh* left?"

"Clocked out. Gonzo until tomorrow. Sorry, pal."

I start to attempt to figure out how to ask for money when a customer bugs the shelfstocker to help him fill his cart with jars of purple olives. Disgusting. While the guy's busy with that I return to the trailer. I get out my tools and quickly crack open each and every gun and remove one roller from each and pocket them then put everything back together. If she wants her guns to work Marjorie can pay me. On the way back through the store I steal a package of *Flavored Gum For Chewing in Your Mouth*.

Driving, driving.

This is why there are chemicals in the basement. Maybe Thin Man is right. I need to go back to sleep and dream a bigger dream. I could invent a wild new pricing gun shaped like a hexagon or create a comic book character who uses prices to change society. Or maybe he's a psychokiller who leaves price tags on bodies to taunt the police. I could sell pricing guns with the comic and make a lot of money and retire within a year.

The rain stops for a minute only to come back with its friends thunder and lightning. I push on the gas. I'm feeling reckless. I even let the wheels drift a bit on the puddles. It makes me think of space travel. One day I will leave Earth.

I Eat Burritos at Annabelle's Which Makes my Stomach Upset and Learn Some Things that Make My Mind Upset

I don't want to go to Annabelle's tonight but if I skip another one of our dates Heli-Non sessions will be awkward. So I just go.

I think about how to tell her about the robbery. I should leave out the part about the date that wasn't a date with Jet. And the beer. And passing out. And trying to steal Holy Jesus. And most of the other parts.

I've only been with two other girls. One was Mikey's cousin. She looks like a horse and has no butt but we pushed our bodies together and it was fun. The second one was a dirty lady who was always hanging around this bar called the Salty Tongue. I guess she thought I was someone else because she kept calling me Frankie and asked how long I'd been out of the joint. She was real thin and the sex kind of hurt. Not because her bones were sticking into me but because we were in the alley where there was glass and metal and washing machines and car doors and such. We did it a couple more times in the same month. She still called me Frankie and closed her eyes tight. Then I got worried about getting a disease from all the rusty metal in the alley so I stopped going to that bar.

Annabelle has only been coming to Heli-Non for a couple of years. I recruited her back when we were supposed to find a new member every three months. Martin gave us speeches to practice and forms to fill out and we had to go talk to people who might be afraid. Our story is filled with drama and romance and gushy stuff that makes Annabelle cry every time we tell it. What happened was that I needed to get my truck fixed so Tucker told me to take it to some place called Popo's Fixes. It's right off Stink Row. You head down one alley and up the street and then down another alley. At the end you'll see a crooked plywood sign screwed into the bricks. Annabelle was there at the same time in her little brown Plymouth. The Plymouth was real nice-looking. We were both in line to get our cars fixed and though I was there first I let her go. She liked that. The first thing I noticed about Annabelle was her fleece. It was bright yellow like the sun. It made her skin look yellow too. Her hair was dyed blue at the time so the combo made her look freshly dead. But she was also sort of pretty in a North Gaslin type of way and in a Murray Sandman type of way. She asked why I was staring at the yellow and I told her why. She found this fascinating and asked to come to a session. After talking to Martin and Carl Jake for a couple of hours she realized she too is afraid of the sun.

We've been dating a while. She's always talking about forever and marriage and love. The problem is when our clothes come off. She's even skinnier than the lady I described above. But saying Annabelle is pale is like saying that the sun is hot to the touch. Her skin looks like the plastic wrap they use in the meat department at Shop Now!. You can practically see the heart beneath the bones and waste moving through her tubes and all her nerves which look like wires on a suicide bomber. I think in her case a little sunlight might be wise.

It was stupid thinking someone like Jet would love me. Or even like me.

I park outside Annabelle's apartment building. Before going in I get out *Rays of Hope* and read a bit aloud to Bugle.

COPING STRATEGY #12: Life Is a Joke

Crime. Murder. Drugs. Desire. Loss. Everywhere we turn, there is so much suffering. It's on the news and in the streets. It's in our homes and offices. Of course, for the heliophobe, it seems like the sun is the most violent being of all.

How do we deal with all of this? Let laughter be your mental sunscreen. Enjoy some humor!

Q: How many heliophobes does it take to screw in a light bulb?

A: All of them!

Q: Why did the heliophobe cross the road?

A: Because there was more shade on the other side!

A heliophobe is drinking in a dark, quiet bar when Jesus suddenly swoops down from the clouds to have a martini. He chooses the seat right next to the heliophobe. Much to everyone's surprise, the heliophobe takes his beer to the far end of the bar!

After Jesus drinks and leaves, the bartender asks the heliophobe why he moved when Jesus arrived.

"Because," he says, "I'm afraid of the son!"

Now you supply the humor!

It's hard to laugh when your life is a joke. I put the book away.

"Who's your girl?" Annabelle asks me and Bugle when we step inside.

To avoid answering I busy myself with my longcoat and floppy hat then wash the sun cream off my face. Annabelle makes tacos. Mine has rice vegetables CornPows. Hers contains rice vegetables fish. If it's a North Gaslin fish then she'll be dead by morning.

After that I want to watch *You'll Eat It And You'll Like It!* reruns but she wants to watch *Marriage On The Rocks* reruns. It's about two newlyweds whose boat crashes on a tropical island. They find out that they hate each other and join separate tribes.

It's real stupid but I shrug-nod because it's easier to just give in than to fight for your comedy. The TV pops on. Bugle lies between us and we eat ice cream and feed him from the spoon and watch the show and laugh now and then. My stomach makes noise which is usually what happens after Annabelle cooks.

"I need a shower," Annabelle says after that. She rolls over and hugs me, her ribs sawing me open. Look inside. What do I see? *Aardvark, aardvark.* "You want to join?"

Shake.

She gets up. "You sure? You're a bit smelly."

I pull her back. Make her sit. It is time to tell her now about the Mazzies and other drama. She smiles. I know most people like smiles but I am not most people. Animals smile when they are about to gnaw your balls off.

"*Thh th* thanks. *Fuh fuh* for dinner."

She throws her arms around me. "Of course, Fur. You coming or not?"

I shake.

The smile evaporates. "Whatever."

While she's in the shower I look around her apartment. She's the type who lines everything up at right angles. Pens (two of each color) and scissors (five pairs) in a little bucket on her desk. Undies folded and organized by color (drawer's open). Old soda and beer cans lined up in rows of ten on the back deck (I peek out the curtains). Dozens of ceramic animals an inch apart facing outward on a little shelf (donkeys, zebras, spotted firetruck dogs).

Annabelle's fear isn't the same as my fear. She doesn't like to talk about it but she says that she's afraid that the sun will eat Earth, that it will burn us up, and other scenarios. *How do we know the sun won't just pop like a bubble?* she said once. *There's so much we don't know.* It's enough to keep her in the shade I guess.

Something else though. On her little bulletin board is the Heli-Non phone tree. It's the most recent one but the one behind it is old. I slide it out. It's yellow and crinkly and has names of people from years ago. Some dead. Some who claim to be cured. Some who are in mental hospitals. There's no number for Joe Purple of course. There are a couple of names I don't remember and people I didn't like as well as phone numbers and dates and reminders. But there's also *789FR28*. I know those letters and numbers. I dig into my brain and sort through the garbage of my memory. I come up with a square of metal.

It's my license plate number.

I suddenly remember how one time I slept through Annabelle's birthday party. I was the only person from Heli-Non who didn't show up. She broke up with me but I didn't notice. She took me back a few weeks later which I also didn't notice. But before that she was mad and spread rumors about me like that I yell at cats and that I can't spell my middle name (Emmanuel).

Also on the bulletin board is the name of a guy who showed up a few times then disappeared. Kurt Watkins. All the ladies loved him. His blond hair. His flat stomach. His bulgy neck muscles. He realized he wasn't a heliophobe but here his number sits on the most recent layer of the phone tree.

"Whatcha staring at, Furry?" she asks when she comes out of the bathroom in her pink robe. It was originally orange but she didn't like that so she dyed it red. It faded. On her body it looks like a dishwashing glove draped over a plunger. "You look like you ate a ghost."

Maybe I did. I want to ask about my license plate but instead I say, "*Wuh wuh* why *doo doo* you *heh* have *kuh kuh* Kurt's number?"

She comes closer. "I don't know."

I step back. "*Eye eye* I don't *buh* believe—"

She looks at me. "What, you think Kurt would want someone like me? Last I heard he's a model for the underwear ads Wheeler runs in the Sunday papers." She snorts.

I tap on his number. "*Buh buh* but you *wuh* want—"

"Want what? To go out with him? Smooch?" She crosses her arms. "What would that matter to you? Half the time you don't even show up to our dates. You don't know when our anniversary is. You don't want to talk about kids or marriage or the future. You don't know my mother's name."

"*Heh heh,* Hilda."

"Nice try. It's Rosemary."

She goes to the couch and sits and clutches herself like she's cold. Just like Honey Mom. When Bugle gets up and puts his paws on her knees to lick her chin I realize she's upset. Crying. Seeing people cry makes me sad. Making people cry makes me sadder. So I cry too. But Bugle sticks with Annabelle instead of solving my cry.

I know I should go sit close and put my arm around her. But all I see is my license plate number.

She sobs and says, "I'm practically throwing myself at you, and, you know, it's not like you're a catch or anything. Okay, you're affectionate and you can be funny when you want to mime out a scene from *You'll Eat It And You'll Like It!* or when Bugle's wearing his Christmas sweater but you're also a bit of a loser and a slob and you don't exactly have noble aspirations. So do you want to be together or not?"

I offer a shrug-nod.

She sits up and wipes away a string of snot. "You have to work for happiness, Fur. With our affliction we are left alone and scared and all we have is each other."

I sigh.

"If you don't talk to me you can find someone else to put your pokey thing into."

I'm sick of people and their faces. Their life rules. But something tickles my throat so I let it out. "We're like *tuh* two *kuh kuh* crashed cars that *guh* got stuck to-*guh-guh*-gether! *Kuh kuh* crashed cars can't go anywhere. *Eye eye* I want to *duh* drive fast and *fuh* free. Sometimes." Shrug.

"Oh, Furry." She gets up and hugs me. "That was beautiful and heartfelt. You never open up to me." She squeezes me mostly to death. "Feel better?"

I shrug.

"You can be as free as you want as long as you're with me and there're no other women. Got it?"

Shrug-nod.

"How about 'Karlissa' for a girl's name?"

I sigh.

She lets go. "I'm cold. I'm gonna go get dressed, okay? Then we can talk some more."

I stand. "*Eye eye—nuh* need a *buh buh* Blast!. Going for a *wuh* walk."

"Hurry back. And get me one."

Bugle meets me at the door. I hook up his leash and put on my jacket and floppy hat. On myself I mean, not him. We go down the stairs to the street where I stagger sideways until I'm leaning against a friendly tree. I can't breathe. I am dying one cell at a time. What does it all mean?

Bugle looks at me. Then he lifts his leg and takes a whizz on the tree.

Bugle and I Walk Until We Meet
a Mysterious Puker and then
I Have Deep Thoughts

It's a chilly night. The way all nights should be. My coat flaps in the breeze. I turn and look back at Annabelle's apartment and fight off deep dark thoughts until Bugle pulls me along. A couple of times he gives off little howls when certain stinks excite him.

I go into a bodega. They don't have Blast!. Only the much cheaper and grosser soda called Bango!!.

I consider getting some cereal too. For a long time I've wanted to try a different kind. Like Brix O' Wheat or Brantastic. But whenever it comes time to decide I freeze up. Also I don't like the weird mascots on the other boxes. I like Slammin' Sammy who is a billy goat with an attitude.

Sadly I only have enough for a soda. I get a weird one called Mega-Prackle which has a green alien for a mascot.

I drink and walk. It turns out that Mega-Prackle is grosser than Bango!!. I toss it in a trashcan but my stomach tells me it is too late. Soon we turn onto a nicer-looking street. Someone is sitting on a bench under a streetlamp, leaning forward with his elbows on his knees. He's wearing a long brown trench coat, fancy brown hat, brown shoes, dark brown pants. The lenses of his eyeglasses are tinted at the top so that you can barely see his eyes. He doesn't look like a private detective but maybe someone who got kicked out of the private detective academy and joined the other side.

Right when Bugle and I are about to pass by the guy bucks like a bronco and spews big-time onto the sidewalk. I'm not a total wimp but immediately I feel a sympathy puke coming on. My stomach flips inside-out and my mouth fills with Annabelle's cooking. I try to stop it with my hands which means it spurts through my fingers and splatters on the concrete a few feet from his. Bugle yanks to the end of his leash and watches in horror.

"Fuck," the other puker mutters. He takes out a handkerchief and cleans himself up then offers it to me.

I take it, wipe, hand it back. He says to keep it and gestures for me to sit. I do. Bugle stands between my legs.

"I mean, hellfire," the guy says and leans back. He has scars, a painful expression, a story in his slanty crime-smile.

I know it's rude but I stare. I have a good feeling about this guy. He knows things. I want to ask him questions. Such as how to find crime people and play the crime game. I missed my chance with Alphonse Polish at Flipjacks but here's a better candidate. With his help I could become a player myself and learn things that could help me pay rent and get the chemicals out of the basement and track down the Mazzies. Then I could split my time between fixing pricing guns and being a crimer. Maybe I couldn't be a chief crimer or major hoodlum but I could be a thug or goon or a leg-breaker like Paddy the fat drowning guy once said. I could be a lookout and do important side tasks like guard the getaway car and steal library books about science stuff so we can stop alarms from beeping. I could bring my bug spray and a pair of rubber nunchucks.

This plan sounds good. I prepare to ask. But as my mouth opens the guy's beeper beeps. A shaky hand worms it out of his coat pocket.

"Fucking shit." He puts it away, stands. "Good luck, kid. I hope you feel better." On shaky legs he weaves down the road and into the foggy blurry night.

What am I thinking. I couldn't even get into Mazzie Corp.

I sigh and we head back to the truck. As we're walking my smushed-up beeper beeps. I don't have to look to know it's Annabelle. Her beeps are angrier and out of tune.

I dig for my keys. Instead my fingers find the scrap of paper.
hi murry   fuk u!

In one hand I have the sweary note and in the other puker's handkerchief. Both are light yet the history of the world's crime can be found in the folds of both.

And I think about what Laramie Bob said.
Price. Gun for you.

I lift Bugle into the truck and climb in. Driving, driving. And thinking. Such as about the time Thin Man said, *I want to tell you something, asshole. We are made from chemicals and dust that comes from stars. The sun is a star. You, therefore, are the sun. What are you really fucking afraid of? That you will die too? That's too simple, even for a simpleton dumbfuck like you.*

I'm pretty sure I shrugged at that point.

You need to understand what you're truly afraid of. Is it of failing or losing? Ha! You're already a loser. Like Chef Pierre you have to embarrass yourself every episode, not for cheap laughs but grand gags. Be bold and go big or die a lonely loser like me.

The thing is, Pierre also has a cast of characters in his life. The camera changes angles all the time and follows them home and to prison and to the military laundry facility. But I only see the other heliophobes in one dimension. Their fear. Maybe I need to know what their dirty laundry looks like. Who their first girlfriend was. If they have safes in their bedrooms. If I am in their diaries. I don't know if it's the answer but I guess it's something to do until some smartness or luck shows up.

I hit the brakes. Thanks to puking near a stranger I now know what I need to do. I need to get stuff out of other people. Like facts. Crime information.

Then I hit the gas. I was already heading the right direction.

When I take a hard right into Malaboose Plaza the truck feels like it's going to split in half. In the middle of the lot a bunch of teenagers are standing around a steel drum with a fire inside, their faces glowing. I veer wide but someone still hurls a full can of beer. It bounces off the tire then spins and explodes.

Shop Now! is open 24/7. At night the light hits the shelves nicely. All those rows of shiny products waiting to be adopted for a few dollars and then taken home and devoured. I love it here. I would stock shelves again if only I didn't have a criminal record as a result of such a job.

I find Mikey on a little ladder in the frozen foods section.

"There you are," he says. "Been wondering what you've been up to."

"*Nuh nuh* need to *tuh* talk."

"Can you fix this first?" He hands me an old Fortran, a rugged but problematic A-80 X-Tra model. The trigger is stuck.

"*Tuh* ten bucks."

"Screw that. You can have one Praline Promise."

He's talking about the oval tubs of diet ice cream filled with bits of artificial candy. I put my hand on my stomach and shake my head.

"Forget it then."

He reaches for the gun but I juke sideways and bang it against the freezer door.

2@$2.99! 2@$2.99!

"Thanks, you big weirdo."

"*Luh* look *hoo hoo* who's talking."

Mikey gets back to work. Cool air pours over us as I hand him tubs of ice cream to put on the high freezer shelves.

"So what's up? And what the hell are you wearing?"

I look at myself. "*Wuh wuh* onesie. It's *kuh* cool."

"You look like a homeless clown."

A cart turns the corner toward us, an old man pushing it. He's got a diaper on under his pants and his cart has a wonky wheel that goes *whimp whimp whimp* the whole way. It contains eight boxes of tin foil, two boxes of black garbage bags, lots of cat food, and enough bottled water to bathe a donkey. Which I did once. This guy could be me in twenty years. If I live that long.

When the guy is gone I say to Mikey, "*Th* things are *ruh ruh* real bad."

He gets us popsicles from a torn box and leans on the ladder. The PA system is playing music with all the words replaced by flutes and clarinets. It makes me want to sleep not buy stuff. I perch on the edge of the freezer and fill him in as best as my mouth will allow. Including the date, Jet, the dinks, the note, the license plate number, the stuff people have been saying, the price tags.

"I agree with Tucker that it wasn't the college dinks. You probably just got burgled by some scummy. Did you call the cops?"

As I nod and tell him about Conrad Flowers the top half of my popsicle tumbles off. I want to cry. I'm not very different from the retarded girl from the parking lot. Except I don't even have a cool tricycle.

"Oh, Murray. You're just going to have to explain to Mazzie what happened. You won't get the job but you'll feel better and can move on. Right? Maybe they'll even be forgiving but you have to be upfront."

Terrible advice. Mikey is dumb. I reach into my pocket and rub my fingers on the puke-filled handkerchief. "Can you *uh uh* ask *juh juh* John Boy or Billiam? *Th th* they know *luh* lots about *kuh kuh* crimes."

"My brothers are all on probation. I would love for them to go back to prison but they claim to be going to church and staying clean and all that."

For effect I wipe my eyes and nose with the handkerchief. Some carrot bits fall out.

He sighs. "Don't fucking cry. What do you need?"

I tell him not to laugh. Then I tell him my plan.

He laughs.

My Investigation Takes Us to Martin's Where I Learn Some Weird Stuff About Him

Martin lives in a basement apartment in Southwest North Gaslin. I went there a couple of times in the early days for Heli-Non sessions when the schoolhouse was shut down for asbestos. His place has one slitty window looking into dirt.

"Tell me again what I'm supposed to do," Mikey says with another sigh. It's Tuesday evening. Safely after dark.

I park the truck. "In—*veh veh*—vestigation. He's the *luh luh* leader of *hee hee* Heli-Non."

The truth is that I don't know much about Martin. He's mysterious. Like a planet no one visits very often. That's why I need Mikey. Everyone likes Mikey.

"*Eye eye* I'll *kuh* keep him talking. You *luh* look around."

"For what?"

"*Muh muh* Mazzies. Or *kluh kluh* clues."

"What kind of clues?"

I glare at him so hard my forehead gets a cramp. "Finger-*puh-puh*-prints. *Zhh zh* genetics."

Mikey sighs so hard he steams up the window. "Right. Genetics."

We get out and shuffle up the sidewalk to the entrance then go down a hallway to a staircase and descend belowground. I knock. Martin comes to the door in a hoodie and sweatpants so big I could use them to cover my truck at night.

"Well hello, Murray! And friend."

"I'm Mikey. These are for you." Mikey hands over two tubs of Praline Promise. A whole cooler of it sits in the back of my truck.

"A gift? Thank you, kind people."

"It's melting."

"No problem. Perfect timing. We're just finishing dinner."

He gestures across the room. Sitting in a white T-shirt and underwear at a table covered in papers and Golden China Bell Dragon Tail Pay-'n-Chow Buffet food cartons is Jung. When he sees me he raises chopsticks full of noodles and smiles. But when he sees Mikey his face clouds over and his eyebrows pinch together.

Mikey looks at me. I shrug.

Martin clears off a cushy chair and half the couch. I take the chair. It smells like sour feet but not much worse than me.

"This is quite a surprise," Martin says.

"*Wuh wuh* we—" I gesture toward Jung.

Jung laughs and raises his chopsticks again.

Martin scoops ice cream into four bowls. It takes about ten minutes for him to make his way around the room and distribute them. By now the Praline Promise has melted. I sip. It tastes like powdered milk mixed with stomach medicine but with slivered fake praline candy floating around in it. Jung and Martin dig in. Mikey sets it aside and studies Martin's place. I've assigned him a tough job. The clue could be stuck to the bottom of the garbage bags rotting by the door. Or behind the exercise bike covered with Halloween decorations. Or in the stacks of papers and magazines. I wonder what Martin does all day and what he does to pay his bills.

"So is everything okay? Or did you just pop in to say hello?"

"*Heh heh* hello."

Jung laughs and raises his bowl of ice cream.

"Well, that's great. Here, I think you should have this. I was about to eat it but I think it was destined for you." He hands over a fortune cookie.

I open it.

Common sense accomplishes nothing. Simply become insane.

"*Th* thanks."

I eat the cookie while Mikey looks at the old Christmas cards taped to the back of the door. I notice that Martin has lots of photos of robots. Including two big framed posters in which they are doing battle.

"*Yuh* you like *row row* robots?"

"Why yes! I build them myself. Do you like robots?"

I'm about to shake my head when Mikey says, "Sure he does. In the car he was like 'I am a robot, I am a robot.'" He does it in a funny voice while moving his arms up and down. Martin laughs kindly but Jung looks mad enough to assassinate Mikey with his chopsticks.

"Excellent! Let me show you a couple." Martin waddles off.

Mikey pokes through some papers on the couch. "Haven't read today's news yet," he says in case Jung is suspicious.

Jung's face sours but he looks away and switches on a little radio held together with packing tape.

You could make millions in the aluminum siding business. The industry is ripe for horrendous unadulterated snuff straggle down-pour fashion grandiose buffalo klondike foible hiccup…

Martin comes back and hands me a robot. It's a foot tall and spray-painted silver. Wires emerging from its back lead to a controller. He shows me how to make it move and punch. My robot is named Caligumor. His is Tyrannopoc. We sit on the floor and make the robots fight.

"You like robots?" Mikey asks Jung.

Jung switches the radio over to music and turns toward the wall.

Mikey lifts the cushions and peers beneath. He doesn't like what he sees, puts them back.

"Jung doesn't really have any hobbies," Martin whispers to me. "I've tried to get him into robot wars but mostly he likes titty magazines like *Jugga Jugga*."

My jaw drops. It's like hearing your grandmother fart and belch at the same time. Martin takes this opportunity to punch my robot in the nose. Then I punch his in the groin. We jerk the controls back and forth and swear and spit. I laugh but Martin's sweating. When I punch Tyrannopoc in the throat he falls over.

Martin sets it upright again but now it won't walk. I punch it in the ear. It falls over. Victory.

"Son of a bitch!" Martin's huge fat hand turns into a ball and smashes the robot. His face is so red and puffy he could go as Mars for Halloween.

No one moves.

"Oh well. I have others."

"Gonna use the bathroom," Mikey says. "If that's okay."

"Of course, of course!" Martin says to him. Then he says to me wants to play chess. I don't know how to tell him no in his own house so I sigh angrily but he's already sliding on his belly like a walrus toward a wooden box near the sofa.

We lie on the floor and he tells me what all the chess pieces are for as he puts them on their home bases. All the priests and fortresses are hard to understand. I'd rather play Owl House or Rat Race. For now though I breathe heavily on the chessboard and think hard. I decide to move my horse but I guess you can't put two pieces on the same square even if they're on the same team. Martin taps on the square he wants me to move to and then eats the horse with his fortress.

"Think ahead three moves," he says. "That's a metaphor for life."

I try to do that but when you don't know any moves it's like trying to guess your name before you're born.

A half hour later Mikey comes back wiping his hands on his pants. "Whew! Rough one. Well, Murray, we've got to go see your other friend now, right? He wanted some Praline Promise too."

"Already?" Martin says to me.

I nod sympathetically.

"Who's the lucky recipient of the rest of the ice cream?" Martin asks. "Someone I know?"

My tongue dries up. I look around while trying to picture all those weary cold faces sitting in a circle in the dusty schoolhouse. For some reason Channing pops into my head. "*Chh—*"

"Channing? Oh, that's nice. You'll be seeing his mother's new house, I assume."

My blank face is my answer.

"It's the lovely gray one on Myrlply Drive, as I'm sure you know."

I did not think my face could go blanker but apparently it does.

"You'll see the garbage truck out front. Did you know he drives one home every night? Well, let me see you out at least."

It takes all of us to get Martin off the floor. Now he's tired. He plops down on the couch and just extends his hand for a shake.

"It was so nice to have you stop by just to hang out. We'll have to do it again."

Nod. I wave to Jung. He smiles and waves.

"See ya," Mikey says to him.

Jung glares like Mikey just wiped boogers on his mom's casket.

We run up the stairs and down the sideway and dive into my truck.

"Jesus, Murray. You've got quite a crew of friends."

I stare into space, panting.

"That guy is as soft as an old grape, inside and out. I don't think he could ever do anything malicious."

The truck needs gas. I remember that now.

"However in the bathroom I found a stack of books he wrote. I tore out the last page. It says 'Martin Smithley is the co-author of twenty-seven books, including *Stone Cold: The Everyday Guide to Placophobia* and *Playtime's Over: Raising Children While Battling Pedophobia*. He has degrees in abnormal psychology, business management, chemistry, and French. He has overcome numerous fears, and so can you.' So basically he just writes these things and runs these groups and makes a little money." He reads it to himself again. "Pedophobia. What is that—fear of kids?"

Shrug.

Mikey thinks hard. "But he's only the co-author. Who's the other writer? It doesn't say." He shakes his head. "Regardless they peddle in fear—of anything. But you, your phobia takes the cake. Fear of the goddamn sun. That big orange thing in the sky." He shakes his head.

I try to start the truck. It sputters.

"You know gas is just sunlight stored up in the earth, right? And it's running out. Just like time. Now *there's* a fear."

His words remind me of a quote from *Rays of Hope*, the Testimony section.

> *The fear never goes away. It just softens over the years. Like an old knife in your pocket digging into your thigh. You get a little fatter and the knife gets a little duller and the days roll along. Otherwise you bleed. And bleed. When you're all drained out, the fear will finally end.*
>
> — *Jane, a heliophobe*

So what now?"

"*Ch ch* Channing's house."

"You're serious about seeing that guy too?"

I give him Bugle eyes. "*Eye eye* got *uh uh* arrested for you."

He steams up the windows again. "I know."

I turn the key. There's just enough ancient sunlight in the tank to get it running.

"Turn on your headlights, Murray."

Going to See Channing Is About as Fun as that Time I Accidentally Ate Octopus at Golden China Bell Dragon Tail Pay-'n-Chow Buffet

Channing lives with his mother on Myrlply Drive just like Martin said. The house is indeed easy to find with the large Waste-B-Gone garbage truck hulking out front. We park. The neighborhood is so quiet you can practically hear other people's dreams.

"Let's get this shit over with," Mikey says and heads toward the porch.

I ring the bell. The door swings open. The mother answers. Her eyes perform a skit, jumping from me in my mechanic onesie to handsome Mikey and back. The mother is not ugly and does not look like the mother of Channing: long blond hair, an actress chin, legs that could walk all day. "Pleased to gain your acquaintance," she says, offering her fingertips. I assume we need to kiss them but Mikey just gives them a jiggle. She stares at him and his muscles with big intense eyes. To cancel any confusion he acts extra gay by cocking his hip and bending his wrist.

The mother's face changes but she's not angry. Just learning. "Oh," she says then turns around and screams, "Channing!" then turns back toward us. Says, "He's probably jerking off." She then walks over and opens a door leading into darkness and screams again. "Channing!"

We hear thumping. Soon Channing emerges from the base-ment. He's wearing army pants and a T-shirt with the stomach part cut off. His glasses are smudged. "What the fuck—oh, Murray. What the holy shit is this? Did someone die?"

I shake my head.

Mikey says, "Murray just wanted me to meet some of his friends. So we're stopping by." He offers Praline Promise.

"Wow, for me? Hey, I have root beer. Janice, make us some fucking floats."

"Okay, sweetie." The mother takes the Praline Promise to the kitchen.

Channing shuts the door and brings his ugliness in close. "You have never once stopped by, Murray. What the fuck is this all about?"

I swallow a bit of puke, say, "*Fruh fruh* friends." I add a shrug for effect.

His head moves up and down. "Right. Okay, well, fucking cool then, I guess. Come in. We just got a kitchen table and it's nice as shit so don't scratch it."

The three of us sit at the table and wait for the floats even though I've just barely recovered from the last bowl of the goop.

Janice the mother is humming as she works. Scoop, plop, scoop, plop. Her butt is round and fun and moving in rhythm with the scoop and plop. Done, she slides one to each of us, a cherry on top. She sits on the counter with her ankles crossed and slurps up her own. She says, "Interesting choice of ice cream."

"*Speh speh speh—*"

"It's on special," Mikey says.

I nod.

"I guess it'd have to be," the mother says, raising an eyebrow. She's got the cherry in her mouth, her big blue eyes watching the three strange man-boys at her table. When she spits the stem into the sink along with a white stream of Praline Promise I almost have an accident in my pants.

"Well, I like this shit," Channing says.

We slurp, suck.

"It was nice of you to visit," the mother says. "Channing doesn't get too many visitors."

"Janice, shut your fucking pie hole."

Mikey and I look at each other.

"It's not like it's a big secret that you spend most of your days around dump truck drivers and live in your mother's basement where you play War Beasts and have phone sex all night."

"Goddamn it, you're such a cunt."

She makes a face at the Praline Promise and pushes her float aside. "So are you boys part of that silly group?"

Channing spears his spoon into his float. "It's fucking anonymous, Janice! *Gawwwd.*"

"Okay, sorry!"

"I'm happy to say that I'm normal," Mikey says.

I make a snorting sound.

"And you, Murray, you're afraid of the sun too?"

Shrug-nod.

"Well, I don't like spiders," Janice says.

Channing and I lock eyes. Then we break into laughter. Channing says, "Fucking spiders. A Type-4 phobia. Doesn't even take time off your lifespan." We laugh again.

The mother sighs. "*Marriage On The Rocks* is on. Who wants to watch it with me?"

Mikey stands up. "Hell yes." The mother hooks her arm in his and leads him to the living room, both of them giggling the whole way. The TV comes on so loud you can't hear your teeth crushing the pralines.

"Come on, Murray. I'll show you my lair."

We take our floats and descend into the basement.

The walls of Channing's lair are bare concrete. There are a few rugs on the floor and there's a big L-shaped desk in the corner with a comfy but serious chair and a couple of computers on the desk. Cables and wires and cords go every direction and papers and game cartridges and disks and toys and dead snacks lie all over the place. Sexy Valentine's Day lights hang from the ceiling. Channing drops into a beanbag chair that makes a giant farty sound. His little belly bunches up where part of his shirt is missing.

"What the fuck is this shit really about?"

I sit on his bed. He has a giant tiger-shaped pillow. I notice now that his feet are in fuzzy purple slippers. Channing's I mean, not the tiger's. "*Wuh* wanted *tuh* see what *yuh yuh* do."

"Stop lying, you big asshole." He uses his straw to make bubbles in his float. "This ice cream's really on special?"

Nod.

"I need this diet shit so I can get buff and score with chicks, like your friend. Not like you. No offense. I used to be something. Now my fear has made me soft and weak. Hey, you want to see something?"

Shrug-nod.

Channing starts digging through boxes and drawers. "I know the fucking thing is around here somewhere. I mean, fuck. Goddamn it. There you are, you fucking son of a bitch." He brings over a stack of photos and hands me one in particular showing a curvy woman in a golden bathing suit with red hair and boobs the size of small bowling balls. "That's Marlene. Can you fucking believe it?"

I hold the photo close to the tip of my nose and stare. "*Wuh* where you *guh guh* get this?"

He takes it back looking ashamed and says quietly, "From her house. I was there once. We screwed a couple of times. Just kidding. She's like a second Janice to me."

He glances at a couple of other photographs then starts to put them away. I jump up. "Wait." I hold out my hand.

"What?"

He doesn't put up a fight as I take the photos. In the stack is a picture of Channing, Moses-Marie, Liza, Manual, Marlene, Laramie Bob, and FX standing in a club. They're all smiling.

"*Wuh wuh wuh*—"

"Oh, that. We went to see some comedian. It was *hee-larious*, man."

"*Wuh wuh* why *wuh wuh* wasn't *eye eye* I invited?"

Channing takes the photos and throws them in the drawer then kicks it shut. "It was a long time ago. I don't fucking know. Would you have gone? We know how you are. You think you're better than us. That's why you're so quiet all the time."

I hear his words but don't know what they mean. Like a foreign language from the other side of the moon.

"We know that you like to keep Heli-Non separate from real life. Except for the whole Annabelle thing. What's her mouth feel like, by the way?"

I shove him. He shoves me back. I want to punch a hole through his throat and grab the back of his shirt and pull it through the hole so that he chokes but instead I swat the air between us.

"You're so fucking special, aren't you, Murray?" He snorts. "It's funny. The real fear is you. We worry that one day you just won't come back. Ever. Then what will we do?"

I stare at him like he's talking upside down.

"You don't fucking like me, do you?" he asks.

Shake.

"That's fucking fine with me. I don't give a fuck." He sits in the beanbag. It gives off a massive fart. I giggle. Channing doesn't. He stares at his fuzzy slippers, tears bubbling in his eyes.

I saw Tucker cry once when we were kids. He'd left his bedroom door open by accident. Usually it was locked but I guess he'd broken up with some girl named Ashlyn McGovern and was so upset he forgot to flip the latch. I was heading to the bathroom and saw him sobbing and went in to give him a hug and that only made him more pissed off and he punched me in the arm so hard it didn't work for a week. I learned my lesson. Don't hug sad people.

"*Wuh wuh* why were *yuh* you at *muh muh* Marlene's?"

"None of your business." Then he shrugs. "For fun."

"Tell me, *zzh zh* jerko."

"Fuck you, spazzmouth."

I swallow his words like the tiny bugs they are, letting them dissolve in my belly. Channing gets up, the beanbag sighing in relief. He goes to his desk and turns on a computer television. Does some computery stuff. Writes some words on a scrap of paper and adds a drawing of a penis shooting pee or sperm across the page.

"Go see her."

"*Hoo* who?"

"Marlene, dipstickburger."

"*Wuh wuh* why?"

"You think you know us but you don't. She's down in Carke."

"*Th th* thanks."

He sits down again. "Fuck off."

I get Channing's Praline Promise float and hand it to him. He sticks the straw in his mouth. I leave him there, sucking.

Tucker Hates Scummies and Just About Everything Else Except Roxanne and Money

Scummies are never on time. They don't wear watches, don't follow a code, and don't have scruples. What they do, though, is work for almost nothing, doing nearly anything, without complaint.

Tucker turns down the heat in the truck's cab. The sun's not up, his lights are dim, and he's idling two blocks away from the construction zone. His coffee is not only gone, it seems like it's about to clear his system. He's getting bored too, and when he gets bored he gets irritated and when he gets irritated he feels the need to stomp scummies rather than hire them.

He takes out his wallet and removes the newspaper cutout for the hundredth time. He turns on the cab light and examines the photo accompanying the article. It's a puff piece about a guy named Sydney Hart, who has been working with some small-time chamber of commerce on the other side of the country. It says the guy has a troubled past but that there's nothing concrete on him, only that he has a knack for pumping life into desperate ventures. Tucker can't say for sure it's Big Man. There's only a thread of resemblance, and the beard is so vast and dense it's impossible to tell what's behind it. But the lines around those eyes tell many stories about cigar smoke and road glare and raised fists. Tucker wants to believe it isn't him. He wants to ball up this article and throw it out the window and let it decompose, just like Big Man should be doing.

Someone raps on the passenger window and he just about pisses himself.

"Oh-fucking-kay, already!" he barks at the glass, then folds the article and puts it back in his wallet. "Over there." He points toward the construction site, and the two scummies lurch off while casting him wary, sullen looks.

He turns his truck around, backs into the dirt lot, then hops out and drops the tail. He and the scummies quickly and quietly load the truck bed with lumber, boxes of nails, concrete mix, pipes, power cords, and whatever else is lying around.

One of the scummies is a little guy with big ears and insanely large clothing. In addition to being toothless, he doesn't seem to have any fingernails and has a face that only a mother could love. Not Tucker's mother but someone else's, perhaps. The other guy is an older chap wearing a denim coat so big it could double as a bathrobe and baggy pants that pool over untied brown sneakers. His mouth, topped with an unruly gray mustache, is in constant motion, but he's not talking, just twitching and waggling his lips. Tucker likes them; he likes his scummies quiet and compliant. Fifteen minutes into the job, no one has said a word.

He wonders what Big Man would say about a brazen yet cowardly theft like this. It was Big Man who gave Tucker his first hammer—which had someone else's initials carved into the handle. *A.P.* "Found it," was all Big Man had said. That hammer now follows Tucker everywhere, stationed under the truck's seat.

"Fucking fucker," he says to himself.

The scummies stop mid-load and glance at him.

"Sorry. Nothing. Get back to work."

He wonders if he should give the hammer to his brother, along with the article, then send him in search of Big Man. Not that Murray could go through with such a thing. The kid cried every time he was forced to eat a steak, and then he simply stopped eating animals entirely, which pushed Big Man's rage toward him past the point of no return. Suggesting that Big Man might still be alive would only screw up his already screwed-up world.

"Asshole."

This time the scummies ignore him and go on working.

"Fifty bucks each, as agreed," he says, pressing the bills into their scummy hands ten minutes later. "Just clear over my tracks as soon as I leave." The older fellow's mustache twitches. Tucker climbs into his truck and rolls out. When he glances back in his rearview mirror, he sees the scummies on their hands and knees, sweeping the dirt like Jain monks or something.

He rolls back into North Gaslin, and as the sun creeps over the horizon he creeps toward the old metal shed in the field behind his mother's house. He backs up to it and unloads everything except the lumber, which he needs for completing a garage job on the other side of town.

There's a light on in the house. He imagines she's already wake—or hasn't even been to bed.

Once he's done unloading, he enters the house through the back door. He doesn't knock anymore, since she never answers anyway. He checks the stove (the burner is usually on) and thermostat (it's usually set to freezing) and heads for Big Man's office. The door is ajar.

It appears much like it did when the old man occupied it, structured in a way that only he could comprehend, a system that is as lost or dead as the man it once belonged to: bills, invoices, letters, books, and cancelled checks stacked in no apparent order. Some near the top are as old as the house itself and yet just beneath them are others from the days before he left. Papers sit on shelves, columns totter along walls, and through it all are narrow paths. Perhaps the layout resembles Big Man's mind—or perhaps it was meant to betray any sense of what thoughts occurred there. The horror of dissecting it all is too much for Honey, who keeps the room intact and the door open in the hope that one day she'll spot Big Man sitting there among the papers, contrails of cigar smoke circumnavigating his head.

As the years rolled past and it became clear that would never happen, Tucker started sifting through the stacks for evidence. There was nothing except a few antique firearms and coins, all of which he sold to help keep Honey in the house.

Maybe there's a reference to someone named Sydney Hart though.

He rifles through a few papers, flips through some books and ledgers, and opens some cabinet drawers, but he finds nothing. On the far side of the room, a column tumbles over on its own.

Big Man would have smacked him for that—just for being in the same room when it happened.

"Goddamn it."

He's had enough. He makes his way toward the doorway and flips the light off.

He immediately flips it back on.

Something has caught his eye: a picture on the far wall. It's of Big Man with Ol' Bitch, the first long-hood big rig he ever owned. It was always breaking down and it was ugly as hell, but it was Big Man's ride and he loved it. Tucker goes and takes the photo off the wall and sits in the hard-as-fuck wooden rolling chair with his feet up on Big Man's desk. He takes the article out of his wallet and holds it up to the photo. Both Big Mans are out of focus and fuzzy, and it's just one blur against another—but he notices for the first time that there's a face in the cab of Ol' Bitch. It's big dumb little Murray. It looks like he's hiding, waiting, biding his time, knowing that Big Man is going to disappear one day.

Tucker read once that to a man with a hammer, the whole world looks like a nail, and for their father, Murray was that nail. He even said it: "Murray is dumb as a fucking nail." Tucker was quite sure Big Man had broken Murray's cranium at one point, hitting him like a dead soldier in a never-ending roofing job.

He closes his eyes. "Don't," he says to himself. "Just don't."

He doesn't.

He wishes he hadn't hit Murray so much either. He's pretty sure the blows only made the kid weirder. Dumber. More stuttery. But seriously, that fucking kid. It was like he weighed the proper decisions in his mind and always, always chose the one that made the least sense, perhaps out of a sense of adventure, perhaps because he had some sort of decision-making dyslexia, or perhaps because he was just plain fucking idiotic. Whatever the reasoning behind it, it drove Tucker mad. And since Honey was a heap of madness and sadness herself, that left him to step in and say, "Magoo, why the fuck do you have to hang out with the one deaf kid and the one queer kid in the whole fucking school? Don't you think you have enough problems?"

Murray'd just shrug, which always warranted a kick.

Tucker closes his eyes. "Don't," he mutters to himself.

He kicked too hard. Too often. "Where'd you get those bruises, Murray?" his mother would ask at the breakfast table, and he'd just shrug—which made Tucker's heart twist and made him want to kick him again.

Don't.

Sometimes he gets so confused, like Murray. A common activity for him at times like this is to try and arrange a timeline in his mind. Was Murray fucked up before Big Man left? Did Murray get better or worse as the years went on? Was the kid ever happy? Why did he hate being outside so much? Is he one of those people who is afraid of public spaces?

"Tucker?"

He jumps up. "In here."

Honey's tattered robe appears in the doorway, her shrunken body inside it. "What are you doing here so late?"

"You mean early. I couldn't sleep so I got up to get some work done. I'm storing some junk in the old shed. Don't touch it and don't tell anyone, especially Murray. Anyway, I want to clear out this room. We'll have a bonfire."

"Now?"

"Not right this minute. Whenever."

"You don't need to do that."

"I'm going to, whether you like it or not. Do you need anything today?"

"I don't know. Tea?"

"When did you last eat?"

"I don't know. Supper?"

"Are you asking me?"

"I don't know. Am I?"

He sighs. "I've got to get to work. If you need anything, have Murray pick it up."

"Dried fruit."

"How about a big plate of spaghetti? Some bread. A cake. Just tell Murray."

"Have a good day."

She escorts him to the back door, lets him out, slides it shut, waves, and fades back into her ghostly state.

As he heads toward his truck, he glances back at the house, lit up yellow and orange by the rising sun, almost like it's on fire. And if it were, he wonders if he would try to save her.

Tucker opens the door to his truck, slides out the hammer from beneath the seat, and kneels in the dirt, just out of view of the house.

"Kill you!"

He pounds away breathlessly until he's made a face-shaped indentation in the earth.

"Kill you! Fucking kill you!"

The hammer feels like an extension of his very being. When he's done he smacks himself on the head with the handle. Once, twice, hard.

"You little pussy. Don't. *Don't.*"

We Learn that Jet Is a Computer Frogger and Has Told Everyone Our Secrets and We Wonder if We Should Hire a Hitman or Just Flee but I Still Like Her

On Wednesday afternoon a special session is called but we cannot go to the schoolhouse. It is being used for an Allodoxaphobia Network meeting. The fear of opinions. They argue for two hours and then go home and watch the news.

Instead we have to meet in the basement of a church. It's dark and water is dripping into a bucket. There is no bug juice, no crackers, and barely enough light to pray. But there is a large beige computer on the floor that Channing has brought along with some telephone equipment and cords. A bunch of heliophobes are kneeling or lying in front of the television part reading something. I crouch with my hands on my knees breathing loudly through my mouth as I squint to see the little green word-worms squiggling across the page.

"It's a weblog," Channing says to me. "Turns out that Jet is a computer blogger."

I look at him with a shrug on my face. "*Kuh kuh—fuh* frogger?"

"It's like journalism but free because it's on the internet where there's no one to say you can't say this shit or that shit or use real names or whatever. Just fucking read it."

NOT AFRAID OF THE DARK:
The Plight of the Modern Heliophobe

An exposé by Jeanette Horowitz

Heli-Non, a local heliophobia support group, meets in an old schoolhouse whose main doors are welded shut and painted blue. Attendees enter around the back, up a Z-shaped wheelchair ramp. By now most of them know every hall and stairwell in the building. Some have even seen the belfry, accessed by shimmying up a secret ladder in the supply closet. One attendee said there was nothing up there but bird droppings and some old eggs that failed to hatch; there wasn't even a bell, only sunlight breaking through the slats—which didn't frighten him, he claims. At least not right then. He claims it's more complicated than that.

These are the types of things I was told when I infiltrated the group for a single mind-numbing evening followed by a series of one-on-one interviews and a deeper investigation. Most obliged to my request; I will use only their initials unless they gave explicit permission to cite their names.

"This is a cureless sickness," says Carl Jake Dunham, helio-phobe, Heli-Non co-founder, and co-author of Rays of Hope: Living with Heliophobia. "While forty percent of visitors to your home will snoop in your cabinets, one thing they'll never find is a box of pills that says 'anti-heliophobia pills.' Perhaps to some it seems like an irrational sickness, an illogical one. But it's a profound one. A wraith of an affliction."

Heli-Non isn't the only group that meets in the former Maple Bluffs Elementary school, now owned by North Gaslin Church of Christ. There's also Dentophobic Anonymous, which addresses the fear of dental work, and Hexakosioihexekonta-hexaphobia Network, whose members share a profound fear of Satan and the number 666. Heli-Non, however, is the only sun-centric phobia group in the state, if not the region or country.

"Despite our size, our group is diverse, both in terms of age, gender, ethnicity, and background," says group leader and co-founder Martin Smithley. "The fear doesn't know skin color or body type and can strike anyone, anytime. A tribesman may suddenly look up into a tropical sky and think, 'This is going to end badly,' the same way a scientist studying solar flares could be forced to come to grips with the inevitable cessation of the lifeblood of our galaxy—the mother who giveth and taketh life on a daily basis. I mean the sun, of course."

When asked why a collective group couldn't be formed to address a wide range of phobias, Dunham says, "Every pho-bia has its particular discourse, its members their particular temperaments and needs. A heroin addict generally does not attend AA meetings and a sex addict generally does not attend a gambling support group. Right?"

M., like many of his fellow heliophobes, totes around a battered copy of Rays of Hope at all times. Having sold 190 copies so far, Rays of Hope contains such maxims as "Dealing with a fear of something one hundred times the size of Earth is like digging a grave from beneath the ground: paralyzing, solitary, and seemingly endless but not entirely impossible."

Doesn't a constant preoccupation with the sun only worsen the anxiety about something that one simply cannot change?

"Perhaps but unlikely," Dunham says. "It's sort of like being taught to swim when your father tosses you into a lake. One in a million children will drown. The rest will swim for the moon."

Rays of Hope isn't the only item M. relies on. Like many of his fellow heliophobes, he armors himself with a wide-brimmed hat, a long brown coat, and goggles. M. also suffers from a debilitating stutter that, along with childhood trauma, affects conversations and relationships. Most questions are answered with simple affirmative or dissenting gestures. He hasn't had a solid job in three years, and he spends most of his days watching television reruns with his dog and sleeping.

His fellow Heli-Non members have nothing but kind words for M., however, indicating that the group is not only holding him back, it hinges on his oppression as some sort of emblem of the legitimacy of the fear—and the group.

"The guy is gold," says a well-known local musician and fellow heliophobe who prefers to remain anonymous. "One time he rescued a baby mouse from the snack closet. He buys me a card on my birthday every year. Last time it was a musical one by this obscure band Jibberbarf and the Bosses of Vomit. Only he would think of something like that."

So is M.'s fear of the sun a simple matter of displacement, or is he a bonafide sun-fearer?

"The sun is an easy target," says social psychology professor Lee Hope, who has studied atypical fears in contemporary contexts for over thirty years. "If a person ascribes all of his or her fear to one particular object or idea, there is likely a disconnect between the phobic individual and their true emotional state. Usually, someone such as a heliophobe or adherent to an obscure and irrational phobia will have a host of other problems to deal with. I, for example, have a bad back and dislike dark-colored snakes. A generous correlation can be made between those two if need be."

Other members have abandoned promising career tracks or otherwise had their lives derailed by their phobia. The musician abandoned a national tour after one gig despite the certainty that it would have been a massive career boost. Fellow heliophobe A. was on her way to a new career in the textile industry when a nervous breakdown sent her fleeing Chicago back to North Gaslin. Other Heli-Non members share tales of lost jobs, devastatingly broken relationships with family and loved ones, and an innate inability to cope with stories of national and global tragedy. Some attend the "sessions" wearing masks that never come off—both literally and figuratively.

Heli-Non members are also encouraged to undergo a controversial procedure known as "Retrieval," which Dunham and Smithley describe as "akin to the theory of abandonment in search of a higher sense of self... like how one's other senses are heightened after looking into the sun."

But Professor Hope is concerned.

"*Their methods are disconcerting. Whenever someone is coerced into facing their fear in such a traumatic fashion, there is often an underlying motive, such as acquiescence to a code or belief system.*"

Dunham and Smithley, along with most members of the group, insist that Heli-Non is neither bullying, manipulative, nor cultish. It's a safe space, a place to seek help and lay out one's deepest worries.

But is it? This, you see, is where I come in. My father was one such member of Heli-Non, and our family watched over the years as his fears manifested, moving from a minor grievance with bright sunlight to an all-out fear of venturing out during the day to a maddening descent into conspiracy theories and voices and paranoia. He lost his job, poorly paying as it was, then us—his family. He took to the streets. We've seen him only once in the past seven years, and he will only come out of his hovel at night. We fear for his sanity.

The last time I spoke to him, he wavered between deep resentment for particular members of the group and comfort in knowing that others still share his fear. But when I pressed him, asking if they really did share his fear or if they were simply enabling one another's irrational displacement, he clammed up. Like the other heliophobes I talked to, most do not want to confront their "affliction" or else it might, in their words, burn the eyes right out of their heads.

As you can imagine, I bear resentment toward the group as well, and I went into that room prepared to expose their darkest secrets and worst traits. After spending a few hours with each of them, however, I could do no such thing. Save for certain individuals, I found them affable, flawed, and oh so human—very much like my father. At the very least, they have formed a community of their own in this grim, oppressive town. In the end, it was I who was conflicted.

"I didn't expect Heli-Non to cure me," says Manual, who has survived two types of cancer, "but it provided support when there was none. The only glimmers in my life came not from the sun but from my family and my friends. Sometimes they forced me to face things I didn't have the strength to take on alone. They taught me there is another side to everyone. To everything. Even the sun."

"*Whore whore* Horowitz?"

Channing nods. "Her father is *the* Wiley fucking Horowitz. I thought for sure he was at the bottom of the river by now."

Martin uncaps a protein shake meant for swimmers and guys who jump motorcycles over canyons and guzzles long and hard then says, "This is defamation. I think."

Laramie Bob squats over the computer and makes a farting sound. Some people laugh. I notice that Joe Purple is not here. Which makes sense. No one knows his phone number. Nor is Marlene. Nor is Carl Jake which is ultrasuperweird since he never misses anything. One time he broke his ankle while cleaning his antenna and he paid the ambulance people to drop him off at the schoolhouse on his way home.

"What are our options?" FX asks. "Can we find her? Make her take it down?"

"She's using an IP mask but one day we'll find her and, you know," Channing says.

I don't know and I don't care but I like that she uses a mask. Like Joe Purple.

Martin sneers. "You all talked to her outside of the group. From what I understand you were all flinging your number at her."

I don't mention our date which wasn't a date. Or that I like Jet's computer frogging article. But I also feel bad. Wiley Horowitz and I got along well. For a while. He was a lot older but he had funny puns and was like a goofy uncle. I thought I saw him in a dark alley a couple of years ago but when you see an old friend in a dark alley at night you generally don't stop to say hello. Maybe I should have.

Laramie Bob gets up from the floor and leaves. Then Annabelle, who is mad because I talked to Jet alone in a bar, glares at me and slides out. Channing unplugs his computer and phone gear and waves goodbye but no one waves back. One by one everyone else slips free. Only I stay behind. I know Martin needs help getting up the stairs.

"Thanks, Murray. You're true blue through and through."

"*Zzzh zzzhh* Jung?"

"I don't know where he is tonight. To be honest, I'm glad. We need some time apart. I've been letting him stay in my guest room for nearly a month now. It's just a cot in my office but he doesn't seem to mind."

I stuff him into his Datsun then wave goodbye. *Meep.*

My truck is nearby. I float toward it on a cloud of ugly self-hatred and anger while thinking about Jet and Wiley. Then I spot an orange glow in distance. It's a cigarette burning in the mouth of a driver in another car. When I open the door to my truck the light bounces off the cop decals on the hood and the boxy lights on their roof. I can almost smell him from here. Conrad Flowers.

If I get in and drive he can pull me over and give me a ticket for the baby spares or the missing headlight or the cardboard window or the hole in the muffler or the leftover poop or anything else he might find. He might also find out where I live. He'll sniff the chemicals in the basement and maybe shoot Bugle.

I close the door, lock it. I walk.

He follows.

When I turn a corner he does too but with his headlights off. We are close to Main Street. It's the business district. Some stores are still open. I turn down an alley and Conrad Flowers slows at the top of it then races around the corner to meet me when I come out. I turn around and go right back down the alley and he zips around the block. If I do it again I will be more suspicious than a naked one-armed scummy rapping on the street corner with a chicken on his shoulder. Which happens from time to time in North Gaslin. Thus I turn right and head into the first store I see.

It's a craft store. This is not good.

"Uh, help you?" the lady at the counter says. She's wearing a dress that looks like a picnic blanket and eating a foot-long sub while sorting beads into little bags.

I shrug and browse. Now and then I glance out the windows to see if I can spot Conrad Flowers. All I see is my ugly reflection staring back at me. I tour the aisles. Needles. Yarn. Glitter. Expensive pens. Boring paper and photo albums. Scrapbooking stuff. I like that. I could make a Bugle Book or Astro Fire Cop collection. But these things require money. I only have like ten dollars left to get a Blast! and pay my rent. There's only one other customer in the place. He's tough-looking and dark-skinned and keeps glancing over at me. I assume he's a security guard. He could be a bead-robber though.

When I think I might fall asleep and stab myself on the shelf hooks I just give up and go back outside. "You come back now," the lady says without looking up from her beads and sandwich.

Walking, walking. My feet hurt. I need new shoes. I am hungry. I will get a burrito and Blast! from a GasStop.

No. Conrad Flowers turns onto this street. I halt. I turn around. I walk again.

I pass a barber shop. There's a gumball machine in there. My mouth is so tacky and gross that the gumball machine calls out to me like a miniature lighthouse. I find a quarter in my pocket. But when I go in to buy one the barber gets up and sweeps off the seat and spins it toward me.

"Trim?" he says.

I look at the guy. The quarter's burning a hole in my hand.

"Buzz?"

Shrug.

"A shave?"

Shrug.

"Ya gotta help me out, pal."

"*Ch ch* Chuck *ruh* Rollins-style."

He motions for me to sit. "Young or old Chuck?"

"*Kuh* cool *ch* Chuck."

"All right."

His name is Massimiliano. A whole sentence in a word. I know I'll never be able to say it. He has a white mustache with a personality of its own. We listen to some old people music,

William Wilson and the Wild Williamson Sisters and their ancient ditty "Have Some Pie." Or is it Ralph and the Chicken Wizards with "Try Not to Cry"? It's hard to tell with the crappy radio. Massimiliano hums and snips and I sit back and hope Conrad Flowers gets bored with watching my thick greasy hair slap onto the plastic floor like eels from the sky.

My mind floats like a paper airplane in a tornado. For a while I think of all the haircuts I've ever gotten. That's boring though and even my memories get sick of the idea. Then I remember the time I stopped going to Heli-Non. It hits me like a piece of cheese you ate but then puke up a few hours later and it tastes like dog food. Also a haircut was involved.

This was back when my toilet wasn't flushing and gray scum came up through the tub and sink. I told Tucker but instead of fixing it he got me a membership to the North Gaslin Recreation Center. I'd go there late at night when no one was exercising and would take showers in the empty locker room. A couple times people came in anyway and saw me scrubbing my undercarriage but what could I do.

One night before Heli-Non I went there to get a free haircut that some barber students were offering. After they'd fucked it up real bad and then shaved my head to cover it up I went and sat in the TV room and watched *You'll Eat It And You'll Like It!*. I even remember the episode. It was the one where Chef Pierre climbs the Eiffel Tower like King Kong. He is covered in flour and pigeons try to eat him. "Lard soup! Lard soup!"

By the time the janitor banged into the sofa with his sweeper machine I had slept right through Heli-Non. I knew that if I went home there would be a bunch of messages from Annabelle and that she'd also probably stop by to yell at me so

I grabbed Bugle and drove around instead. We ended up going to the neighboring town called Woolhaven. It's a different world out there. Like a Christmas pageant with people saying hello to each other and not asking for drugs or food afterward. People stopping when the light's red and not screaming at pigeons or humping a parking meter for no good reason. It smelled like warm sugar and maple leaves. Buildings there are made from wood and bricks. I realized the world can be pretty if you go to the right place.

It wasn't only Annabelle who left messages on my machine while I was gone. Martin and Channing too. I didn't call anyone back though. I took Bugle to see Thin Man and hung out there to avoid Annabelle. There were even more messages after I skipped the next session and the one after that. A whole month went by and I felt strange but okay. I opened *Rays of Hope* once or twice but that's it.

I was visiting Honey Mom, sitting on the back porch and staring out across the weed field, when someone broke into my house. At least I think so. It wasn't really breaking and entering, just entering. Nothing was missing or smashed but I could tell things were different. The TV was at a weird angle and my blankets weren't on the floor like normal but on the bed. The weirdest part was that someone had opened my silverware drawer and put the spoons where the knives go and the forks were facing down instead of up.

It was probably someone from Heli-Non playing a prank but I had no proof and I didn't want them to be in my home so I went back to the sessions. When I walked in they all jumped up as if I'd just sat up at my own funeral. They hugged me and patted me on the back and got me a plate of cookies and some bug juice and even let me skip cleanup duty.

I haven't missed a session since. But I didn't sign up for Retrieval that year. Or ever again. And I almost never talk or do the assignments. I like the bug juice though. And I like the other heliophobes. Not Carl Jake and definitely not Channing but the others. They're like family you don't need to buy presents for.

"Alright, son. You are handsome again."

Now I've got a hairdo that twists high in the front and is slick on top and neat on the sides. Massimiliano pushes my head forward and sweeps my neck and ears. It tickles and I sneeze.

The haircut costs $8. On the way out we shake hands. I forget to get the gumball.

Flowers is gone.

I Visit Honey Mom and Try to Wear My Father's Shoes then Feed Thin Man and Gift My Box to a Yokel then Learn Something so Shocking I Nearly Swallow My Brain

I notice my answering machine is blinking. I tap the button and the tape jerks and squeals like a gassy pig and a nasally voice goes *Mr. Murray Sandman, this is Janine at Mazzie Corp. I'm Max Codpoodle's assistant. He's expecting your final report and for the prototypes to be returned. He will be in town Monday and would like to meet at the Book Barn at two p.m. If you have any questions please scribble sudsy potluck mayday tasseled parliament...*

That's five days away. I have to go see Marlene next—as soon as Bugle is done dropping a massive poop on the dirt patch in front of Mrs. Johnson's trailer.

My beeper beeps. Because it's cracked from when I fell it makes a creaky dying grasshopper sound.

It's Honey Mom.

"Looks like we're gonna visit the old lady," I tell Bugle. He looks at me. I know, I know. The dog is the only one I can talk to like my mouth is normal. And sometimes Channing.

My visit to Marlene's will have to wait.

Honey Mom sleeps a lot. She's also awake at weird times of the day. I put Bugle in the truck and look around for Conrad Flowers. I don't see him. He must be at home punching kittens.

The house is dark when I pull up. I keep Bugle close because if he gets a scent of the rabbits he'll bolt into the fields and be in Zimbabwe by noon the next day. I go to the front door and knock and she is already there. "Go straight to Thin Man's," she says and hands me a plastic sack. We're still in the dark and I don't know what I've got. "He's not feeling well." She hands me a key. "Don't lose it. I'll stay up." She shuts the door.

"This way Buges." We cut through the field toward the Box. I punch in the code. Up the stairs. Panting. Panting. I slide the key in and get a shock. "Ow."

I release Bugle. We find Thin Man on the couch wrapped in a few blankets. The TV is on but silent. I open the bag Honey Mom gave me. Inside is tea so old it might have a diploma. Also a brown banana. Some cinnamon oatmeal in a packet. A half-eaten chocolate bar.

I heat water and make the tea and oatmeal. When I return to the living room Bugle is sitting on Thin Man's lap and he's stroking his ears. I mean Thin Man is stroking Bugle's ears. I shoo Bugle off and put the tray on Thin Man's lap and feed him. He's too tired to insult me or push me away. He moves his mouth around and swallows. When I make him sip the tea his face scrunches up.

From Honey? he asks with his fingers.

I nod and make him sip. He winces but doesn't dump it on the floor like a toddler. Then his fingers go *Nice hair, you douche bag. Who you pretending to be?*

I think about that. And I want to ask him the same. But he has a tummy ache so I don't.

Thin Man is as similar to Big Man as I am to Tucker. He was once a professor at a college out west where people ride horses to their classes which are in cabins on top of mountains. Or so I always imagined. Thin Man, whose real name is Huey Anton Sandman, taught history. He knows who started Earth and who was the first to swim across the ocean and all that. He had a pretty wife and two stepkids. I never met them but I saw a picture once and they all lived in a nice house with swings and a big family car and a cat named Jockles. Then Thin Man got throat cancer. Which was probably from drinking sunshine. He lost his voice parts and was in the hospital for a long time. When he got out of the hospital he couldn't teach anymore so he lost his job. His wife didn't like that so she took the kids and went even farther west to where people live on surfboards and sing to dolphins every morning. I guess it wasn't such a good family after all. He came back to North Gaslin and couldn't talk with his hands yet. I had to show him how. It was weird being a teacher for a teacher when you're still trying to write your name correctly. No one else learned it, not even Big Man.

When he's done eating he points at the little table near the doorway. On it is his Murray Art Box. I get it and bring it to him and he shoves it against my stomach.

Go after your dream, you big baby idiot nutjob.

I nod only because he's a sick old man who can't speak.

Now he gestures behind me. A *You'll Eat It And You'll Like It!* rerun is on. Probably the dumbest episode ever. Pierre and his upstairs neighbor Mrs. Dadu-Ghipa get trapped in an abandoned motel during a hurricane and they have to make gourmet meals with vending machine food. "Lard soup! Lard soup!" Turns out Mrs. Dadu-Ghipa is a serial killer with a heart of gold. She learns that Pierre is a fraud but promises not to tell anyone as long as he doesn't tell the police she eats people on weekends.

We watch it but don't laugh once. By the time the credits roll Thin Man is asleep.

On the way back to Honey Mom's I take a detour to the river. A river so putrid and lame it doesn't even have a name. I bring the Murray Art Box with me. Bugle and I sit under the lamplight on a rotting fishing pier and watch things hurrying along in the current. Shop Now! bags. A headless squirrel. Corn cobs. A small boat too with a yokel standing in the middle and casting and reeling an old wooden rod. A lamp shines near his feet. There aren't many fish anymore and most of them have faces where their tails should be and eyes instead of stomachs.

When the yokel sees me and Bugle he paddles over and parks in the mud and hops off with the lantern in his hand. He doesn't say hello or g'day or anything, just climbs onto the pier and sits with me and my dog who sniffs his hands. Hands black with grease. Brown shoes curled up like the tongues of the dead horses you see in cowboy movies. He takes a long hard look at the box in my hands. I take off the lid and show him a drawing of Astro Fire Cop. He laughs at it, *Hyuk hyuk hyuk*, his shoulders rising and falling like he's got hiccups.

Astro Fire Cop is just a regular guy named Titus John Mercury. No special skills. He's just brave is all. He's constantly battling these guys called the Blood Brothers. They have machines that pump blood out of their bodies and mix it together to form an evil potion. They then spray it on their enemies and turn them into mind-slaves and get them to start fires throughout history. It's hard to prove though. Only Astro Fire Cop understands it. He crosses paths with them through various wormholes and on other planets. He's always armed with his Infinity Hose which he keeps on his back. It turns air into water.

I sent some pages to a few comic publishers but they said it was a silly idea. Traveling through time to put out old fires. Changing evil history. They are probably right and Thin Man is wrong for once. I crumple up the drawing of Astro Fire Cop and toss it in the river. I toss each drawing one by one. Then I hand the box to the yokel. He looks like he's going to cry. He runs his hands across the shiny silver skin which is just dumb old foil and we watch the papers float away.

Back at Honey Mom's I go inside to put the key on the table. The radio's on, going *The leader of the small Asian country was arrested yesterday for groping a ten-ton griddlecake tracer palimpsest unsubstantiated by topnotch tampon…* Honey Mom is at the stove making waffles from scratch, not a box. "These are for you," she says. I did not realize I was so hungry and since I can never return to Flipjacks I sit down. She gives the first one to Bugle. He snarfs it in two bites.

The next one is mine. It's as large as the plate. The syrup is real but so ancient it's basically sugar.

"You have a new haircut," she says and raises her hand as if she might touch me. She doesn't. "And new clothes."

I nod-shrug. The lunchbag pants and striped shirt are new to me but someone might have died in them.

"You look good, Murray. Those shoes are terrible though. Don't you know how to tie laces?"

I know how but it takes time and is boring.

"Get some from your father's closet. He never wears them."

I eat. Bugle curls up and whimpers in his sleep. Honey Mom sits and picks at the edges of a pancake but that's it. Then she sighs. It's nine at night. "I suppose I should turn in. Lock the front door when you leave. I'll clean up tomorrow."

She never cleans up though. The dishes always pile up until Tucker or Roxanne comes over. Once she's gone I do it myself. I fill the dishwasher and run it. It makes a sound like a pheasant with its tailfeathers caught in a vacuum cleaner but that's nothing new.

I guess some different shoes wouldn't hurt. I edge closer to Big Man's office. Big Man kept all his clothes in there instead of the bedroom. It's weird but if you think about it not that weird because I keep all my dirty ones in a pile in the living room.

The office looks different. I have a good memory for weird things. Like how the red book about seeds on the shelf was always upside down. Now there's a dust track showing that it was moved. I can tell that Tucker has been in here. He opened the drawers and sorted through a couple of piles and played with the framed photographs on the wall. I study them. The one of Ol' Bitch is a tiny bit askew. I see myself in the cab of the truck.

What no one knew was that I'd stolen a package of chocolate chips and was eating them one by one.

I try on Big Man's boots and shoes. They don't fit. That's one of the funny things about him. Big Man's feet were clubby, blocky. I kick them back into the closet. Then something crashes behind me and I jump so high I nearly hit the ceiling. Bugle has knocked over a tower of ledgers.

"Buges, *wuh wuh*—come on, *duh* dude!"

The ghost of Big Man haunts this place. And my mouth. Bugle looks scared but I don't want him to be so I make him feel better by toppling a tower. Then the next. A couple of minutes later the entire floor is covered with papers and books and I'm sweating.

Something tickles my brain though. Another photo Tucker moved. I get a chair and drag it to the corner where there are frames on a high shelf along with fishing and lawn dart trophies. Beside the one of Ol' Bitch is one showing our family. Big Man's not smiling but squinting. A cigar in the corner of his mouth like always and a trucker's cap tilted on his head. I scooch the chair closer to check out a photo of Mikey and Tucker and some kid named Benny Monagee who I think is dead now. Mikey's clinging to Tucker. Tucker has always liked him back but pretends not to.

But this isn't what interests me. This junk has been hiding another photo that's fallen over and is covered with an entire body's worth of dust. It has a purplish brown frame. I don't recall ever seeing it. It depicts Big Man's bowling team The Lightning Sharks. Guys who once came around to lean against Ol' Bitch and spit into the grass. All of them are wearing matching shirts with their initials on the pocket.

TM: Thin Man.

WA: Whimpering Arnold.

BM: Big Man.

4BJ: Fourth-Born Jerry.

NNNN: Not-so-Nice Nick the Numbskull.

CJ:

My heart screeches like a needle on a record. I bring the photo closer. He wasn't as bald as he is now. He wasn't wearing ugly white sneakers and wasn't round like a beach ball that's been sat on. But that face. That smile. Like he has all the answers and just wants to blend them up and pour them into your ear.

The other day I read that our universe contains a star 3,000 times the size of the sun. You could fly beside it all your life and you'd never get past it. And of course it's dying. It probably has already exploded by now. I think I can feel it.

"Murray?" Honey Mom asks from the doorway. "What did you do?"

I step backward off the chair. There's nothing there to catch me. It's a long way down.

I Pop in to See Marlene at Her Place of Work and Boy Do I Feel Stupid Once I Figure out Some Things

The new news which is old news about Carl Jake gets me stirred up. Even though it's late I take a risk and head to the town of Carke where Marlene lives. Like most heliophobes she's probably awake. But first I stop at Tucker's to steal some gas and some cash from his golf bag.

Carke is south of North Gaslin. I've never been there, only heard of it. It's the type of place where men stand on their lawns in purple and gold robes and talk poetry to the trees while sipping from a glass of boiled wine or something. Then they shoot their sleeping families in the face and run off with the local librarian. Marlene must be a maid or something at one of the big houses. A housecleaner maybe. She wears rags most days and seems to be allergic to combs.

I use some old gas station maps to get me to her area. It's still confusing so I stop to ask for directions from a woman walking a dog that turns out to be a cat and Bugle goes nuts so I have to roll up the window and shrug at the woman then drive off real fast. I find my way to Marlene's road. First I have to pass through some gates. They're tall and iron, the type of thing a vampire would have in front of his castle to keep out religious salesmen like Zeb from Shop Now!.

The house is large and made of bricks and tiles and stones and is three stories tall. The roof has a bunch of high points and bold windows where the old poet must stand with his dinky out as little people like me mow his lawn. The lights are on. A bunch of cars are parked in the driveway. Both nice ones and crappy ones. I park and hook up Bugle to his leash.

The front door is open. A girl is standing outside it talking to herself real loud. "Yah. Yah. So I'm like—no, I'm like—yah. No. I'm like—shut up. Yah." No, not talking to herself. She has a large gray cellular phone in her hand. I have heard of those. They have an invisible cord and you can basically carry them everywhere. I need one. When she sees me she steps aside. Either out of fear or because she thinks I'm here to mow the lawn.

I go in. The house reminds me of the mansion from the episode of *You'll Eat It And You'll Like It!* when Chef Pierre travels alone to a remote island to cook for a wealthy madman who just wants someone to listen to his bad jokes. The twist is that Chief Pierre thinks they're good jokes and can't stop laughing. His stomach starts to hurt so much that his innards almost burst. The irony is that for the first time in his life he makes a good tasty meal all by himself without Laurencio's help. Then he has to leave because the madman goes insane and chases Pierre away. Pierre is sad at the end but you don't know if he's sad because the jokes have stopped or because he can never again make the recipe.

A large man in tall boots and green pants walks past but when he sees Bugle he stops and says, "You da dog guy? We ain't hunting til nine o'clock."

I shrug.

"That's a beagle idinnit?

"Is *muh muh* Marlene *heh heh* here?"

"Of course she is," he says and walks off.

Bugle and I walk around the huge rooms with fancy floors and decorations. It's like an art museum you live in. Other people are doing stuff like singing and laughing and going up the stairs and entering rooms and then leaving them. Somewhere someone is playing a synthesizer with a drumbeat background. I recognize the tune. It's from the commercial for marshmallow tacos.

Then Choo the Dachshund comes spiraling around the corner and charges at us like a furry missile, barking, and yapping. He puts on the brakes early but with the wooden museum floors he slides like my baby spares on ice and skids right up to Bugle who's got his hackles up. Bugle howls once and Choo flops onto his back and shows us his dinky. I scratch his belly. He's nice. I should get a second dog.

"Murray?" Marlene says. She comes around the corner with a glass of steaming tea in her hands. She's wearing a long sweater with a belt and some big weird blue pants that swallow her feet. Glasses are perched on her head.

"*Huh* hey."

"My gosh, hon', what the hell are you doing here?" She comes over and hugs me long and hard, her boobs smashing against mine. "This is so—unusual?"

I nod. "I—we—" I gesture at Bugle.

"I didn't know you know where I live."

My scalp tingles. "*Luh luh* live?" I look around.

She laughs. "Um, yeah, hon'. This is my house."

An older woman walks past giving me the hairy eyeball.

"That's Ma. Ignore her. I love the new hair, by the way. It makes you look so *debonair*."

I blush. Even though I don't know what she's saying since I don't speak German.

"Come on. Do you want something to drink?"

I want something to drink but not tea. She leads me to the kitchen. It's as big as a restaurant. The refrigerator is large enough to hide ten bodies inside. Not that I would know.

"How about Blast!? You like that stuff." Before I can answer she cracks the can and pours it into a glass.

I take it, sip. It's very tasty. Like all Blast! colas ever.

A young boy walks into the kitchen and opens the refrigerator and takes out a Blast! too then walks off without saying a word.

"Little shit. That's my nephew. I don't know his name. These people show up and hang out and stay for a while and eat from my refrigerator then leave. What can you do?" She shrugs and mugs like Chef Pierre.

Choo and Bugle dance around one another and playfight as Marlene leads me through a room she calls the parlor. It's too fancy to sit in so we go to a different one made of glass at the back of the house.

"This is the sunroom. Obviously I only come here at night. And before you ask, no, my family don't know anything about me and Heli-Non, so be careful what you discuss. They think I'm just a night owl. Which I am but not for the typical reasons. As you know."

We sit on comfy chairs surrounded by plants and fancy furniture. Choo lies at her feet and Bugle sits panting while staring at Choo. The piano song somewhere in the house changes to something twinkly and soft and it makes me nervous for some reason.

"*Chuh chuh* Channing *guh* gave me the *aaa aa* address. I *thh* thought you—you—*kuh* clean the *puh puh* place."

She smiles and opens a drawer on the little table beside her and gets a cigarette out and lights it. Carl Jake says cigarettes are basically sunlight you force into the darkness of your lungs and for once I can't say I disagree. "I know. I don't look like a wealthy entrepreneur. No, this is mine."

"*On on*-entre-*puh-puh*-preneur?"

She sucks fire into her lungs, nods. "Do you know the shopping network that sells things like Boat-in-a-Can and Travel Chalkboard? I started that channel with my late husband. He died but I continued on with our work. He was holding me back, to be honest, and I thrived once I was in control. The business grew and grew." Her hands dance in the air, smoke twirling around her head. "But then I burned out. The fear overtook me. I sold everything and retired and here I am, happy and surrounded by ignorant-ass family who won't leave me alone. At least I think they're family."

My jaw is hanging so low I can't talk.

"But what prompted you to get my address from Channing?"

I look down. It was a stupid idea coming here. Before I can come up with an answer a guy enters the room with a beer bottle in each hand and sits behind Marlene but at an angle and pours one beer into the other bottle then stares at the back of her head. "Who's this guy?" he asks.

"My friend Murray. Murray, this is one of my nephews. Charles or Chuck or something."

"Jim."

"Jim. Right."

I nod.

"Who's Murray?" he asks while staring at the side-back of her head.

Marlene says to me, "They're everywhere, these cousins and nephews and nieces. I think it's time to change the locks, don't you, Murray?"

I shrug.

The guy continues to stare at Marlene. "What's his deal? Kinda late, isn't it?"

"Murray and I are friends, Chuck. This is what friends do."

"Jim."

"Jim what?"

"That's my name."

"I don't care. When are you leaving?"

"I just got here. You said I could stay the week and find a job and maybe clean the pool and such."

"*Puh puh* pool?"

Marlene squints while exhaling. "They love the pool. The ultimate bourgeois symbol, isn't it?"

I shrug. I stood in a pool once. I couldn't stop peeing.

"So how do you know this Murray guy?" Chuck/Jim asks.

"We share a mutual interest."

"Is it a sex thing?"

"No, it is not a 'sex thing.' We belong to a... a club."

"Right. A sex club."

"No, it's an intellectual pursuit. Therefore you would not be invited."

He scoffs and sips his beer. "By the way I know a guy who's looking for a nice lady with, you know, means."

"No thanks."

"He's an investor who used to play pro baseball."

Marlene says nothing but her face lights up a little bit and her eyes shine. Choo senses it too and looks at her. Bugle is still panting and staring at Choo.

"He comes through here on his private plane," Chuck/Jim says. "Pretty much the only one to still use North Gaslin Airport."

"Oh," Marlene says and puffs her cigarette more sexily.

Carl Jake once said that not even money can cure our fear. I don't think that's true. If I had money like this I wouldn't be afraid of anything. Except for the fear of losing the money.

Now that he knows I'm not here for a sex thing with Marlene this guy Chuck/Jim is able to look at me. He says, "So Murray, what line of work are you in?"

I take a sip of Blast! and say, "I *fuh fuh* fix—"

"Murray is a consumer-focused retail resource technician," Marlene says.

It's the nicest thing anyone has ever said about me. I nod.

"Wow," Chuck/Jim says. "Dunno what that means but it sounds complicated."

"And *yuh yuh* you?" I ask with great bravery.

He sits back and starts to answer but Marlene jumps in for him too.

"He's a grifter, Murray. He puts a lot of effort into getting other people to hand him money for no reason at all."

I nod. He snorts. I think I like this guy a bit. I feel stupid being here though. Now I just want to leave. But I have to pee. Even though I've barely drunk half my Blast!. I ask Marlene for the bathroom and she tells me where all of them are but it's like listening to instructions for putting together a space helicopter.

I walk slowly through the house. Bugle plods along beside me on his leash. Two children are playing tag. That's what happens when you drink Blast! late at night. When Tucker and I did that as kids Big Man joined our game. Except that when he caught us he tagged over and over on the ass then threw us on our beds and told us to shut our goddamn traps.

The house has lots of shelves and nooks with items on them. Some are nice like vases and sculptures of naked people but others are cheap and weird. These are from Marlene's shopping network. Things like the PeppWrench which is a wrench that also grinds pepper for your spaghetti and the CrimeCroc which is a big inflatable crocodile for scaring off crime people. It's not hard to picture the Mazzies on a shelf here. I get down on my hands and knees and say to Bugle "Find the—" but right then a door opens and someone's legs appear and just like that I lock up. "—*maa maaa*" my mouth goes while I'm on the ground with Bugle. "*Maaa maaa—*"

"What the fuck?" they say with a huff and sigh. "You know what?" the legs' owner says, the girl with the phone, "I don't want to know." She leaves.

We go up a level. I hear voices in bedrooms so I avoid them. There's a big room with a giant TV and massive movie chairs with coolers beneath them for drinks. Why we don't have Heli-Non birthday or Christmas or anything parties here I don't know. We could call it "Darke in Carke." "Carke and Cake." And so forth.

Another room is a big office with a massive desk and some patents and certificates on the walls. Its shelves host more plastic items like a fancy metal device that lets you put on band-aids without hands. I tell Bugle to sniff around here. I stop short of opening drawers and doors though. It feels weird. I like Marlene and she likes me. Or at least she's nice to me. It's weird that she has money and family and knows people from other towns. She's not a recluse or crazy and doesn't dig under her movie seat cushions for change so she can buy cereal. It must be weird to be successful and afraid of the sun. The rest of us are losers and afraid no one will remember our names after we die.

"There you are," someone says. Bugle and I jump two feet in the air and have a heart attack but live. Standing in the doorway is one of the kids. She's scowling and has a toy in her hands. "Jim said you could fix this." She holds out a game. It's not a fun game but an educational one where it tells you meanings and you find the word or it tells you numbers and you make math with them.

"I *duh* don't know how," I say. The words come out pretty easily. Kids are basically dogs but weirder and more unpredictable.

The girl looks tired and like she might cry. I don't like it when kids cry. Bugle usually goes to them and rubs against their legs and that makes me jealous but also sad.

"Okay," I say.

I have my repair kit on me, in the inner pocket of my longcoat. Always do. I turn on the desk lamp and sit there in a big brown heavy wheeled chair and spread out my kit. The toy machine is clunky and colorful. I don't know electronics but as soon as I start opening it up I can tell the problem is food. Snack gunk from the girl's hands has made the buttons stick together and the wire connections crummy and the speakers gummy. I clean it all and blow out the speaker with my little handheld device and use my pliers and flathead screwdriver to clamp the wires back into place. I get some new batteries from a device on the wall called the Electric Banana Slicer which is exactly what it sounds like. I put the machine back together and turn it on. Immediately it's asking me for the square root of the capital of Libya.

The girl is so happy she hugs Bugle. Then she sits on the floor and plays with the game and it's weird how smart she is.

"Having fun?" Marlene says in the doorway, scaring me all the way to death again.

The girl explains what I did. Marlene smiles and crosses her arms and leans against the door frame. "So why are you really here, Murray?"

I get the note out of my pocket and show it to her. It's been crumpled and opened so many times you can barely read it.

hi murry   fuk u!

I tell her then about the Mazzies and the crime. And how things are not going well for me in life. Like how I need a new beeper and a window for the truck and tires and rent and clothes and to get the chemicals out of the basement. But also that I suffer from heliophobia just like her and this makes things difficult. Romance. Crime solving. Travels.

Marlene thinks real hard while scratching her left knuckles which are bloody and raw like she removes the skin for a hobby. Then she taps the center of my skull which is what Big Man would do when mad. *Use that little mung bean of yours* his throat would grumble. But Marlene's finger is softer and she says, "That spelling is atrocious and the handwriting is chicken scratch. Do you recognize it? It looks familiar."

I stare at it. Then I remember once how Laramie Bob played a prank on April Fool's Day by putting an old wasp nest in my truck. A note was stuck to it. Was this it? Maybe it fell beneath the seat then got kicked up during the robbery. Or maybe that's what the prototype pricing gun thief wants me to think.

"You guys are afraid of the sun?" the little girl asks without looking up from her game.

Marlene looks at me then at the girl. "Um, well, sweetie— what's your name again?"

"'Helio' is sun and 'phobia' is fear," she says. "I know what it means. That's a weird fear to have. I'm afraid of stinkbugs and rats—but the sun? Come on, Marlene."

"Are we related?"

The girl shrugs and continues dividing words into shapes. It feels like time to leave but I have another question. I ask what she knows about Carl Jake.

"He's friendly but odd. I suppose that sounds silly since we're all odd. But with him I tend to just block him out like irritating white noise. You know, like an alarm clock going off in a room but you're not sure which one so you try to live with it?"

Shrug. I hear him even in my sleep.

"Why do you ask?"

"He *nuh nuh* knew my *fuh* father."

"Your father—what happened again?"

"*Duh*-disa-*puh-puh*-peared."

"Oh. I'm sorry."

I shake my head.

"Do you think Carl Jake knows something?"

Shrug.

"Do you want me to go see Carl Jake with you?"

Shake. I can fight my own battles. Like Astro Fire Cop. No one knows the flames like me.

"I'd bet my money that Joe Purple had something to do with it. But good luck finding him."

I don't think she's right. But who knows.

"We're always here for you, Murray."

I squint at her. Here for me how? They don't buy me birthday presents or bring me snacks when I'm sick. They don't tell me I'll one day achieve my dreams or stop being afraid of the sun. They mostly like to keep me around to point and laugh at. So they can say, *At least I'm not that guy. Just look at him. Murray Sandman. Mister So-So. Moody Stinker.*

Marlene and Choo escort me and Bugle out. Jim/Chuck can be seen watching us from a window on the third floor. He either has his dinky or a beer bottle in his hands.

Marlene hugs me and tells me to let her know what happens.

We drive away. I pass through the gates. The radio's on. It's going *Yesterday Mr. Jones was walking to the bagel store when a sluggard bicycle hypnotized the mopping scofflaw paperback sourdough...*

Bugle falls asleep halfway back to North Gaslin. As soon as I cross the town line I see Conrad Flowers in my mirror.

Conrad Flowers Chases Me
to Honey Mom's Where I Talk Like
an Adult with Tucker

I head to Honey Mom's with Conrad Flowers on my tail. I approach the property from the back. There's a dirt track Tucker uses to sneak in and out. He doesn't know that I know he hides stuff in the shed. One time I found three turquoise machine guns there.

I take the turn hard and hope the baby spares don't explode or fold. Then I flip off the headlights and jam on the gas and hold Bugle close as we veer onto the dirt track which has a tall berm at the lip. We almost leave the ground but not quite. The truck slaps into the dirt and goes all squirrelly but I straighten us out. We barrel through the grass toward the shed and park behind it.

Conrad Flowers' patrol car goes up and down the street a few times. I hold my breath. Bugle goes back to sleep. When the coast is clear I drive up to the house and park. I'll sleep here.

The sliding door on the back deck is unlocked as usual. We slip inside. I make myself a peanut butter sandwich in the kitchen and one for Bugle. It is delicious. Even Bugle says so. My old toothbrush is still in the bathroom upstairs but I don't want to wake Honey Mom. I sprawl out on the sofa in the den. We sleep. Eventually. It feels good.

"Cut in straight lines Magoo," Tucker is saying to me in my dream. I'm mowing a lawn on the moon. It's difficult because the grass is made of fire. "Magoo." A space rock beams off my forehead.

I wake up. Tucker is tapping me between the eyes.

"Have some coffee." Tucker takes a cup out of a cardboard tray. "New café just opened up. Young people, chess boards, blankets and shit. It's all the rage."

I sit up and sip. It's good coffee. Doesn't taste like it came out of a rusty drainpipe behind a tire shop. "*Th* thanks."

Tucker's dressed and ready to go build a skyscraper or something. It's weird how good-looking he is. It's also weird how he's being nice. "What the fuck happened to Big Man's office?"

I shrug. "He's *duh* dead."

"Maybe. Maybe not."

Bugle rolls onto his back and Tucker scratches his belly.

"Magoo, we have to talk."

I look at him.

"I'm selling this place and putting Honey in an assisted living home."

"*Wuh* why?"

"It's like a tomb filled with ghosts. But not even scary ghosts. Just, like, dead ones."

"*Wuh wuh* what then?"

"I'm going to raze it and get the whole lot rezoned for commercial use. Turn it into a chemical plant or something."

The ceiling creaks. Honey Mom is walking around upstairs. She has a sewing room where she makes clothes for her childhood dolls. We think. No one has been in there in years.

"Don't give me that look, Murray. You tried. I tried. Fuck it. It's decided." He sighs and sips his coffee. "You'll get your cut from the sale. I'll take a small cut too and the rest will go toward putting Honey in a home." He stands and digs into his pocket and pulls out some money. Now I feel bad for raiding his golf bag. "Buy Honey and yourself some food. And I suggest if there's anything you want here you take it."

He lifts a hand. Thinks about putting it on my shoulder. Doesn't. Leaves. By the time he's gone I remember to ask about Conrad Flowers. Why he's a terrorist who's ruining my ugly life.

There's nothing left to eat so I walk Bugle to GasStop. Sugar Slams. Milk. Bread. Tea for Honey Mom. A piece of weird fruit shaped like a star. A chewie for Bugle. He and I sit in the shadows behind the building. I eat the fruit which tastes like Blast! but without all the chemicals and think about Tucker's weird nice mood. It makes me nervous when he's nice. But I also feel bad for him. Having to make these decisions because I won't. Can't. I eat the fruit all the way through and my mind goes places like usual.

One time Mikey and I were riding in his uncle's van on a straight flat road when the door flew open. The wind sucked Mikey out like a feather and the road scraped off half his skin, leaving behind a face that looked more like tomato sauce than flesh.

When Big Man heard about Mikey he said, "Something not right with that kid." Like it was his fault the door opened and the road ate half his face.

Most of my memories of Big Man are like that. There is only one almost-good memory that I hold onto which surfaces in my brain at strange times. Just like the things in the water we saw that day.

*   *   *

"Want to see a fucking beast?" Big Man asked me one afternoon after appearing out of nowhere in the doorway of my room with a cigar in his fingers. Honey Mom and Tucker were at the fair. I hadn't wanted to go. All that bright sun and sweaty yokels rubbing up against you while eating turkey legs the size of babies. But now I wished I had so that I wouldn't be cornered by Big Man.

"Come on." He tossed some shoes I hadn't worn in forever onto the bed, old canvas things with no laces. By the time I got to the front door Big Man was in his gleaming black antique Chevy pickup truck. He'd spent years restoring it. It's what he drove off in when he disappeared.

When I climbed in he handed me a brochure.

"Found it in a puddle."

Ferocious lizards still walk among us it read. It showed some gray-green alligators.

"It's a goddamn sign is what it is."

"Of *wuh* what?"

"That we should go see some ferocious fucking lizards."

"Kind of *fuh* far. *Heh* Henryville."

"We're not going to Henryville. That's just for reference." He tapped the brochure with a big dirty finger. "Look at those fuckers. You ever see one?" He spit. "When I was a kid there were yokel families who made a living giving boat tours just so tourists and fat cats could see them. Those were meager livings for sure. We used to drive past and throw rocks at the creatures. Hated them. I don't know why. For that reason I never saw these wretched beasts up close. Damn it. Damn it!" He beat the steering wheel with his fist then petted it softly. "Sorry, baby, sorry."

Driving, driving. We followed the river. It split off for a while then later joined a bigger river. After a couple of hours of this he pulled off the road. We got out and sat in the grass and looked at the water. "Keep an eye out. Though I imagine that such creatures are used to such inquiry into their lives and have taken to the shadowed banks or are floating indiscernible among those hunks of sodden wood drifting past."

He talked like a textbook whenever he was angry. Sometimes when drunk. But this was different. His stomach was growling. Mine too. He put his hand on my shoulder. It felt like a brick wrapped in sandpaper.

"Our will must be irreducible, Murray."

I shivered.

"You can be a good kid. I don't know why life is such a struggle for you but if you keep trying, things will, you know, achieve equilibrium in the due course of time. You understand?"

It was always easiest to just nod. Like when someone's speaking Spanish to you at the bus station.

We heard footsteps in the grass behind us and turned around. An old man in huge overalls and a red shirt stood behind us. His lip was filled with brown goop. "What you guys doing?"

"Looking for gators."

"Not gonna see 'em here."

"Where are they hiding?"

"Boats'll take you out to see the tame ones. Even let you touch a couple of the old fat buggers. But that ain't right. I know where the real ones are. I kin show you for twenty bucks."

We followed. His truck. Our truck. Weaving down roads dark with drooping trees. Moss hung all over everything and the roads were lined with smashed bottles. Every road sign was shot up. Along a muddy stretch of river the gatorman killed the engine. Under a tattered old tarp lay a metal flat-bottom boat with a small motor. We climbed in. I had to wear a life jacket. Big Man insisted on rowing so we could keep quiet but then he got tired.

"Been awhile since I've been on water," he said, clutching his chest.

"I kin tell," the gatorman said. He yanked the engine on. The riverbank was lined with whole dead trees. Their roots stuck out like monsters' mouths, fangs and drool and all. He steered us up a narrower side river and turned off the engine. He told me to paddle softly and not to splash. "They'll come." I rowed. My arms jiggled. It was getting dark and I hadn't eaten since breakfast. "That's good." I pulled the oars in. We sat there for a long time. I was so hungry that I stopped being hungry.

And then it came. A splash. Big Man's eyes bulged like supernovas. His hands gripped the edges of the boats. A tail swished past.

"Jesus hellfire monster cabbages!" Big Man said. He pulled his hands into his lap.

The gatorman chuckled. I wasn't scared. Not when sitting between Big Man and the gatorman. Even though I was always afraid of Big Man and generally afraid of strangers. Even though it was dark. Even though we were far from home and monsters were inches away. I felt okay. The moon stalked us from behind the trees. More creatures swished in the water. Two small ones floated by so close I could have named them. Then a monstrous one squirmed past. There was barely enough room for all of them in that little river. I thought they might climb atop one another and into the boat and tear us to pieces but the animals just floated.

"They'll follow now."

The gatorman paddled us back toward the main river. I counted twelve alligators but there could have been more. A couple of ducks took off when they saw them floating behind us. There was oil in the water and it swirled around the lizards and made weird rainbow paths.

"A thousand brilliant poisonous colors," Big Man said, "with the eternal moon wobbling in the center of it. Yes, just two fortunate stones, the moon and the Earth." He swept his arm toward the sky. "Two among the billions dying and exploding and joining to become one."

"Been drinking?" the gatorman asked Big Man.

Big Man stared into the water. He mumbled a little bit. Saying that the world was big. There was another him out there. A better him. "Perhaps the other me is an alligator," he said and laughed. I never told anyone about this. Never will.

The real alligators squirmed and swished. I still wasn't scared.

And sometimes I remember the other thing Big Man said after Mikey fell out of the van. That Mikey's uncle was a wretched sonofabitch so drunk he often wore his shoes backward. That he needed to atone. No one has seen Mikey's uncle since that day.

And we haven't seen Big Man in so long I can barely remember his face. Sometimes I close my eyes and see only an alligator.

The alligator is my friend though. I feel safe with him. Like he ate me and I'm warm inside his belly.

*   *   *

Honey Mom is at the kitchen table when I get back. "I'm sorry I don't have food," she says as I put the groceries down.

I get myself a bowl. I dump cereal into it. I flood it with milk. Milk is gross if you think about it. Something from another animal's boob. I try not to think about it.

"I wasn't expecting company. No one ever visits so I stopped buying fancy groceries."

I try not to slurp. It's almost impossible. "*Wuh wuh* we *vuh* visited. *Muh* me. Mikey."

She's drinking cold pale tea from a big black mug. The same dead tea bag, not the new stuff I bought her. "You did?"

"*Yoo yoo* you were *sss* so sad. Didn't *tuh* talk."

"I'm sorry I'm such a failure. A terrible mother. Maybe that's why..." She doesn't finish. Just looks out the window. I do too. A bird lands in the yard. It doesn't like what it sees and takes off.

I finish the cereal and wash the bowl and put it away. When I turn back she's gone.

I Call Liza on the Phone Which Goes Poorly but She Realizes It's Me Right Away and Says Just Come Over Which is What I Wanted but then I'm Nervous Like Do I Bring Gifts

Bugle is howling at a leaf that won't fall off the dead tree in the back corner of the yard. I would like to have a video camera in my eyes for such moments so I can hold on to them forever but then I realize that my eyes are basically the same thing and my brain is the recorder. It's not a recorder I can trust though. I learn this a few minutes later when heading to the kitchen for a snack.

While standing in front of the fridge I notice that the Heli-Non phone tree has slid to the bottom because of a weak magnet. The tree is getting splattered with Bugle water so I slide it up.

That's when I see Kurt Watkins' telephone number in tiny print along the edge.

I don't remember it. I guess I was wrong for accusing Annabelle of wanting to love him.

I scan the other names and numbers. People I'll know for the rest of my life and some I'll never see again if I'm lucky. But there's also Liza. I sigh. Then finish my snack.

I put on the lunchbag pants and red striped shirt. I leave Bugle.

"I heard you were making the rounds," Liza says when I show up at her doorstep. The orange porch light is glowing and a gazillion bugs are throwing themselves at it like aliens hurling themselves into the sun because they're confused and idiots. "I just figured that since you hadn't stopped to see me you didn't like me."

I like Liza. It's just that she reminds me of my fourth-grade teacher Ms. Zimmerspin. Not that they look similar or are alike in age. Ms. Zimmerspin was white and about fifty but looked at least fifty-two. She wasn't a warm lady or kind especially when you got math numbers wrong but she was smart and healthy. She was always doing crossword puzzles in Chinese or running triathlons with a rifle strapped to her leg. She'd come to class all sweaty and then tell us to do math numbers and because we were afraid of exercising we shut up and did our work. Also I think Liza would never steal from me and wouldn't know crime people because she's nice and has good teeth and manners.

I can't say any of that though so I hand her a six-pack of Summery Lemon-Flavored Soda and she smiles and says, "I've got just the glasses for these." What she's referring to are limited edition *Marriage On The Rocks* cups from the Fast Munch chain which we don't even have in North Gaslin. I learn about these cups as I follow her into her kitchen. It's nice but a bit messy. Based on the items in her cupboard she likes cereal like Sugar Slams too as well as Chips With Salt and foods you can stick in your pocket on the way out the door. She reaches into the freezer, gets ice, cracks the cubes' spines, drops some into two cups. *Clink, clank.* She hands me one.

"Is this about your burglary, Sandy?" she asks. She has a nickname for everyone which is another thing I like about her. FX is Foxy. Martin is Marty. Annabelle is Belle of the Ball. Channing is Canned Laughter which is funny. Carl Jake is Carpe Dumb-Dumb which I only half understand.

I nod.

"Marlene told me as much. And you think I might know something?"

I shrug, then shake my head. How to explain.

"I wish I did hon' but I don't and I'm sorry to tell you this but I'm on my way to work. I've got an extra shift since there's no meeting tonight. You know, a j-o-b? That thing you do when you're not a bum?" She laughs and touches me on the shoulder.

I smile and nod and sip the soda. It's good. Liza doesn't sip hers though. She gets food together for work.

I step into the living room. The couch is orange and old but scratchy and you wouldn't want to sleep on it but I don't plan to. There's also an old coffee table where she's been working on a puzzle with more pieces than all the pebbles in the world.

"Oh, that," she says. "It's some ancient church in God-knows-where. Someplace I'll never go because you won't get me on an airplane again."

I've never been on an airplane and only on a train once so I nod because it's true. I'm also not a big fan of puzzles but in a sense a puzzle is the easiest thing in the world because the answers are right there and you just have to turn the pieces the correct way and try each one a few hundred times and eventually you'll get it right. You don't even have to be smart. Just patient.

As Liza starts putting on her work stuff and jacket I hear music coming from down the hallway. I also smell glue. And paint. As I listen harder I can tell that the music is a rap song called "Crack(er) F(r)iend" by Slick Sprout and the Five Fidgets. Is Liza married? Does she rent rooms to rappers? Is she being robbed too?

"Can you take this to Eddie?" Liza asks.

"*Wuh wuh* what?"

She hands me the other glass of Summery Lemon-Flavored Soda. "He's old enough to stay home alone now but it wouldn't hurt for him to have some company."

I take the other glass and because both my hands are occupied I can't defend myself when Liza grabs me. She squeezes me weirdly around the shoulders and says, "Thanks, Sandy. We'll have to catch up at FX's show." I don't know what she's talking about but she's gone before I can think about putting together a question and consider asking it.

I turn back to the hallway. A light is on in the room ahead. The beam stretches out and touches my feet. Like every house in North Gaslin the floors are creaky.

"Ma?" someone says.

The roommate has a nickname for Liza. Because I don't like roommates I freeze.

"When we eatin'?"

He quits talking and goes back to humming along with the music. *Your momma a kitten, not a pussy. And you a muthafuckin' wussy.* I hear scratching sounds, banging, and a machine running. Now I am curious. I shuffle into the light and lean forward and put my honker into the room. When I see a huge head-shaped thing with horns made from chrome pipes my eyeballs start slipping out of my head.

There's a kid in there. Tall, skinny. Black like Liza. His hair is long and he has on big stomper boots but he can't be older than fifteen. Which is about how old I feel most of the time. He's making something out of dark-gray fabric with a sewing machine. He stops to hold it up to the light. It turns out I've discovered my first secret identity because he is Cosmic Immortal. Is he also Joe Purple?

"Uh," my voice says without me wanting to and this guy Eddie turns and looks at me. His eyes are wide and dark and I can see Liza in them and I realize she too has secrets.

"Whoa. 'Sup, pal. That for me?"

He means the soda. It's getting flat so I shuffle closer and hand it over.

"I thought I heard someone come in. You one of Ma's weird friends from that group?"

He's not Joe Purple. I ignore his question and lean over him and his sewing machine. I no longer think that sewing is for girls and I wonder if Tucker's wife Roxanne has one and maybe I can—

"You like it?" Eddie asks.

"*Kuh kuh kuh* Cosmic *imm imm*—!"

"—Immortal. Cool, right? One of these years I'll work up the courage to go to Hell-o-ween. It's only a couple days away. You ever been?"

I nod. "*Fuh fuh* five *tuh* times."

He looks at me. "No shit."

Shit.

"You going this year?" I start to shake my head but he says, "As what?"

My mouth moves faster than my brain. "*Wuh wuh* witch." It's what I've always gone as. It's an easy getup. Fake nose. Pointy hat. Cape made from an old black sheet. Some green goop from the basement for my face.

"Bro, you can't go to Hell-o-ween as a witch. Come on. What's your dream costume? Within reason."

That's easy. I tell Eddie. He looks at me a moment, then makes a square from his fingers and closes one eye like he's directing a movie and scans me over.

"Got it. We're gonna need a fuckton of cardboard. You got a car?"

I nod.

Eddie claps his hand, finishes his Summery Lemon-Flavored Soda, then turns off the lights. "Don't tell Ma about this. I'm not supposed to go out after dark. Not since that thing."

I nod again but I don't know what thing he means. I hope it was a good thing. I get my keys and wonder if Annabelle is right. We should have kids. As long as they come out like Eddie.

Mail Arrives as Does Bad News
from a Guy in a Yellow Tie

My doorbell rings the next afternoon. I didn't even know the bell still worked. Bugle howls like crazy.

I peek out and see a short guy with no shoulders in a baggy suit with a yellow tie. I hate yellow. I hate ties. I hate men with no shoulders on my doorstep. He waits a minute while listening to Bugle bugling then goes over and stuffs the papers in the mailbox. Then he climbs into a shiny silver Chevette and zooms off.

I'm still in my pajamas because we were up late working in Eddie's room. I left right before Liza came home. I slide on my slippers and put on my floppy hat and dash to my mailbox. It's maxed out with bills and notices that are accordioning and tearing and spilling onto the ground. They're all bad news telling me to pay this, pay that. I feel dizzy. I taste fried rubber. The thing to do is to call Tucker but he always says, "Pay your rent and then we can talk about toxic chemicals in the basement."

I notice among them something with the Heli-Non stamp. I tear it open with my teeth.

"FATHERS & SUNS" RETREAT

This special event just for boys and men takes place on the spring solstice of every year. We meet for three days at The Cap, a retreat cabin in Spry Poi. The event culminates in the "Reconciling with Your Sun" ritual. The event always fills up fast, so be sure to register with your Heli-Non rep ASAP!

Pricing tiers:

• One full day of "Masculinity & Manifestation," including a full day's access to group sessions, audio therapy, Minor Retrieval, and a limited-edition audio cassette version of Rays of Hope: only $97.79. Drinks and snacks included, along with all Suitable Materials.

• A two-day pass, plus a bonus hour of Face to Face with one of our trained Heli-Non reps: only $174.22.

• Bonus third-day stayover and Exploration, plus the audio cassette and one Ultimate Retrieval session: only $249.41.

For more information, applications, and to remit payment with a credit card, please visit: http://www.martinsmithelyproductions.com/pages/manifestation_retreat/users/information.

I crumple it up. But I don't litter. Because a cop car is parked at the end of the street. A shiver runs from the tip of my nose to the tip of my penis to the ends of my toes.

Back inside I lock the door and check all the tape on the curtains. I take my cereal to the couch and eat it dry while listening for sounds of footsteps on the porch but all I hear is my heart pounding in my nipples.

To calm myself I focus on the postcard tacked above the wall beside the TV. I found it on the street years ago. It's from a guy named Earl Sharkey, to Ms. Grace Rickman. It shows a cabin in the snow at the top of the earth. Carl Jake said that up far north the sun doesn't rise for half the year. I would take Bugle and move there right now so I wouldn't have to face Max Codpoodle or Conrad Flowers or Tucker. Even if the North Pole doesn't have a Heli-Non chapter or Blast! cola or *You'll Eat It And You'll Like It!*. I'd have a purple snowmobile and some goggles that let you see at night. I would have my own igloo and a hot tub. Strange women would come and go. I wouldn't know their language. They wouldn't know mine. We would screw in silence. They'd like the whiteness of my body. Its squishiness. Like a furless polar bear.

> *Glad you're not here! It's so cold the toilet water freezes and then you need the plunger to free up your caca! It's so cold you can write your name in your breath as it hovers in the air. It's so cold your thoughts freeeeeze annnnddd youuuuu caaannnn't—ha ha ha, just joshing, Gracie. I do miss your warmth though! See you soon, dollface. – Earl (Sharkey)*
>
> *P.S. I saw a three-legged rabbit!*

But I'm not going anywhere. That's what happens when you have cynical depression and you throw your dreams into the river.

I peel back some tape and peek outside. Conrad Flowers is gone. I sigh and extend my foot and turn on the TV. *You'll Eat It And You'll Like It!* will be on soon. It takes away all my pain.

Before the show starts my beeper beeps. It's Larson. Weird. Has never called me ever. I go to the phone and call back. He picks up on the first ring and says, "Yeah, it's cool. We're just not meeting this Thursday because I guess we're gonna go out and socialize for a change on Friday. Some sort of pre-Halloween special session, I guess. You in? It's at the Low Hand."

I get the intel and hang up.

Heli-Non has only been canceled two other times. The first was the time Martin was alone in the schoolhouse, pouring bug juice and setting up chairs, and a guy banged on the door. He'd driven through the fence across the street and into the cemetery and crashed into a headstone. *Winifred Sullivan, 1934–1991.* One arm was dangling and blood dripped through the gaps between the ramp's boards. Martin fainted and got wedged in the doorway. The car accident guy had to go to the church five blocks away and call for an ambulance and firetruck to come help Martin and also to save himself.

The second time when there was lots of snow on the ground.

My hands are tingling. I don't think a bar is a good setting for me right now. Or ever again.

The phone rings again. It's Larson. Says, "Oh yeah and keep this quiet. Don't tell anyone else."

I nod. Then hang up.

Special FX and Strobe Lite Live
at the Low Hand

A horde of scummies stumbles past. FX tosses his guitar back into his van, locks it, and puts on casual airs while waiting for them to clear out. He hasn't been jumped outside a club in a couple of years, but the last incident was traumatic. Weeks of pawn shop visits ensued, but he never saw that guitar again. It was his favorite, a gift from venerable blues madman Meatus Boone, long since dead and gone.

They move on, rifling through bins and crates, searching out quaff.

FX knows the feeling.

The Low Hand is already filled with smoke. FX hasn't played a gig in months and doesn't really want to, but he's tired of painting ceilings and doing long-haul furniture delivery at night and thus agreed to a one-off appearance. He wishes he hadn't. Once he pierces the veil of smoke, he realizes the clientele is the same old motley array of crushed souls drinking their way toward the middle—people who have never known true joy, who have never gotten an award or a raise or even a tepid congratulations, people whose goal for the year is to save up for a new television. His people. His ears, his souls. They are people who make the best of it, he tells himself—and sometimes the best of it happens at a wobbly table in a little brick-and-beam hideaway.

He and his drummer Strobe Lite set up with haste. Strobe Lite adjusts his kit and dampens his high hat while FX tunes his guitar and prays that the D string doesn't break. It's already as frayed as his nerves.

"Alright," Strobe Lite says to FX, and FX swallows his bile, sheds his leather jacket, and perches on his stool. When FX gives Strobe Lite a nod, Strobe Lite smacks his sticks together four times and FX leans into the microphone and draws his pick across the strings.

The sound of his own voice always startles FX at first. It sounds like an animal trapped in the bottom of a cave, either crying for help or driving would-be invaders away. It always takes him a minute or two to get used to his own voice, trembling with so much fear it's practically a musical accompaniment.

Maybe Carl Jake is onto something. The other day Martin was trying to explain to the group that everyone needs to live in the present, to be happy today, and not worry about what the sun might do tomorrow. But then Carl Jake jumped in to say that wasn't correct—"now" is actually the past because our eyes are too slow. By the time "now" enters our brains, it's already gone. We're in the future already, constantly, forever. The past is an idea and nothing more.

What's on FX's mind as he scrabbles through those first notes though, is the memory of the time he walked into the schoolhouse on the wrong night. He encountered a different group of people in the seats where he and his friends should have been—and Carl Jake was among them, though his back was toward the door. A woman in a denim frock was leading the group, behind whom, on the chalkboard, was written "Phobo-phobia." FX waved his hands and shook his head and backed away before the goon could twist around and eyeball him. He zigzagged down the ramp, dissecting the scene in his head. The fear of phobias. Was that what Carl Jake had now? Was it what he himself had? But isn't that a paradox—aren't you afraid of the fear of fear itself, thereby negating its existence and ruling yourself immune?

He couldn't say. Still can't. The song pulls him back. FX muscles through, and music happens. Two guys and some crappy beat-up instruments on a warped stage with leaden acoustics, and suddenly the city has a spirit to speak of. They don't even pause between songs and instead orchestrate a seamless segue from one arrangement to the next. FX alternately groans and sings, his fingers riding the strings as if fated to each note, sliding swiftly and precisely from fret to fret. It's almost as if the strings go right through his wrists and into his organs, meaning that if the music stops, he'll stop. Behind it all is the hiss of snares and clatter of high-hats and continuo of bass. Strobe Lite, as small and wiry as his sticks, floats above his trap set.

The noise takes over the crowd. The bar fills. People leave their chairs. Bodies collide or cling to one another, the haze soon so thick that dew forms on the ceiling.

The last song of the set is slower and darker, deeper, throaty and pained, the lyrics sexy but North Gaslin sexy—gritty and unholy, featuring the type of sex that could shame a coyote, screwing that'd take place in a busted-up trailer home or in the foreman's office on a night so cold it seems like the lovers might break off each other's parts. Women cloister close to the stage, sipping at their beers but really drinking in FX. It isn't his looks, which are simply so-so. Look deeper and you'll see the red lines of distress in his eyes, the tell-tale signs of weary middle-aged madness. His clothes are a tad baggy and need a wash. His skin is bad, his hands gnarled. But women find that vulnerability, that rawness, alluring.

"You're not a poet just because you read some poems, and you're not a musician if you just sing someone else's song," he once told a reporter. "It's a crazy lifestyle. Might as well go insane."

"Gonna take a short break," he tells the audience. He slides his leather jacket over his sweaty shirt and makes his way toward the bar.

"Orange juice," he tells the bartender.

"And?" the bartender says. Gina. Someone he dated once. All they did was drink and screw.

"And ice."

"And?"

"And a napkin."

"And?"

"And make it fast."

"Whatever."

He leans back and drains the glass. It burns in his scorched throat. He gets another. And another. Gina finally just gives him a pitcher and he's about to carry it to the dark edge of the stage where he can drink it in peace when he notices a bunch of idiotic faces leering at him from the far corner. At first they don't register. The setting is entirely wrong, as is their demeanor. They look... normal. Almost.

"What the hell is this?" he says as he ambles up to their table.

Everyone rises and swarms him, saying, "Wow, just wow," and "FX the maestro," and "I knew you were good but not that good."

He's embarrassed and proud and feels like he's in high school again, sinking three-pointers while his grandmother watches from the front bleacher. "Why didn't you tell me you guys were coming?"

"Pretty sure you wouldn't have allowed that."

"You're probably right."

"Come on, have a drink with us."

"I've got this," he says, hoisting the pitcher of O.J.

"Good enough."

Liza indicates the open seat next to her. He hesitates a moment, then accepts. "This is so fucking weird," he says, taking them all in. Huge Martin. Weird little Annabelle. Mysterious Murray. Beautiful Liza. Slumping Larson. Cross-eyed Laramie Bob. Execrable Channing. "No Carl Jake?"

The others exchange looks.

"Thank God," FX says.

"Don't thank Him," Larson says toothily. "Thank us. We kept it on the down-low."

"I appreciate it."

The venue seems even more crowded now. FX drinks another glass of juice and wonders where he's going to find the vigor for a second set.

His fellow heliophobes stare at him, beaming.

"So," Martin says.

"So."

"Lovely music."

"Thanks."

"What was the name of that one song," Annabelle says, "about the devil in the tree when you're walking through the forest of life?"

"'Devil in the Tree.'"

"Yeah. That one."

They're still staring at him.

"'Devil in the Tree.' That's the name."

Everyone nods. Liza takes his hand under the table, soaking up his sweat.

"That one was great," Larson says.

"Yeah."

"Yeah."

FX laughs and wonders if this is the weirdest moment of his life, where his two greatest fears have intertwined like barbed wire and... more barbed wire. He turns to scan the room to see if anyone of note is witnessing this scene but instead comes eye to eye with Murray. FX smiles and waits for him to mirror it, but he doesn't. Normally the guy has the softest and most delirious countenance on the planet, but right now it looks like he's going to drive a rusty fork into FX's cheek.

"You okay, buddy?"

He shakes his head.

"One too many?"

"What's up, Furry?" Annabelle says, leaning against him.

Murray's trembling hand rises up and stretches toward FX. FX thinks Murray is going to try and feed him a peanut or pretzel or something but instead the fingers land on the lapel of FX's jacket.

"Dude, what are you doing?"

The others laugh and ask Murray if he's feeling okay. When FX tries to lean away, Murray grabs hold of the jacket as if it were a dog's scruff and comes away with a tiny white sticker.

"*Muh* Mazzie," he says, holding up a price tag: *$9.29.*

"What?" FX says. His face is red. "What's going on?"

"*Muh* Mazzie!"

"We heard you," Larson says. "What's wrong?"

"Yeah, what's going on, Murray?" Martin asks.

Murray shows them the price tag. "*Muh* Mazzie *tuh* tag!"

"Yeah," Laramie Bob says, "it definitely looks like a price tag."

"Not these fucking pricing guns again," Channing says. "He's telling some fucking story about—"

Marlene swats Channing to shut him up.

"*Luh luh* look at the *kuh* corners. *Nuh* no one *buh buh* but Mazzie does this."

They stare blankly as if watching a live train crash in slow motion on television: helpless, inevitable, all that momentum.

"I'm really fucking sorry I have a price tag on my coat, Murray. Sometimes I buy stuff."

Murray's mouth stretches out and the flesh around his eyes reorganizes itself until it's a crumpled mass of anger. "*Wuh wuh—heh heh—*"

"Murray," Martin says, "take a breath."

"*Wuh wuh—*"

"Take it easy, brother," Laramie Bob says.

"*Shh sh* shut the *fuh* fuck up!"

"Furry!" Annabelle says.

"No, you shut the fuck up!" Channing, on the verge of tears, says to Murray.

"*Wuh* where *ar ar* are they?" he says so close to FX's face that FX can see the tooth missing from the back of Murray's bottom row.

"Where's what?"

"*Muh muh—*"

"This is embarrassing, Furry," Annabelle says.

"*Muh muh—*"

"Have another beer, Murray."

"*Muh* my *guh* guns!"

"Whoa, Murray," Laramie Bob says. "Just whoa."

"Guns?" FX says and laughs. "Come on, Sandman. Hey, did you ever—"

Murray shoves his hand into FX's jacket and pulls out his keys, then pushes away from the table, his chair toppling. He grabs his hat and coat and stomps out into the night.

When FX and the others find him, he's in the back of FX's van, tossing things left and right, sorting through crates, digging under cushions and magazines and boxes.

"Dude, come on," FX says.

"Murray," Martin says, "this isn't rational."

Murray glares at Martin; Martin looks down in shame.

"Furry, this is really weird."

Murray glares at Annabelle; she looks down. Murray digs and tosses and kicks and spits and swears and mutters. Finally FX and Channing haul him out like a frantic toddler.

"*Maa—maaaa—*Mazzies."

"Man, you are whacked," FX says. He's going to miss his second set. Which comes as a relief, if he's honest.

"*Eye eye* I'm not *arf arf* afraid."

FX lays his hand on Murray's chest. The knuckle on his right thumb is tattooed with NO and H-O-P-E on the other four fingers. "Good. Then quit Heli-Non and move on with your life. To be honest, I don't think I need the sessions myself, but the whole vibe keeps me low and dirty. Know what I mean? Without it, who would I be?"

"*Nuh nuh no.* I mean—*fuh* fuck. I'm not *arf arf* afraid to tell *yuh* you what I think. You big *luh* loser. *Guh* go be big. A *muh* music *ss* star. A star, you *fuh* fuck! Be a *ss* star!"

"Shut your face, Murray. You don't know what you're talking about." FX turns away, but Murray says:

"*Yuh* you're an *eck eck* eclipse."

The other heliophobes gasp. Liza steps forward to mitigate the situation, but FX brushes past her. "I'm not an eclipse."

Murray nods. "You're your own *duh* darkness. *Buh buh* blocking your own *sss* sunlight. *Yuh* you're a *fruh* fraud. *Wuh* worse than me."

So it's true. When the guy's had enough to drink, he can almost express himself in full. "Fuck you, Sandman."

"Yeah, look who's talking," Channing says.

"Ha!" Murray barks.

"What?"

"Ha!"

"I heard you. Dick."

"*Yuh* you are a *buh* basement baby. Momma's *buh* boy."

"Says the retarded mushmouth. My mom was nice to you."

"And you're a *zzh* jerk to her."

"So? She's my mom, not yours. Yours is cuckoo."

Murray shrugs, then points at Larson. "*Luh* lush." He turns to Annabelle. "You *aw aww* orbit yourself. You're *nuh* nosy."

"You're a slob with no prospects."

He nods and turns to Martin, but Murray just stares at him until Martin looks down. Murray turns to Laramie Bob instead. "*Zzzh* jerk. Twenty *puh puh* percent on a *luh luh* loan for a friend? Eat your vig! Jerk." Then he shifts toward Marlene. "Rich and *ss* selfish. *Muh* me and *muh* Martin pay for snacks and *yuh* you eat them all the time. *Wuh* what have you got to be *aff aff* afraid of? All that *muh* money? A home theater!" He waves his arms in the air. "All of you. *Eck eck* eclipses!"

FX grabs his acoustic guitar from the back of the van and raises it high like he's going to brain Murray, but Murray simply turns toward him with his arms raised, welcoming it. FX loves the guitar though, and he sort of loves Murray, and he can't do it. He tosses it back into the truck and starts to gather up his gear.

The others help, then either drift back toward the club or down the street. Murray disappears into the shadows of one alley or another. It's over.

FX closes up the van. His hands are shaking. He's just about to go back inside and tell the crew he's done for the night when someone strolls up with his hands in his pockets while making a sucking sound with his mouth.

"What'd I miss?" Carl Jake asks.

We're Going to Hell-o-ween

Tonight is Hell-o-ween.

I told Mikey I didn't want to go because I haven't solved my pricing gun crime and because of the Honey Mom sadness stuff and the Heli-Non weirdness stuff and the money stuff and every other stuff but Mikey says a good time will help get my mind off things. I guess he's right. I've spent all day in bed writing an imaginary speech to present to Max Codpoodle. Now it's time to go sip yet another beer and turn into warm liquid happiness and eat a bunch of Chewy Corn. I won't have to think about the Mazzies or paying rent or the ballfondlers and buttsmackers and templejabbers who've made me sad and sore all my life.

Plus I have a good costume. Too good for a Heli-Non gathering in someone's apartment building rec room.

While I'm putting finishing touches on the costume my beeper beeps. Again. This time it's Martin. Everyone is trying to get in touch with me. I don't want to talk. Don't want visitors.

Last night I put a chair in front of the door which was dumb since it opens toward the outside but it probably would have scared someone when it fell over. Marlene stopped by today and knocked and knocked. Even though Bugle barked I ignored her because I thought she would be mad and never hug me again. Instead she left bug juice and cookies. They're cheap generic Shop Now! ones but that's what I like. FX called my machine too and played a lick from a song about bees. That confused me. Forgiveness is unnatural.

Mikey says I should open my heart to the other helio-phobes but it seems like if I do that they'll just steal my blood. I know what I did, what I said. Something about seeing FX play music on stage set me off. Seeing him in his natural habi-tat. Like a wild animal licking its balls up in a tree. Historically he was the second heliophobe after me. Back in the old days he wrote songs about the sun and deep stuff about death and life and vampires. He had energy. Hope. Anger. Now he looks like he got kicked in the head while asleep and only woke up halfway.

The real kicker was the Mazzie price tag though. I realized later it came off his roll of duct tape. But by then I'd said what I'd said.

I sigh and shake off the bad vibes. I've got a party to attend.

Bugle gets a long walk and extra treats and special hugs. Then I put on my costume and lock my door with the key. I drive. I park across the street from Wiggles, honk. Wiggles is a bar whose name is really The Wigwam. It isn't a gay bar but Mikey and all his friends go there and the owner likes the money so he lets them do whatever they want. There's a big party going on inside. I honk. *Meep meep.* Rain is falling.

Mikey appears, jogs over. He's wearing a taco costume. He climbs in and pounds the dashboard.

"Fuck yeah! Hell-o-ween here we come!" He looks me up and down. "Wow, Murray. Look at that fucking thing. You finally put your skills to use. Amazing!"

I look at myself but I already know my costume is amazing. I'm a Sugar Slams box but also a robot. Cyber Slammin' Sammy. Luckily it hinges at the middle so I can sit and go pee and stuff. I smack the steering wheel and try to peel out but we only slip and skid. Mikey leans his head out into the rain and howls.

Another thirty minutes later Mikey still has his head still out the window because he's asking some guy dressed like a punk for directions to the main party. The punk knows which house, says it's the one with the gnomes. He flings a cigarette into the back of the truck and climbs in next to Mikey. Turns out it's not a costume. He really is a punk. "Turn around, man."

I do a U-ey on someone's lawn and knock over someone's barrel. The lid gets stuck under the truck and makes a sonic scrapey noise. It's funny but no one laughs except me. The punk directs us through Knifepoint where the streets are arranged like a burrow dug by a badger on cocaine. We see fires and hear explosions. I drive slowly. Mikey's eyes are as big as headlights. Mine itch from the smoke. The punk squints like a cool guy.

Along the way we pass smaller parties and battles and crimes. People lie alongside the curb, soaked. Bonfires snap in the rain. Fireworks arc overhead. Old men and teenage girls in weird costumes or in their underwear stroll past. Some people leap into the path of the truck or pound on its hood or climb into the back. It's like a war zone. Not that I've ever been to war. But I bet it'd be safer than Hell-o-ween.

"Fuckin' a, men," the punk says.

It's not raining that hard but the wind blows through the cardboard across the back window. The music gets louder. The crowd gets thicker. Costumes get wilder. People are on stilts. People are on fire. A guy stops and stares at us as we slide past. He's wearing all black except for a silver mask that looks like dripping metal but with glowing misshapen red eyes. My sphincter clenches and I belch. Finally he turns away and moves on.

"That there's the place you're looking for." The punk points at a house with glowing gnomes on the roof. I don't like gnomes much but it gives me a good idea for a new Astro Fire Cop story. Alien Elves from Hell. They could all travel in an intergalactic sleigh. I suddenly regret sending my drawings downriver.

"The mailbox says *B. Mona.*," Mikey says as I slow down. "This is definitely it."

The punk climbs out and hurries off.

Someone's crawling down the middle of the street.

"Well, let's hope that they have beer on tap."

I park at an angle like all the other cars. We get out and adjust our costumes and approach with caution. Mikey raps on the screen door. No one answers. The gnomes are watching us. A new fear: automatonophobia. He shrugs and I shrug. We enter.

The music sounds like someone's plugging a lamp into a socket over and over. *Bzzt, bzzt, bzzt.* I close the door and we stumble over a pile of stinky sandals and torn-up canvas shoes and scuffed-up combat boots. We're not even past the foyer and the air is hazy like someone's car is running in the basement. We step into the kitchen where pink and purple Christmas lights blink out of synch. Two guys are holding each other's opposite arms and trading slaps to the face as people lay down bets. It seems like the party stretches forever through the house. We slide along the hallway into a living room decorated with lots of rugs and junky tapestries and weird art. Here a girl sits on a beanbag. There's a bulbous glass tower attached to her face. I can't tell if it's a bong or one of those things for playing funky songs on the sidewalk. Or even better something that Astro Fire Cop might use in deep sea warfare or a space rescue. Five or six other stoners are bobbing their heads to the music. *Bzzt, bzzt.* Most look like they've never shaved but still can't grow a beard. I've seen nicer flannels and jeans on scarecrows. Their costumes are silly cheap masks from Dollar Zone. Cats, presidents, diseased monsters. One of them finally realizes we're standing there. He pushes his clown-cop mask onto his head and his eyelids peel back.

"Faggot and Maggot?" he says.

My eyes pop out of my skull and memories flood my brain like cough syrup and spaghetti sauce—the worst meal in the world. Mikey's jaw drops so low you could fit Chuck Rollins's foot inside it. My plans for forgetting about the past and all the spankers and ballfondlers have vanished like happiness on a sunny day.

"Benny?" Mikey says.

"*Bee bee—*"

Mikey nudges me. "Is that really you, Benny?"

Benny Monagee was also known as Beaker in high school. He was evil in all sorts of special ways. He was the type of kid who'd steal your fence at night just so you were confused. Another time he stabbed me with a pencil during a really big test. Because I couldn't get the words out to explain why I was screaming I had to go to the principal's office and fail the class and go to summer school where Clinton Kennedi fondled my balls in the bathroom. Beaker carried a briefcase and used it to break kids' noses. He stalked sisters. He trampled flowers. But he was sharp too. One time I ruined his woodworking project by standing on it to reach the two-by-fours and he got everyone to call me Woody Woodfucker for the rest of the year.

"Dudes, I'm sorry. That was mean to call you by your old nicks. Wow! What the fuck are you doing here?"

We cannot move. Everything is upsidewaysdown. "*Heh heh*—" I say then kick Mikey.

"It's Hell-o-ween, right?" Mikey says.

"That's right, bitches!" Beaker says.

Also you never called him Beaker or he'd pour vegetable oil through the slats in your locker or spray-paint your cat. Or just punch you in the liver.

"Look at those costumes. Damn, Murray! You're a Sugar Slams robot. Well, come on and give me a hug."

Mikey glances at me. I give him a micro-shrug. He leads. We step over empty beer cans. Some underwear. A toppled ashtray.

"Oh, wait. Do you mind taking your shoes off?"

We look at our feet. Then shrug. Mikey says, "Sure thing."

I wedge myself into the door frame and slip off my shoes. Then Mikey holds onto my shoulder while taking off his expensive athletic sneakers with pillows of air under the toes. We go back to complete the hug but when Beaker tries to get up he falls backward and says, "Whoa. I'm stoned as fuck."

Instead we just slap hands across the coffee table.

"Well, fuck yeah! It's so cool to see you guys again after all these years."

"This is your place?" Mikey asks.

"Yup. For real. Now sit the fuck down." He waves toward a wooden chair. It's occupied by a monstrous lime-green carnival bear. Stuffing's spilling out the nose where a dog or stoner bit it off. I nudge him aside and sit with my arm around his shoulder. Mikey sits on the floor. "Everyone," Beaker says, "this chubby box of robotic cereal is Murray 'Magoo' Sandman and the big gay taco is Mikey Priest. Dudes, this is a bunch of people."

Nod-wave.

"And this hot piece of ass here is my life partner, Nan."

What I thought was a pile of clothes is a human person in patched-up hobo jeans and a tank top so loose you can almost see her lady parts. Her hair resembles the stuff cats hurl onto your rug. She's got black smears under her eyes like a baseball player and she's wearing a red cap sideways. I can't tell if she's in a costume or not. I nod-wave.

"Quite a party, huh?" Beaker says.

"Looks… lively," Mikey says.

"We'll have knife juggling in a little while and then we'll open the mud pit and mix up some flaming cocktails. I busted through the fence so we could expand into the fields behind us. We've got go-karts, a human-powered Ferris wheel, and a couple of surprises."

"*Huh huh*—" I'm nervous. I don't even know what I'm saying. I think we should leave before Beaker tries to give us haircuts with a box knife like he did senior year right before graduation.

"Ha ha, good ol' Magoo." He holds up the bong thing. "You wanna take a hit?"

"Yeah he does," Mikey says. Before I can say no he's holding the brain destroyer against my mouth and I'm making love to the hole at the top. It's sweet and hot and tastes like rabbit farts. I'm dying. I can't breathe. I hold my breath. I'm not dying. Now I'm dying again. I spew it out. My head swims through concrete. Mikey takes a hit too then passes the machine to a short guy with a huge chest and little stick arms who's wearing a business suit and lipstick. The lipstick transfers to the bong.

"Great stuff," Mikey says.

"*Zhh zhh—*"

"I know, right?" Beaker says.

"*Zhh zhh—*"

"Fucking Magoo. As wacky as ever."

"Well, then," Mikey says slowly like he's on a sailboat and we have months of travel around the globe to have this conversation. "You still doing computer programming, Bea—Benny?"

"Screw that. I'm an entrepreneur now. Goddamn, Mikey. Look at those muscles of yours. Do you tow trucks for a living? Like, with your arms?"

"Sure do. Want to wrestle?" Mikey winks at him.

"Maybe later in the mud pit. Seriously though, this is fucked up." He leans forward. "Your pops was in the clink with my pa for a while. Did you know that?" He sits back before Mikey can answer. "And you, Magoo. Whatever happened to Big Man? Did they ever find him?"

I think I'm shaking my head but I don't know. Everything is spinning like a shot-down spaceship.

"Man, look as us. Three old friends with the shittiest fathers imaginable. Mikey's is the drunk. Mine is the tyrannical asshole. Magoo's is the weird one who either talked your ear off or stood there silently judging you. Until he just, like, went away."

"I guess it explains a lot," Mikey says. "Though my dad is sober now, I hear. One of my brothers saw him mopping floors at a typing school in Woolhaven."

Beaker laughs. "I can't believe I'm getting high with Mikey Priest and Magoo Sandman. I thought you guys were as straight as they come. Except for the whole fucking guys in the ass thing, Mikey."

Mikey and the stoners giggle. I stroke the basset hound's fur. "*Zhh zhh—*"

"Totally, Magoo."

"*Zhh zhh—*?"

"Yeah," Beaker mumbles. He closes his eyes.

"Whew, great stuff," Mikey says. "Did I say that?"

"It bears repeating," business-guy says.

I close my eyes.

"Want some heroin?" someone whispers from the ceiling. When I look up I see only a bulb wrapped in orange tissue. Just to be safe I shake my head a few hundred times like Bugle when he's crawling out of a puddle.

"Cool."

No one talks for a couple minutes. We listen to fireworks. Maybe they're gunshots. The music's going *wee-ooo, wee-ooo.* I'm as high as the constellations. Though Carl Jake said the other day that once you leave the planet there's no such thing as height. Aardvark, aardvark. I can't think about that now. I'm floating like Astro Fire Cop. My eyes follow their own orbit and land on a picture of a cat dressed up like Elvis. We make eye contact for an hour or two until finally his little mouth opens and he says, "Sandman?"

I look at Beaker. He says softly, "So I guess you heard about my accident."

I sort of remember but not really. I glance at Mikey who shrugs and says, "No, what happened?"

"This was about five years ago. I was on my way to Thunder Mountain, you know, the amusement park, with Jerbo. Remember him from high school?"

Jeremy Bowlicky was a math genius. Rumor is that he works for the mob now, moving money under the oceans with computers and stuff. Or he's in an asylum. It's unclear.

"He was driving and fell asleep at the wheel. Drove us right off a cliff."

"No shit."

Beaker nods. "Deep shit. I was in a coma for a couple weeks. When I woke up I had no idea who I was."

"That's awful."

"It was. But it was a new beginning. I got to reinvent myself."

"I'm so sorry, Bea—Benny."

Beaker's face flattens. Mikey's goes white. I try not to laugh. Luckily Benny doesn't freak out or anything. "Anyway. It's all good. It made me a better person. It fucked up my memory big time though. So it's kind of weird that I remember you both since I don't remember anyone from the bad days."

We're quiet for a while until something flies across the room and hits me in the face. No. It's just the bear's plastic eyeball tapping me on the cheek. I laugh. I can't stop. The others join in.

"Is it true, Magoo?"

"*Wuh wuh wuh—*"

"Mikey says you've got the weirdest job one could imagine and that I'll never guess what it is." Elvis Cat is talking through

Beaker now. His tail swishes as he props up the bong on his feet and sticks his mouth on the cakey spit already there. His eyes are glowing. I detect the same old red warning lights signaling that Beaker is still in there behind the scars and hair and shark-teeth necklace.

"No," I say clearly. I start to get up. At least in spirit. My body remains attached to the chair.

"He's a police sketch artist," Mikey says, his eyes droopy and wet.

"What?" Nan the hobo girl says.

"That sounds totally retarded," the stick-arm business-guy says, exhaling brown exhaust.

I don't like that word so I give him a hard stare until he points his eyeballs toward the floor and pouts.

"I always thought you'd draw comics or something," Beaker says. "You could draw real good in high school."

"I thought you lost your memory," Mikey says.

Beaker gives him a pinched slitty look.

"Police, huh?" Nan says. "Working for the piggos to maintain the industrial prison system must help you sleep well at night."

Mikey pushes the taco shell out of his face. "And what do you do for a living?"

"I assist Benjamin with his entrepreneurial endeavors."

"Neat. Is this your team?"

Nan scowls. She's ugly but I'd eat her if she were made of chocolate.

"The gray market is the real market," business-guy says.

My lids creep down. I push them back up with my fingers.

Beaker leans forward. "Serious, Magoo. You could have been something. Look at that costume."

"*Diss-diss*-dys-*luh*-lexsia.*"

"You have dyslexia?" Nan says. "Like Picasso, da Vinci, and Rodin?"

Now I want to fry her in oil. My ankles throb. I scrape them together.

"What else do you recall from the shitty old days?" Mikey asks Beaker.

"Aw, you know. How miserable I was. How everyone picked on me."

"Like who?"

"Everyone. You, Magoo, teachers."

"Uh, just like Murray and his dyslexia, you've got it backward."

"No way."

My mouth goes, "*Thpppttt*," and everyone looks at me. "*Yuh* you once *guh* gave me a *wuh* wedgie so *buh* bad my ass *kuh* crack bled."

Everyone's heads turn toward Beaker.

Business-guy says, "You did that, Benny?"

"Nah."

"You once gave me two black eyes in one week," Mikey says, "with your briefcase."

"That's fucked up!" Nan says. She shoves Beaker away. "Why were you such a dick?"

Mikey says, "He once filled the tires on Murray's bike with cement. And one time he made these kids hold me down in the locker room while he farted in my face."

"No way! Didn't happen."

"Sure did. And who do you think outed me as gay years before I was ready? I didn't want to come out in high school. But

Bea—Benny—put up fliers in the school with my picture on them saying *For a good time call Mikey. Guys only.*"

Carrot-hat guy juts his chin at Mikey. "Why didn't you beat him up?"

"I was small and weak back then. Benny is the reason I started lifting weights. For years I dreamed about beating up Benny, actually. I had this whole scenario in my brain where Murray and I—well, it doesn't matter anymore. It's all in the past."

"Dude," a stoner with buck teeth says to Beaker, "I'm never sharing a bong with you again."

Beaker looks like his grandmother just took away his favorite sippy cup. "I'm really sorry, dudes. I know I was kind of, like, different and all that but I didn't know I was such a terrorist." He wipes his nose. "Things changed for me after the accident, I swear."

We're at a funeral now. Elvis Cat stares down into Beaker's grave.

Mikey flips his wrist. "It's cool. Don't worry about it."

Beaker reaches for the bong. "Start over? This'll be our peace pipe. Unless you want—" He shoves some papers aside and gestures at a silver platter full of needles.

"I'll stick with the natural stuff," Mikey says and takes another hit.

I close my eyes. It feels like I'm orbiting myself. Saturn rings are circling my waist, tickling me. I giggle as everyone drifts away like moons.

When I open my eyes again for a sec I see the guy in the dripping metal mask. Staring at me staring at him. I realize now who he is. The character known as Abstractio. I blink long and hard. Now he's gone. Aardvark, aard…

After We've Done Drugs We Get in Trouble and Take Part in a Violence Competition

The CD switches over to some goofy stuff with flowing water and meowing tigers and chirping bugs. I press my face into the bear's green fur. It's so soft. But Mikey shakes me awake.

"Follow me."

We creep through a dining room filled with upside-down couches and people slumped over them. We open the basement door and hear noises like slapping and groaning and see lots of leather and skin and decide not to go down there. Three people are passed out on the bathroom floor. Then we find a little bedroom-office combo with a photo of Nan and Beaker on the door. Mikey knocks. No answer. We go inside. It looks like someone set off a bomb made out of clothes and flip-flops and stuffed animals. A lava lamp in the corner makes the room spin like a cyborg butterfly in hyperspace.

"This should be fun."

While Mikey rifles through the drawers I hold my head onto my body.

Mikey finds a little paper bag and pockets it.

I hold onto the walls to keep the house from imploding.

He grabs hold of me and shakes me. "This is our chance for revenge, you fool. Look for something incriminating."

I smile and nod and prod my toe into a pile of clothes. I open some cabinets and a bucket that turns out to be filled with crow wings but no birds. Mikey hoots quietly when he finds a bunch of brown bottles filled with pills. He waves me closer and makes me stuff them into the mechanic onesie under my costume.

Then I stop. Because the music has stopped. The house is quiet. The silence is so thick you could pack it in a bong and smoke it. Then it starts up again and sounds like two helicopters having sex. *Whuuuzz. Whuuuzz.*

Mikey picks up a cardboard box. There's a computer underneath it. "Oh fuck yes." He sits on the floor and turns on the television part. It shows a picture of a dinosaur with a big fat doobie saying that he doesn't care if he goes extinct, he's still going to get high.

"*Wuh* what are you *duh* doing?"

"Just seeing what this psychotic asshole has been up to."

While he plays around I crawl into the closet. I find a cashbox. There's money inside.

"This computer's a piece of crap," Mikey says, "but he's got a dirty web search history. Bomb-making supplies. Puppet porn. Briefcase oil. Same old Beaker."

I slump against the closet wall and kick some junk aside so I can stretch out my legs. I can hear some people having a love session in the other room. It makes me wonder if some sex lubricant would help the rollers eject tags more efficiently on the Doo-Har Pricetasker.

Some guilt washes over me for going through Beaker's stuff like this. Even though he was an asshole and hurt and humiliated us he was probably doing it because he was abused by his father. He had a lisp for a long time too. That didn't stop him from making fun of my stutter. It was always kind of funny watch him do his Murray act while sounding like a deflating balloon filled with bees. And there was one year his father moved out. Beaker was really happy. Since none of us got invited to the school dances or parties or anything at all we hung out in Beaker's basement and watched movies and played ping pong and spied on his older sister and her friends. Then his father moved back home and a few days later Beaker poured pink paint in Mikey's backpack and cut the cables on my bike's brakes so that I had to ride down a hill and into the woods where I smashed into the trees. It hurt. I needed stitches but Big Man said stitches are for whiney-babies then showed me a six-inch scar running from his belly button to his ribs.

Mikey stops. We hear noises in the hall. I take this opportunity to crawl backward out of the closet. Murray Sandman. Mad Scrambler. Manic Scamperer. The music starts again. We shrug, poke around more. We find a stack of photos. "Holy shit. This is us." There's a photo from one of Beaker's birthday parties. We were tiny. Beaker's got a bloody nose. In another photo Beaker is building a tree fort that's four stories high. "Remember this thing? What did we call it?"

"*Ho ho ho* Hotel."

"That's right."

The fort even had an elevator made from a crate and some pulleys. The town made him tear it down before a kid could die and sue. The last photo is just of me and Mikey. Our arms crossed, shoulder to shoulder. Looking at the camera like a couple of cool dudes.

The door swings open.

"Whoa," Nan says. She has on one hiking boot. Her boobs are swinging in her shirt like bananas. I realize I'm hungrier than I've been in years. "What's all this about?"

"We were just looking for a phone," Mikey says.

I nod in agreement.

"We don't have one, man. The cops can reverse the line and turn it into a microphone. Duh." Nan cranes her neck past us. "What were you doing with our computer?"

We look down at the dinosaur.

"*Muh muh muh—*"

"Minesweeper!" Mikey says.

I nod. Though I don't know what that means.

"Man, that's not cool, you know, coming in here and, like, I don't know. You know?"

We exchange a look then get up. Mikey inches toward the door and I follow but Nan puts up her hand. Says, "Stay." She returns a minute later with Beaker. It takes a long time for his brain to get back up to speed.

"What's up?"

"These old friends of yours are messing around in here."

Mikey says, "We wanted to order a pizza, that's all."

I rub my cardboard robot belly.

"It's cool, Nan. Hey, guys, we got pizzas on the grill out back. Come on. I'll show you."

Mikey says, "That sounds great. Thanks, Beaker." It takes Mikey a couple seconds to realize what he's done. Then his jaw starts quivering and his face goes white.

"What'd he call you?" Nan asks.

Beaker's face turns into boiled evil. "What'd you call me?"

"Shit. I'm sorry Bea—Benny." Mikey hangs his head.

"If you were my friends, man, you'd know that I hate being called Beaker. I mean, fuck! That was the worst time of my life."

"But—your memory."

"You don't forget trauma, man."

We stand there waiting for the banshee to rise up from Beaker's heart and latch onto someone's face. His other friends appear in the hallway.

"But I'm all about peace and shit now, you know?"

"I'm not feeling so peaceful," Nan says. "We should, like, deal with this."

Beaker thinks hard. He's deciding whether to tear his shirt off and become Beaker-Beaker-Insane-o-Freaker or normal medicated Benny Monagee with his briefcase full of nunchucks and broken calculators. It's clear this is going to end with either vomit or blood.

"Dudes. Follow me."

Our choices are few. We follow.

We push through the dining room filled with a dozen rolling office chairs. Some of which are filled with costumed bodies. Then through a long sunroom filled with plants and cheap broken statues and ugly stoners. The coffee table is flipped over and bottles and mugs are smashed all over the floor. Everyone makes a path for us, knows something is going on. We exit through the sliding doors and out into the little back yard where tables are filled with snacks beer pizza chips zucchini tomato slices and other vegetables. Despite my state of mental health I have an idea. On a whim I grab hold of some chili peppers. Just in case this walk is leading where I think it is.

"Through there!" Beaker yells over the music which is ten times louder than the electronic bleep-bloop stuff inside. He points at the broken fence leading into the fields behind his property. We don't have our shoes but we don't ask about them.

Bonfires fight back the rain. People quickly form a circle in the mud.

"Benny," Mikey says, "what the fuck is this?"

The stereo system outside jumps to a new disc. Louder. Insaner. My head feels larger than the Earth but filled with helium. I wish I could just float away. Someone tears off my upper costume and then my robotic pants, exposing the mechanic onesie. I want to weep. I'm glad Eddie isn't here. It seems like half of North Gaslin is though. Scummies. Bikers. Dweebs. Guppies. They're hooting and rocking from one foot to the other while sipping beers and smoking fat joints and six-inch-long cigarettes.

Beaker signals toward the darkness beyond the fire. "Bring in the Ancients. Let's show my old friends a good time."

The crowd parts. My jaw falls open and rain collects in it as three guys come forward all wearing backward hats and hand-made superhero shirts. Beaker wasn't kidding. They really look like the comic book characters known as the Ancients. Horse-blood. Green Darkness. Swordsnapper. Meanwhile we're still in our socks and mud seeps through our toes all cold and squishy.

"Who's first? Vince? You wanna warm up your knuckles on my friend here?" Beaker shoves my shoulder. "Vince is still in high school. You can take him, right Magoo?"

Vince a.k.a. Horseblood steps forward. He's wearing gray baggy pants and striped sneakers. Curly hair pokes out of his hat. If he's in high school it must be a special one for kids who took drugs as babies and chew on rocks instead of study. "Come on, bitch."

I've been in fights before. One time I had to fight this kid Ralph Bequeba in the farthest corner of the playground where the teachers' eyesight wouldn't reach. I was getting my ribs kicked sideways when my pants split open. The other kids let the fight end after that because it was embarrassing.

I have a secret weapon though, thanks to the snack table. I shove the chili peppers into my mouth. My tongue and lips immediately start burning.

"Let's go, bitch," Vince a.k.a. Horseblood says.

Tears whittle down my face as I chew.

"He's crying!" Beaker says. "Look at this pussy."

Mikey hangs his head. I think he's praying but I'm not sure.

"This guy's a cunt," Horseblood says. "I'm gonna murderize him."

My face turns so hot the rain turns to steam on my skin. I'm thirteen again, cornered in the shadows beneath the stairs in our school. It was stupid thinking I could escape my worries or the past by going to a party. The past is everywhere, like air made out of memories.

"A retarded cunt," Horseblood says. But he sounds like Big Man. That's all it takes. I step forward.

Horseblood squares off like a boxer. I do the same but old-timey with my fists up high. Everyone laughs. They don't know that I have a plan though. When Horseblood comes at me I spit like a cobra into his face. The mess is slimy and thick and red and stinky and goes splat on his nose and eyes. He paws at the mess and that only makes it worse. He makes a whimpering sound as it sizzles in his eyeballs and drips into his mouth. I take this opportunity to twist as far as my spine and belly will allow and swing back around and put my knuckles into his face.

It's not a good punch. My fist slides along the goop and scrapes past his ear and carries me with it. Horseblood and I hug each other for a couple seconds. Then I punch him somewhere on his body. He takes this opportunity to punch me in the ribs. It hurts so much my feet go out and I slump against him. We flop onto the ground together. When we're down there he manages to deliver another punch to my neck. My head bends like a roller coaster track. I hear stoner laughter, *huh huh huh.*

"What a faker," Beaker says. "Hurry up. I'm getting hungry."

Horseblood claws at my face. A finger that looks all chewed up like a dog toy manages to get into my mouth. I chomp down on it as hard as I can. My teeth bottom out on bone but I don't stop. I pretend it's a pretzel and keep chomping.

"Fuck!" He leaps back and holds his stump-finger up. "Aw fuck!"

I get to my feet and spit out the fire-goop and finger piece. Horseblood looks so mad that his thoughts alone could melt a bank vault. When he goes to punch me I let it connect and accept that it's going to hurt a lot. It does. But thanks to Tucker and Big Man I'm used to being punched in the head. I shake it off and drive my heel into his kneecap. He reels back. Once the lights rearrange themselves in his brain I pop my foot out again and catch him just inside the groin. It hurts my toes but it hurts his groin more and makes his leg move funny. I raise my fists but again it's a trick and I go for another kick. This time in the same knee. Just when he thinks I'm going to punch him I kick the knee yet again. Horseblood grabs the leg with the stumpy-fingered hand. Now comes the punch. I raise my fist high like I'm Devil Donkey and bring it down on the side of his skull. It flattens him.

"Get up, you piece of shit!" his #1 fan calls out.

"Don't lose, you loser!" Nan adds.

Horseblood tries to stand but his eyes keep shutting. "What the fuck, man." He buries his head in his arms while rocking back and forth. Blood from the missing finger spurts onto his face. "My head's ringing."

My mouth is burning and my head feels caved in but I also feel like Chuck Rollins in *Metal Devil*, the movie where he jumps his motorcycle onto a moving circus train and an elephant saves him from a lion. It's pretty good but was poorly received except in China. I kick Horseblood in the ribs. Something snaps. I punch him in the mouth. I can't stop. I'm in space, just hurtling forever.

"Stop!" Beaker barks. "You made your point." He sighs. "Well, fuck. That was weird. Whatever. It's your turn, Mikey."

Beaker snaps his fingers in the air. I'd like to bite one off. Mikey stands there staring at the mud. I love Mikey. I want to hug him. Not right now but maybe later. People nudge him forward and egg him on. He cries a bit and shakes his head. Someone kicks him in the butt and he perks up and starts to tug off the taco costume and his shirt. People gasp when they see his muscles. But he doesn't like fighting. He'd rather hug these men.

The music thuds and goes around in circles like a radio in a whirlpool as Green Darkness steps into the circle. He's so brawny and idiotic he makes Horseblood look like a baby pony. Mikey doesn't raise his fists or anything. I haven't seen him so scared since that time a raccoon walked into his kitchen. He walks backward, waiting to see what Green Darkness is going to do. Green Darkness doesn't wait though. He laughs and empties his nostrils of snot and charges. But the mud slows him down and he slips and slides. His arm cocks back and starts a long arc toward Mikey. It's so slow Mikey has time to count the knuckles going past. One two ten. After the fist and arm pass by Mikey punches Green Darkness in the ear. It hurts to get punched in the ear. More than you'd think.

Green Darkness falls into the crowd. He doesn't look so super anymore. The crowd throw him back at Mikey who steps aside as Green Darkness staggers past then kicks him hard in the ass so that Green Darkness goes sprawling into the bonfire. People pull him out before he burns up but his pants catch on fire and then then his shirt and hair. He rolls in the mud then crawls off.

Mikey looks relieved. "It's over, Beak—Benny. Fuck."

Beaker snaps his fingers again and sends in Swordsnapper who tosses his white cap aside and gets into a kung fu position. Now Mikey puts up his fists, blocks a couple of easy attacks.

The crowd yells, "Don't give in!" and "Don't die!" and "Kill the Taco Man!"

"Kill the faggot!" Beaker says.

Now Mikey's mad.

Swordsnapper spins around and hops forward while unleashing a series of jabby kicks. But right when his foot is about to spear Mikey's ribs Mikey grabs a fistful of ash-mud and flings it in Swordsnapper's face. It's hot and wet and goes splat. Swordsnapper lands hard then spins and jumps up again. He goes for a big swinging punch but can't see well now and misses big time. He only manages to spin around and his butt ends up right in

Mikey's face. Mikey takes this opportunity to pull Swordsnapper's pants down. Swordsnapper's junk pops out and his white crack blinks at us. Everyone laughs. He yells and cries and hops off to take care of his problems.

"Fuck this!" Beaker says. "Bring in the God. He'll take care of both of you." I start to back away but Beaker grabs me by the back of my neck and throws me into the circle.

Godkiller steps forth. Gasps roll through the crowd. Godkiller is a character that's half evil and half superhero. He eats angels for breakfast but saves old ladies from planes that are on fire in the sky. It's confusing and makes your heart angry and weepy. I didn't think he was real but here he is. He's wearing all black but his shirt has a purple G in a golden triangle. This guy could actually play Godkiller in a movie. He has muscles that move under his skin like small dogs fighting over bones. He also has tattoos and scars and skidmarks and grease-spatter burns. He has probably killed a god or two in his life. No one moves. For a few seconds it's so quiet you can hear all the blood draining into the guy's hands and turning them into snowplows.

Mikey nudges for me to get behind him. We back away. Godkiller laughs. Beaker laughs. Everyone else looks like they just saw a train crash into a bus full of special-needs babies.

"I will love you!" Godkiller says which is right from the comic book. This is basically the greatest moment of my life. Everything I have ever dreamed of. Except that it's a nightmare. I'm going to hell. At least it will be with Mikey.

Godkiller snorts then stamps and attacks. He's big and lumbering and slow but all I can do is watch and wait to be pulverized by knuckles that look like prongs on a backhoe bucket.

Mikey is a quick thinker though. He shoves me one way while ducking the other. Godkiller's huge fist carries him past us and into the crowd. A few people dare to kick and punch Godkiller and a girl scratches his face. He goes after them one by one and punches their lights out *snap snap snap*. Only the girl doesn't get a facepunch, just a noseflick.

Godkiller turns toward us again. I have accepted that I will die or at least never walk with straight legs again or speak with my already broken mouth. It was a short bad life and I am sad.

Then a hush falls over the crowd.

Out of nowhere Abstractio appears. The guy in the molten metal mask. He snaps his fingers and gestures for us to get out of the ring. Because I do not want to die I do not hesitate. Godkiller laughs and makes a *thhppt whatever* sound.

"These aren't the rules!" Beaker yells.

Abstractio turns toward him with his glowing red eyes and Beaker turns pale. And just like that I know it's Joe Purple in the mask. I see it in his confident and unhurried movements. How he's muscular but not brawny and dumb. The way he can't see behind him but knows everything all the time. Like he's not afraid of the sun but the sun is afraid of him.

Godkiller isn't afraid though. He's bored. He charges with his fists up high. Abstractio jukes sideways but a fist still grazes his shoulder and bounces up and turns his metal mask into a pile of shiny flakes. Gasps and *ooohs* rise up louder than the music. Abstractio shrugs it off and tries for a horsestomp-style kick. Joe Purple is no joker. But neither is Godkiller whose fists keep cocking back and shooting out again and again. Abstractio stumbles backward into the crowd and they shove him right back into the path of Godkiller's oncoming fist. He slips and falls to his hands and knees. Godkiller prepares a haymaker. But while Abstractio's down there he puts his fits into Godkiller's crotch not once or twice but three times just like I did to Horseblood's shin.

Godkiller groans and flinches then wilts and falls straight back like a tree with his hands over his groin. Abstractio leaps onto him and rains down punches like Tucker hammering nails into a tree stump. Which he does when angry. And like the tree stump Godkiller doesn't fight back because his balls are throbbing. This goes on like an endless *Marriage On The Rocks* rerun. It's so ugly that even I can't watch. Someone will die tonight but it turns out it won't be me.

Mikey's had enough violence competition for the night though. He kneels next to the still-punching Abstractio and says something that none of us hear. And just like that Abstractio stops. He looks down at Godkiller who isn't such a killer now. Abstractio backs away. The true god.

Then Mikey does something weird. He lifts Godkiller's hand and pats the back of it as a test. Then he leans in and says something to Godkiller. Godkiller nods. Mikey helps him off the ground. The two of them clasp hands like they're going for a walk on a Sunday afternoon.

"Oh fuck," Nan says.

"No no no," Beaker says.

Everyone cheers.

I wrench my head from side to side looking for Joe Purple but as usual he has leapt into the sky or folded up like an origami bird and vanished. What I do see is one of the pill bottles we stole. It fell out of my onesie while fighting the Ancients. I didn't notice earlier that the bottle has a special price tag. A Mazzie tag with beveled corners and a custom symbol. A briefcase.

"*Wuh wuh* where *duh* did you get this?" I ask while shaking the bottle in the air. "*Buh buh* Beaker."

Beaker tries to flee but the crowd shoves him back toward the pit. Even the punk we gave a ride is there to help.

He crosses his arms. "Fuck you, Mag—"

Godkiller smacks Beaker across the jaw. Beaker spins like a drunk pigeon and falls down.

"Okay, okay! I had some pricers that a guy traded for some weed but they didn't work well in our grow room which is cold and dank. They kept jamming. So I got rid of them."

"*Hoo hoo* who? *Nuh* name."

Beaker rubs the welt on his face. "Some scummy. Wild Horton? I don't know, man. It's been a long night. Just—fuck off."

Mikey shakes my shoulder. But I don't want to leave. There are answers here.

If only I knew how to read mud.

I Say Goodbye to Our Home and Get a Kick to the Balls from Conrad Flowers then Welcome Annabelle into My Life

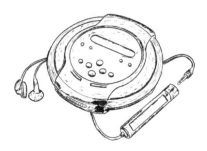

After sleeping for sixteen hours I bathe at the rec center and buy some groceries with the money I took from Beaker's closet. Mikey kept the pills. Then I go home and eat a bunch. Of groceries I mean, not pills. Though pills would be nice too. My head hurts. So does my everything.

Even though I have important things to do like solve my crime and find some money, Bugle and I spend the rest of the day watching *You'll Eat It And You'll Like It!*. They even show my favorite episode, the one with a cameo by Ernie Partridge. He and Chef Pierre go hunting but after a series of follies and goofs a bear ends up with the shotgun. He shoots them in their butts. Pierre can't sit down for weeks. "Lard soup!" he yells. "Lard soup!"

It's real funny but the phone interrupts my joy. I stare at it until the rings run out. The person doesn't leave a message but then my beeper beeps. It shows Tucker's number. Then the phone rings again. I answer it.

"It's time, Magoo. Meet me at Honey's."

I nod.

He hangs up.

It's still raining so I dress Bugle in the rain jacket Honey Mom made him. I wear my longcoat but no floppy hat. Rain spatters my face like frozen sunlight which is the only kind we want.

Driving, driving.

As Bugle and I bounce down the driveway toward the house Roxanne heads toward us in her tiny blue supercharged Pontiac Fiero. I pull over to let them pass. Curled up in the seat beside her is Honey Mom. Roxanne waves but Honey Mom does not.

The rain backs off and the sun threatens but doesn't it always.

Tucker and some scummies are loading trucks with stuff. Some of it is going into a dumpster.

Tucker comes toward me as I park. In his hands is my "MS" box. "Anything you want to get, get it now." He sets the box next to the truck. "You'll be getting a check for eleven thousand dollars. That's more than I'm getting but you've had a fucked-up life and I'm sorry and I owe it to you, I guess. I'm going to sign the East North Gaslin house over to you too but the chemicals stay for now. I'll work on it."

Bugle doesn't like all the activity. I put him back in the truck and lean against it and watch my childhood drain out the front door of our house box by box by chair table dresser nugget knick-knack junk crap dust dead skin. It takes forever and I don't want to be here but when I turn to leave Tucker says not yet. Conrad Flowers is on his way.

"*Wuh wuh* why? He *fuh* follows—*ss sss* stalks me."

"Of course he stalks you. What are you such a—fuck, Murray! I'm supposed to be watching out for you and I don't have time. So I got Flowers to help."

"*Hee hee*—I hate him. A *zzh* jerk."

"Duh! All cops are jerks but this is different. I fucking pay him."

Right then a cop car flies down the driveway like a fireball from hell. Conrad Flowers skids to a stop and climbs out but not before hitting his head on the roof of his car. "Sonofabitch." He goes to the back and pops the trunk and pulls out a bucket. He carries it over, drops it at my feet. Inside is mud. "Sorry, Sandman. Someone found these in the river."

I plunge my hand into the mud and pull out a Mazzie. And another.

Tucker joins us. "That's really what all this bullshit was about? Some junky-ass pricers? I thought you were kidding. Fuck!" He shakes his head, goes back to his important life-ruining work.

"You owe me, Sandman!" Flowers calls out.

Tucker flips him off.

Flowers smiles then bops me on the shoulder. I stagger sideways and fall to the ground beside the guns. His smile drops and he shakes his head then gets in his car and heads off to terrorize someone else but not before saying, "Keep the bucket."

The Mazzie prototypes are destroyed. Rage-sweat streams down my face.

I didn't notice before but Thin Man is standing at the corner of the house. I guess he recovered thanks to all that weird juice and long walks and avoidance of crime and bad things. He's leaning on a cane and watching the scummies filing in and out with our furniture and junk. Like they have a right. Like anyone has a right to sift through my moldy childhood.

I hop up and grab my "MS" box and carry it to the dumpster and throw it in then hurl the bucket of guns into the truck and peel out in the dirt driveway and bounce back toward the main road.

Driving, driving. I head to town. It's dark already. I cruise past Annabelle's building but when I look up at her apartment it's dark. She's at work already. She cleans the Worsley-Bompin, the big glass office cube that was supposed to change North Gaslin somehow. Instead it's mostly filled with people who call you on Sunday night to demand money for old bills or to sell you one of Marlene's gold-plated zucchini mashers. I head there.

The sidewalk is nice out front but homeless people hide in the alley. I don't want them to set up camp in my truck so I park far away and put Bugle on his leash.

The Worsley-Bompin has a security guard. He's bored, trying to walk across the lobby by balancing on the line between the tiles. Like he's practicing for a day he gets pulled over for Driving With Knees. Which is hard to explain to cops when you have a speech impediment or have had too much beer. Or both. I hope I can slip past him since I'm wearing my longcoat and have a dog that looks like a drugsniffer.

"What's up, Charlie?" he says.

I nod and keep walking.

"Where you goin', Charlie?"

I look around. I'm not sure who this Charlie is. "*Aa aa* Annabelle."

"Who's that?" he says and comes toward us. Bugle tugs on his leash to smell the guy. The guy likes the sun. His skin tells me this. Or his ancestors liked it. He pets Bugle and Bugle yawns. The tag on his pocket says Stan Byrd.

"She *kuh kuh* cleans."

"Oh yeah. Annie-belle. I know her. Sweet girl. Always brings me a piece of fruit. Tonight it was a coupla cherries."

I shrug. I don't care about fruit right now.

"I'll take you to her. Come on."

Stan Byrd leads us to the elevator. Bugle's claws tick and clack on the tiles. He has never been in a flying box and I would think he'd be scared but maybe not since the guy escorting us is named Stan Byrd.

"She and a coupla other chicks do the top floors first. That's where they'll be, I surmise."

The elevator jerks us toward the sky. My bones press downward like my body doesn't want to get any closer to the sun.

"Gentlemen, we have arrived at your destination, the twentieth floor."

We step off. I nod at Stan Byrd who doesn't even carry a gun. He smiles and gives us a dorky bow as his hand swishes through the air. The door shuts, leaving us up high in the shadowy offices.

A vacuum is running somewhere down the dark hall. Bugle knows where we're going. I let him take me there. We spot Annabelle. She's got headphones on and is swishing her butt from side to side. I can tell from the words she singing that it's a song by Spaghetti Worms called "All the Kids Eat With Their Left Hands." We watch from the dark corner for a couple of minutes as she wipes down desks and windows and such. Today her fleece is black. Must be new. I like it.

Rays of Hope says that sunlight reflects off everything. We shouldn't focus on the shadows it makes but on the shiny spots, the good stuff about people. Such as how Annabelle is annoying and needy and underfed but she forgives me a lot and is sweet and generous. She loves Bugle too. Martin for another example is weak and confused but he never says anything mean about anyone. Tucker is a jerk and loves money but he's protective and has big goals. Honey Mom is fragile and weird but has strong feelings and I guess that means she needs more hugs. Mikey is obsessed with his looks but after that he doesn't do much wrong, just wants love. When it comes to Carl Jake I don't know how he reflects the sun. He's one big black smear on life. As for me I hope I'm shiny in some way but it's not for me to say. It's up to other people's eyeballs to figure it out.

I let Bugle go and he howls and charges Annabelle. She screams and leaps onto someone's desk, knocking staplers and paperweights and computers onto the floor. It's real funny. When she realizes it's Bugle she is even more shocked. She looks out into the dark for me.

"Furry?"

With her skin flushed like that and her hair spiked up and her emotions spinning through fear and joy and wonder all at once she looks alive. On the verge of pretty. If she tried a little harder at life and got herself away from heliophobes she could do much better than Murray Sandman. Minor Sadsack. Major Screwball. She could go out for tea with someone like that guy Kurt Watkins. Lucky for me Kurt Watkins isn't in this building. I go to her.

She pulls her headphones down. Then she slides her arms into my longcoat and pulls herself against my body. For once she doesn't talk. I wish most people knew not to talk during important moments.

Bugle likes the carpet for scratching his back and while he wriggles from side to side Annabelle and I sway back and forth and listen to Spaghetti Worms playing in the headphones around her neck. The words start quiet then build, going *Sauce, potatoes, monkeys, beets! Rabbits, gardens, artichokes—let's eat!* I kiss the top of her head and she kisses me on the nose and Bugle wriggles. It's really nice. This is how it's supposed to be. Then she says, "Have you ever thought of adopting a child from Mongolia?"

Carl Jake Doesn't Like His Son but Loves the Little Aardvark if only He Had a Brain and then Carl Jake Thinks About that Guy Called Big Man

"Pop?" Kenny says, rapping on the door.

Carl Jake pushes away from his desk and reaches the door in five strides. He opens it, steps out, and shuts it behind him before his son can catch of glimpse of the work underway inside the garage. "What's up, bud?"

"I'm going out. Can I have some gas money?"

"On your bike?"

Kenny nods, his giant Adam's apple bobbing in synch with his greasy head.

"Meeting up with friends?"

"I dunno. Probably not."

"What are you going to do?"

"I dunno. Just cruise."

"To where?"

"I dunno. Around."

"No parties?"

"Nah."

"Girls?"

"Nah."

"Where's Hugo?"

The kid doesn't say anything. Carl Jake wants to slap him sometimes.

Because Kenny reminds him of someone.

"We need to have a talk one of these days, son."

"About what?"

"Your future."

"What about it?"

"It's here, damn it! You're almost a man now. The hammer's falling. Are you the carpenter or the nail?"

"Is that, like, a Jesus parable or something?"

"Aww, come on."

"All right. We'll chat soon. So..."

"Yeah. *So.* How much?"

"Thirty."

Carl Jake digs into his pocket and extracts a wad. He hands him a twenty.

The kid smiles. "That's all I wanted."

"You'll earn it tomorrow. Lots of projects. Big and small. In and out. Up and down. All around—"

"See ya." Kenny vanishes.

Carl Jake retreats to the garage and makes his way back to his desk. He hears Kenny's motorbike fire up and race off. He resumes his work on his computer. But now his mind is racing too. How dumb and boring and typical the kid is sometimes. He eats like shit, worse even than himself, which no doubt contributes to the horror-movie complexion. Could be worse though. Like Martin.

A thought strikes him, and Carl Jake opens his personal copy of *Rays of Hope*. He flips to the section he wrote as a jab at Martin's gluttony.

COPING STRATEGY #45: *Food Is Life*

Krishna tells us, "Men of darkness eat food which is stale and tasteless, which is rotten and left overnight, impure, unfit for holy offerings" but that "men who are pure eat food which is pure, which gives health, mental power, strength and long life, which has taste and is soothing and nourishing."

Heliophobes should take care, therefore, to eat food that makes them feel nourished and happy. Most importantly, eat foods that resemble the sun. The sun provides many nutrients. In the darkness, one does not find nutrients. One becomes a rat, digging in others' garbage. Living in fear should not equal being hungry.

Absurd. He laughs and tosses the book aside. But it leads to another thought. He pushes the keyboard away and reaches for a photo album on the shelf behind him.

The Great Years, the cover reads.

He opens it. The first photo is of his then-future wife.

The second one digs right into his heart.

Murray. You funny little fuck.

Years ago, while getting a new enterprise underway involving Pakistani health supplements, he met a truck driver named

Big Man. It was hard to breathe while in the same room as the guy. His voice was overwhelming, his cigars suffocating, his demeanor oppressive. But Big Man hauled stuff for Carl Jake in and out of North Gaslin without questioning the loads, and the loads Big Man was being asked to haul were indeed questionable. It was only a matter of time before Big Man made a mistake, but C.J. had taken numerous steps to cover his own involvement, from falsified paperwork to double-blind distribution to plain old lying and bribing. It was easy.

"Got a thing this weekend," Big Man told him one day as the two of them stood on a disused landing strip, wingless gliders along the periphery encased in white plastic. The two of them were loading the truck with illicit supplements for bodybuilders. Big Man handed him a card. The cover depicted a monkey climbing a tree toward some bananas. The fruit was drawn incorrectly—growing toward the ground. The text inside read: *Come to my party! It'll be bananas!* Then in chicken-scratch kid print: *Helo. See yu then. Murray Sandman.*

"What time?"

Big Man snatched the card back. "Idiotic little twerp. He forgot a few key details. It's at three, but you shouldn't show up until later, after the activities have reached their inevitable violent conclusions."

"Your son?"

"Yeah." Big Man lifted three boxes. C.J. struggled with one. "He's different. Something not right about him. I was thinking maybe you could work some magic. You seem to have insight into people's, you know, brains."

"I appreciate that. Sure, I'll come."

They finished moving the boxes and shut the truck.

"By the way," Big Man said. "It ain't at my place."

"Oh."

"At a, uh, friend's. The boy's mother isn't really the party type. Never has been." Big Man shrugged, and it was perhaps the first time C.J. had noticed a vulnerability in him. "The friend is cool though. Good with kids. You'll dig her."

"I see," he said, but he didn't really *see* until two days later. When he pulled up to the garage-apartment unit where the party was being hosted, a kid in lunch-tray-green sweatpants and a ruffled polo shirt came through the gate, chasing a stray soccer ball.

"Hey there," C.J. said, leaning on his knees toward the boy.

The kid looked at the paper sack in his hands. "You *buh buh* bring me *sss* something?"

"Maybe. Are you Murray?"

The boy nodded. C.J. offered his paw. They shook. The boy's hand felt like boiled lettuce. They released and each wiped their palm on their thigh. Then C.J. handed over the paper sack. The boy slid out a *CHUCK ROLLINS GOES TO H.E.L.L.!* graphic novel. The boy looked it over, handed it back. "Is it *wuh* worth *eh* anything?"

"Maybe someday. Now tell me, are—"

"C'mon, dickweed!" a partygoer said and promptly stole the soccer ball.

The boy moaned and ran after it. C.J. watched. Each time the boy got close enough, someone would kick it out of range. It was eight kids against one. He tripped; someone beamed the ball off his forehead. They laughed; he bellowed shrilly.

"C.J.," a voice said from the top of the stairs leading to the apartment. "Thanks for coming. Murray, put down the dirt clod."

The boy threw it anyway. It burst open on the kid's face. The kid only laughed and shoved Murray to the ground.

"I had to bribe them into coming here," Big Man told C.J. as they shook hands at the top of the stairs. "Now you know why." C.J. handed over the graphic novel. "Thanks. He'll at least look at the pictures. Say, is there a test to figure out if your kid is either a dumbass or a super genius? Sometimes the TV movies show a kid who's just—aw Christ, watch out."

The boy came stomping up the stairs, soccer ball in his arms, snot bubbling out his nose. He pushed past and walked up to the refrigerator and punched it, leaving not a mark.

"What the hell is going on out here," a woman said, rounding the corner into the kitchen. She stopped short upon noticing their guest. "Oh, hello."

C.J. lit up. "Hello there," he said, crossing the kitchen to take her tough hand in his puffy mitts. She was a wonder. Her nose was a bit twisted and one eyelid drooped slightly, but her body belonged to a Japanese comic heroine: curvy along the sides and pointy at the ends. Her necklace was old and tarnished and depicted a multi-pronged star of some sort. He repressed the urge to lean in and examine it up close.

"This is my business associate, C.J.," Big Man said.

"Nevada," she said. "Nice to meet you."

"No, no, nice to meet *you*." He meant it. But more than anything, he couldn't believe Big Man had invited him here to be seduced by this delectable creature. She was surely out of his league, but Big Man was of no small esteem, and if he had talked up C.J., clearly Nevada was up for it.

She smiled weakly and recoiled slightly. "You, um, thirsty?"

"Much. I mean very. Yes please."

"Have a seat."

He stationed his round keister at the little kitchen table covered with party detritus. Big Man kindly made himself scarce. C.J. watched as Nevada poured some generic soda into a plastic cup. *Fizzy Grape Flavored Beverage for Enjoyment at Parties and Events or at Home.* "Hungry?"

He nodded. But when she unhinged the pizza box, there was only crust inside, floury little rib bones left behind by birthday vultures.

"Damn it. Sorry about that."

He raised a hand, mugged, and said, "Don't *wurrry* about it," like a movie mafia don.

She offered another tepid smile and emptied the dregs of a candy bag into a bowl. He ate it in one mouthful, barely tasting it. He heard Big Man whistling a ditty but wasn't sure where he was.

"So tell me," she said, "what do you do?"

He felt his nerves crackling like power lines in the fog. He badly wanted to sit in her lap. "Well, let's see. I'm a purveyor of peculiar products. A mercantile maestro. A diviner of delectable delights."

"That's cute. Been practicing it much?"

He laughed into his soda. "A little."

"So tell me, what do you do?"

"A little of this, a little of that. Selling, buying, trading. I have my hands in many pots, but to be honest, I haven't yet realized my actuality."

"You like to talk in code, huh. I think I need a guidebook for this dialogue."

He felt stupid. He tried again. "What I want is to delve deep into the human psyche and figure out what it is that makes us into such perfectly disgusting creatures."

She tipped the candy bowl toward herself and frowned. "Like psychology or psychiatry or whatever it is they're calling head-shrinking these days?"

"I suppose it's related but more tangentially."

The boy suddenly appeared. He'd donned a new outfit: a red polo shirt tucked into a pair of khaki shorts. He'd combed his hair and would have looked like a tiny college man were it not for the toy cars spilling from his pockets.

"Welcome back, birthday boy," Nevada said and patted his shoulder like a dog.

The boy ignored her and stepped to the window and set the cars on the sill and started pushing them out one by one.

Nevada called out for his father. He rounded the corner with his zipper open.

"Damn it, Murray. Get the fuck outside and play with your friends who came all this way to celebrate your birthday with you."

He pushed the last car out the window. "They *huh* hate me. They're all *duh* dinks. I *huh* hate them."

"I'm going to count to five."

"One," his father said.

"*Wuh* one."

"Two."

"*Tuh tuh* two."

"Goddamn it, boy."

"Hey!" the boy yelled out the window, then disappeared down the stairs. Half a minute later someone screamed.

"We'd better go play sheriff," Big Man said. "C.J., you any good at horseshoes?"

"I can barely get on my own, let alone a horse's." He leaned back and laughed up at the dusty ceiling fan.

Nevada looked at Big Man. Big Man glanced at her, then took out a cigar, stepped out onto the stairs, and lit it.

When the other partygoers saw the adults coming down the stairs, they migrated to the other end of the yard like geese, where they admired Murray's new bike. While Nevada got to work raking the pits and clearing them of apples and rocks and toy cars, he and Big Man sat on the fence beside the swing set.

"She's a hot little ho-er, ain't she," Big Man said.

C.J. agreed with long, low moan. Nevada was meticulous in her raking. He wanted someone like that in his life, even if included the strange nose. This was the beginning of the next chapter; he knew it. He felt nothing but warmth and friendship toward this man who had brought her into his life.

Murray appeared from the shadows. He strolled over to the partiers, shoved them aside, and freed his bike. It was a gleaming but clunky department store thing that, C.J. imagined, would be tossed in the dump at the end of the year. Murray climbed on, pushed off, then wobbled off, disappearing around the corner of the garage. The kids called out to him. He circled the garage, disappeared. Reappeared, disappeared.

Crashed.

Everyone heard it.

He came back dragging his bike by its handlebars and sat on the stairs and cried. C.J. noticed, however, that as the boy sulked there, he continually edged away from the sunlight and back into shadow. Earlier, he'd even seemed afraid to step across the line separating dark from light. Was he afraid, or was it some neurosis or even a game? C.J. couldn't tell, but he was fascinated.

The other kids taunted the boy and tossed candy at him until finally Nevada told them that was enough and gave them their party favor bags and said to go away.

"Murray," Nevada said, "play against C.J."

The boy shook his head.

"Now, you little ratfart," Big Man said, exhaling cigar smoke. To C.J. it smelled like something an elk might spit up on the first day of spring.

The boy eventually wandered over but again seemed to stop at the edge of the shadows. "*Huh* how."

"You throw the goddamn shoes at the box in the distance. Try and hit the stake."

"I *huh* hate *huh* horses," he said.

C.J. laughed, got up, and offered him a shoe. The boy took an exaggerated lunging step into the shade to join C.J. He took the shoe, held it like a Frisbee, and flung it wildly. It passed over the swings and hooked an apple tree branch.

"Jeez Louise," C.J. said. "Quite the arm you've got."

The boy tossed the second; it fell way short.

Wee, wee, the swing set cried out. Big Man was giving Nevada a push. She laughed and kicked her feet in the air.

"Aim for the dirt," C.J. told the boy. "Just need to get close is all."

"I *huh huh* hate *sss* sports."

"Just watch, okay?" C.J. tossed the shoe. It clanged mightily against the stake. So did the second. "Well, gosh."

"Good job, Dunham," Big Man called out.

"I *huh huh* hate you. All of *yuh* you." The boy ran up the stairs and into the apartment.

Nevada leapt off the swing and took chase, but she tripped and tumbled onto the grass. Both men hurried over, but Big

Man got there first. He helped her up and dusted off those precious knees.

"Dunham, think you can do your thing with the boy?"

C.J. shuddered. He wasn't a—he couldn't even say the word. And he didn't want to leave Nevada's presence. There was so much to talk about, so much to impress upon her… if only he could remember his list of topics. And yet the sun was moving toward him, and so were their eyes. "Sure thing. Keep my shoes warm."

As he went up the stairs, he heard Nevada say, "Who is this guy?"

His soda glass was still on the table, flies occupying its rim. He went to the fridge and dug around until he found a beer. It was dark brown, thick, and fishy. He guzzled it and fought the urge to smash something. Such as the boy's face, which was watching him from around the corner, cake all over his mouth and nose.

"Come here, you."

C.J. handed over a dish rag. The boy wiped his face and dropped the rag onto the floor and walked off. C.J. followed him into the bedroom and found him sitting on the floor chopping up records with a pair of scissors.

"Hey, hey, hey, little man." He took the blades away and sat with him. "Not a very good birthday, was it?"

"*Hoo hoo* who's that *luh* lady?"

"Nevada? Friend of your pop's."

"I *wuh* want her to *duh* die."

"Why's that?"

He shrugged. "I *wuh* want to *duh* die too."

"Come on, buddy. Don't be so down. Life is tough when you're young and a little strange. I was like that once."

The boy looked C.J. up and down. "*Sss* still are."

"Ha ha. Maybe so. Just, you know, stay off drugs and stay positive. Think about the bright things to come."

The boy rolled his eyes and slumped over.

C.J. let him be. He got up and checked out the room: Nevada's dirty underwear in a pile; papers all over the cheap little desk; some gaudy jewelry in the process of being crafted. The bed was just a mattress on the floor with sheets kicked off. A photo pinned to the wall depicted Nevada and some guy leaning into one another. It took him a moment to realize who the dude was.

"What the?"

He hurried back into the kitchen and peered down into the yard where Big Man and Nevada stood snogging. Wait, wasn't Big Man married? C.J.'s head spun as he considered his options. He blinked away tears. When his eyes had cleared, he realized he'd put his fist into the wall.

"*Wuh* what's wrong?" the boy said behind him.

He kneeled before Murray. He held him by his upper arms and said, "The universe is chaos, and humans only want to make sense of it all. When everything starts to stop making sense, I'll be there for you. Got it?"

The boy shook his head.

"I know."

He ruffled the boy's hair, then exited through the garage and climbed into his bright-blue station wagon. Big Man caught up with him as he was turning around. "You forgot your party favors." He tossed a decorated sack onto his lap.

"This concludes our business ventures. I've found my path. Thanks, Big Man."

"What are you talking about?"

He hit the gas and sprayed the garage and Big Man's shins with dirt.

Down the road he encountered some of the partygoers trying to push over a semi-dead tree. He slowed to a stop and held out the bag. "Want some candy?"

They looked at him. "Are you a fucking pervert or something?"

He tossed the bag and drove off, laughing. Someday he'd have kids of his own. Maybe his would be like Big Man's son. C.J. had learned so much from him, he thought his heart was going to explode.

Carl Jake and I Have a Talk Which Ends up with Us both Bathed in Blood

Mikey and Godkiller plan to get drinks next week. Godkiller's real name is Charles Phelps. He works for the animal shelter and collects action figures in his spare time. I am still terrified of him but perhaps we all need a little Godkiller in our lives.

Such as when we're paying a visit to the person we hate most in the world.

Driving, driving.

Carl Jake's neighborhood is fancy, full of safe zones. His house is pretty nice. Red trim. Orange chimney. Green grass. A bush here and there. I park at the curb to wait for a kid on a dirt bike to clear out of the driveway. He revs the engine over and over as a black cloud forms over the house.

I open *Rays of Hope*.

ON DEATH

Some insects live twenty-four hours. Their lives are a blink in the lifespan of humans. Humans are but a blink in the lifespan of the galaxy. Galaxies are but a blink in the lifespan of the universe. We'll all be one again! Dust dancing in the sunlight!

Live for the now.

The kid finally zips away on his bike. I can go in. Can ask Carl Jake all the questions burning holes in my heart.

As I head up the sidewalk a voice behind the screen door sings, "Mr. Sandman, turn on your magic beam. Oh Mr. Sandman, bring me a dream." Carl Jake swings the door open. He continues singing. "Mr. Sandman, you're so alone. Don't have nobody to call your own." He takes my coat and hat. He sees that I've brought *Rays of Hope*, laughs. "Have a seat." He points at two big cushy chairs. "Get you anything? Soda? Beer? Juice?"

He snaps his fingers. Drinks appear on a tray delivered by two thin arms. Behind them are red lips and fancy hair. "Hello, Murray," his wife says even though I've never met her. I think. I wave hello. She puts down all sorts of sweating drinks, leaves. Doesn't look at me once the whole time. I reach out, take a root beer.

The house is tidy and normal. On the mantel are a few cheap trophies including one for bowling. Walls host family photos and motel-type art. A football game is playing on the TV. Some of the players slap each other's butts. The referee makes signals like he's landing a plane and I think about the night at the airport with Alphonse Polish. It feels like ten Murray Sandmans ago.

"I'm glad you finally took the time to stop by. I don't extend such an invitation to just anyone, you know."

The fireplace has plastic wood in it.

"Lay it on me, Murv. How's life?"

I stare at him. On TV someone scores a touchdown.

"Good, good. You know you are a vital part of Heli-Non but it was kind of touch-and-go there for a while, wasn't it? Your friends were worried. You're the glue for this funny little collage, believe it or not."

The sun beams down through the picture window and settles on the shiny spot at the top of Carl Jake's head.

"Are *yuh* you a *huh huh* heliophobe?"

He crosses his chunky white sneakers. The laces are double-knotted. He lets out a little laugh and says, "Listen, do you remember your first session?"

The TV shows some cheerleaders flying through the air, their pom-poms like colored smoke. I sip some root beer. I can't remember what the date is. What month. What season. Aardvark, aardvark. But I remember the night I walked up the ramp into Heli-Non. I was actually looking for the ham radio class. I ended up in the wrong room with a huge weird guy named Martin looking up at me like I was delivering a pizza made of gold.

"That was our first session too. You see, we weren't sure anyone would ever show up." He lowers the volume on the TV. "Until then it was just the big guy and me. Martin was terrified to be seen in public and he got this idea in his head that heliophobia was the root of his anxiety. So we borrowed the classroom to work it out. We put up a flier to make it look official so we wouldn't have to pay any fees. Then, of all people, you showed up. I was out in the hallway, by the way. On my way back from draining the ol' lizard. When I looked in through that cloudy little pane of glass and saw you there, well, it was pretty much the highlight of my career. Or its genesis, as it turns out. Everything had come full circle, reuniting us."

"*Duh duh* do you know *buh buh* Big Man?"

He takes a long pull on a beer, finishing it. The lady comes back and whisks his bottle away and hands off a drink with ice. Her nose is crooked like she's trying to sniff behind her and one eyelid is weird but she's pretty. Maybe I do know her.

Carl Jake adjusts his cushy chair and leans forward. "Manual Foote called Martin, by the way. He wanted to come back to Heli-Non. Martin told him he was more than welcome. Unfortunately Manual had a relapse and is back in the hospital. It's not looking good." He rattles the ice in his glass. "To answer your question, yes, I knew Big Man." Carl Jake laughs. "Kind of a strange fellow, your dad. Cigars, no deodorant. I can't tell you where he is but I'm sure it's not a very nice place. He wasn't much for beauty. Told me he preferred coal pits and saloons to living rooms and cocktail lounges. And I'm sure you've been wondering why he left. I don't have that answer for you. I'm sure he doesn't either." Carl Jake pushes a button. The football players blink out. "Come. I've got something to show you." He stands up and stretches, farts. "Whoops!" He laughs.

I want to laugh too. For a second his face looks real. But then I'm left with his dumb smirk and the stink of his rotten gas.

We walk down the hallway. He opens the door at the end. It's dark inside. It smells like gasoline and cheese.

"Step inside, pal."

I hesitate. Outside the dirt bike slows down, turns, zooms off again.

"Go on," he says. "This is what you've been waiting for."

I don't know what he means but I'm curious. I step down. It's colder there. There's no light or air or space. The door shuts. We bump up against things.

"Be mindful," he says. "You're in my museum now."

A flashlight is flipped on. The beam bounces around. It's a garage with enough room for two cars but it's just stuff. Everywhere. Wall to wall and floor to ceiling. Stacks of paintings. Magazines and books leaning this way and that. Sculptures. Boxes of little plastic things. Pottery. Melted candles. Electronics. Records and tapes. Antiques. Stuffed dead things. Bugs. A whole miniature pony, preserved. Everything organized but messy. Carl Jake shuffles through to the other end and sits at a fancy wooden desk and turns on a lamp. I can only see his hands and a tiny computer. His face hides in darkness.

"Have a look. Explore. Rummage. What you find will reflect what it is you are truly, deeply searching for."

I don't know which way to move.

"If the thing you're looking for is hard cash you won't find it. However I'm willing to give you some money if that's what you need. All I ask in trade is for you to take part in some psychological experiments. Nothing painful. No contracts. No video. These tests could really help us understand the inner workings of someone who is prone to irrational tendencies such as yourself. I promise there'll be no touchy-feely stuff or jargon or goofball exercises. Just you and me."

My butt knocks something onto the floor. Carl Jake tilts his desk lamp toward it. It's a grocery sack full of kid drawings. *1-2-3 You Can Draw*-type stuff. I feel sick. Like I'm drowning in dark air. I kick the papers aside.

"This is the inside of your mind. These are your thoughts. I know you, Murray. I can help."

I try to spin around but trip and fall onto my hands and knees. Big Man once said, "You must have an inner ear problem. Meaning the thing between your ears doesn't work so good." I feel around with my hands and grope a bicycle wheel. When I stand up I stagger and knock over a box. There's just enough light to see them spilling out: pricing guns. A couple of Fortrans, a few Montgomerys, even a Doo-Har Pricing King 1212. Everyone thinks it's a crap gun but you just have to lube up the trigger mechanisms every couple of hours and it delivers price tags like Astro Fire Cop's hose delivers air-water.

"Murray, be reasonable. Those are junk. The future is all digital. You need to adapt."

He's right. Pricing guns mean nothing to me now.

"Listen, if there's something in particular you're looking for in life, you might have to dig deeper. People like you tend to take the nearest item from an eye-height shelf. Sugar Slams for instance."

"*Eye eye eye—*"

I open a box. Inside are hundreds of pens, all different. Chewed. Dry. Black. Foreign.

Carl Jake's chair creaks and he giggles. "You're a strange duck, Murv. All of you heliophobes are. No, I'm not like you guys. I'm the brains. Martin's the people person, the one who can relate to the phobic mindset. Getting him over his fear was one of the greatest moments of my life. It became an addiction of sorts, studying others' pathologies. Still I didn't think it was a fruitful venture until the day the prodigal son walked in. Hallelujah! We moved forward with you as our bona fide sun-fearer until FX and the others showed up. We even used you as a model for *Rays of Hope*. So have a look around. Find the answer. Maybe find *all* of the answers."

"*Duh duh* don't *wuh* want the answer." I back up toward the door or where I think the door was. My mouth tastes like a pus-soaked band-aid. Root beer gurgles in my gut. "*Luh luh—*"

"Right," he says.

"*Zhh zhh zh—*"

"Uh huh, exactly."

I smash into something. Tiles or marbles or dice clatter on the floor.

"*Fruh fruh—*"

"Whatever you say, Sandman." Carl Jake tilts the light. The things on the floor are teeth. I want to float away like Astro Fire Cop but can't move. Carl Jake gets up and stands beside his desk with his hands in his pockets, the thumbs on the outside like he's Chuck Rollins at the climax of *Peace or Death*. On the floor the teeth seem to be moving. "Look, if you promise to keep coming to Heli-Non and take part in my studies I'll give you what you really came here for." He opens a drawer and takes out a piece of mail and hands it to me. "I don't know if it's still good. It's the last mailing address Big Man used. He requested that I send him some essentials. It was fifteen years ago but it could still be legit."

I hand it back. "*Duh* don't *wuh* want it. I'm not *arf arf* afraid anymore."

"Oh, Murray. Of course you are. I practically raised you. I turned your affliction into a system, a science! It became so real that some members of the group lost their minds beneath that truth. Amazing! All thanks to you. Well, and me."

I've heard enough. I hop over the teeth and exit the garage. I head down the hallway and get my longcoat and hat and sun-goggles. *Rays of Hope* is on the coffee table in a hot pool of sunlight. When Carl Jake rounds the corner saying, "I remember how at one point you wanted to be a police sketch artist so I know you want to help people. And these tests—" I drive the spine of the book into his face. He reels backward then looks up with bright red eyes. He lunges for me but the coffee table is between us and his shins smash into the edge. "Aw, fuck. You broke my legs!" While he rubs them back to life I bring *Rays of Hope* down on the back of his skull. It's not that hard or anything but I guess harder than I thought because he drops straight down and his chin pops on the tabletop. He bellows and spins on his knees and punches the air. Drinks leap off the table and spill across the carpet.

His wife appears from nowhere. "You're animals!" She disappears. I remember who she is now. Which only makes me madder.

Carl Jake catches me at the door. I pop him on the ear with the book and punch him in the gut and he shoves me against the coatrack and knees me in the thigh while knocking my skull with his elbow. My ear goes numb and I can't hear anything except an alarm clock and a swing set and the sound of Big Man slapping me on the forehead and the echoes of every sound I've ever hated in my life. We tangle and grapple and push and shove. It's nothing like the fights Chuck Rollins had. Our battle is a mess of bellies and soft fists and kicks and stomps and spitting and panting until the door opens and the motorbike kid walks in.

"Dad, what the hell is this?"

Carl Jake peels himself off me. I wipe blood from my mouth.

"Kenny. Just having a friendly afternoon tussle is all." Carl Jake grabs his knees. His skull is red and veiny. His eyes are bleary and broken. He waggles his finger in the air, says to the kid, "Don't let him leave," then walks off.

I stare at Kenny. Skinny. Ugly. Weird. The type of person you want to stuff into a toaster. His shirt depicts some sperm and has the words *NG Swim Team, First Place, Breast Stroke*.

Carl Jake comes back with the piece of mail.

"This envelope's a ticket to nowhere," he says. "When you're ready to step out of the darkness... I'll be here for you. You moron."

I Leave My Zone and Go Looking for a Guy Yonder and My Life Changes Forever

After Big Man disappeared Honey Mom hired a detective to find him. He spent a year making phone calls and sending letters and driving down dark dirt roads at midnight but he didn't even find Big Man's antique truck. He told us Big Man must be dead. Murdered maybe. Might have been tangled up with some bad people.

"Death is the ultimate liberation," Larson once said. Meaning when you're dead you finally stop worrying about the sun.

That's why I'm driving to Spry Poi. The mail Carl Jake gave me said Big Man was there. A long time ago but still. You never know. I might find his bones which is something I've imagined for many years. In a grave, under a rock. Away from the sun. I especially like to picture his skull because skulls are always smiling, always laughing. I can pretend I told Big Man a joke or drew him a cartoon and he finally enjoyed it. We'll share a good laugh and I'll head home.

Spry Poi is a hideaway up in the hills where scummies make drugs in their attics and steal farm machines and bang rocks together for heat. You only go there if you need a special kind of vegetable or if your neighbor's wife has been kidnapped. It's almost an hour away and I've never been. Here's me, driving higher and higher. Not higher than airplanes and eagles but higher than I've ever been for sure. I've lived a low life. Never traveled, never strayed. A couple times Tucker and Honey Mom and I went duck hunting but I refused to shoot the stupid ducks. And we didn't have a dog so I had to wade in to get the dead birds. Tucker would spank me if I cried, said we need to eat don't we asshole.

Driving, driving. I ponder. Which is a fancy word for think. I ponder where I am and how I got here. I don't come up with an answer so I keep going. My sungoggles are on and the windows are down. I'm listening to a weird radio station with some singer called Lady Diamond Future. *Bathe yourself in golden light! Say my name! Say my name!* On the steep uphills the truck works like mad, the engine pinging and knocking as usual. The brakes burn up on the downhills and the baby spares slip in the corners. It's scary but I keep going. That's life.

When I run low on gas I pull over beside a big truck. Men in orange clothes are standing in a cherrypicker and cutting branches off a tree. There's nothing they can do from high up. I grab their gas cans and drive off long before they can lower their cherrypicker and chase after me in their huge slow truck. Then I remember that I have money now and I don't need to steal gas. But it's too late. The crime's already in my mirrors. At least the mirrors I still have.

It's hard to believe all this is so close to North Gaslin. And what's beyond this? More hills? Mountains? Oceans and deserts probably. Arenas, museums, offices. Nice stone buildings hosting better-organized Heli-Non groups maybe. Doctors and lawyers and better radio stations. People who can change things.

I almost miss the exit for Spry Poi. Then I have no idea where to go. I drive real slow and look around. It's worse than North Gaslin but in a prettier way if you know what I mean. Spry Poi people live in junky trailers and rotting houses but there's nature and stuff around the crappiness. Goats stand near the road waiting for someone to pay attention to them. Since my truck's ready to quit I pull over and open the hood. I push on a hose and tap on the wires to let it know I care about it. While it's cooling down I check out the goats.

I realize that the truck is just low on gas. Turns out that the gasometer doesn't work anymore. While I'm filling up with one of the stolen cans I see a car coming. It's brown and tan. Inside is a sheriff. I am afraid Conrad Flowers has called in a favor or the cherrypicker guys put out an APB on me. The window drops. I look around, wondering which direction to run. Probably toward the goats. He says something but all I can hear is the sun screaming chainsaw music at me.

"*Sss* sorry?"

"I was asking if you checked out the Trucker's Plate at The Sawtooth. Pancakes as big as tractor tires and eggs like they was shit from an ostrich's ass." The cop's been chewing on a pen and has blue smears on his lips.

Shake. "*Nuh* no. *Guh guh* good stuff?"

"Yep," he says. "It's only good til two though so best get it before long."

Nod. "*Th th* thanks."

"Things all good here?"

I nod. He puts the pen back in his mouth and waves and is about to leave when I say, "*Sss* Sandman?"

He thinks a moment. "Is that a business or something?"

I get out the piece of mail and show him the address. It says *Ldunew Lane*. I don't bother trying to say it.

"One click thataway." He points.

"*Kuh* click?"

"Less than a mile. Follow the road back that way and take a right on Ldunew Lane. Go up the gravel drive. The shop is beside the fire station. Can't miss it. If you do then you need to see an eye doctor."

"*Th th* thanks."

"Be careful. That area—them boys—well, you'll see."

He zooms off. I nearly pee myself.

I find Ldunew Lane. I go up a real narrow road and take a sharp turn then go up an even narrower one. Like the wheel-chair ramp at Heli-Non. I see the fire station up ahead, the repair shop, a bunch of beat-up old cars sleeping in the grass. There are some apartments above the tire shop and some stairs going up but a couple of dudes are hanging out on the bottom steps. They're smoking and drinking and spitting into the weeds. They look like they shoot people for fun after work. People like me. Their muscles are not like Godkiller's but the kind you get from throwing spears at mooses or rocks at werewolves.

"*Huh huh* hey."

Neither of them moves.

"*Ecks ecks*—"

They chortle.

I push my tongue against the roof of my mouth, move some spit up my throat. "Get the *fuh fuh* fuck out of my *wuh* way!"

The mooses look at each other. Then one spits a gob of orange puky stuff into the grass and scooches aside.

"*Th* thanks."

I go up the stairs. I hear loud music behind a door and knock. I wait. The music stops. The door flies open. It's a tall old skinny dark-skinned guy stirring a bowl of batter or maybe napalm. "You selling religion?" he asks.

Shake.

"What can I do for you?"

"*Sss ss*—"

The guy sticks his finger in the bowl and samples the napalm.

"*Ss*—Sand—"

"Salvatore?"

I show him the piece of mail that says *Bart Wilson Sandman.* Which is my father's name.

"The only Sandman we got here is Salvatore. One door down."

"*Th* thanks."

He shuts the door with his foot. The music starts again. I hesitate. What if there are more mooses? Then the door opens again. "But he ain't home," the guy says.

Relief.

"He's out in the cars."

Unrelief.

The guy points with his wooden spoon and napalm drips onto the floor. "Yonder, beyond them trees."

"*Th* thanks."

"It's nothing."

The mooses are gone when I head back down the stairs. There are some tracks where a truck drove through the fields. I follow, my longcoat going *swish swish* in the grass. To my left sits a pile of refrigerators filled with rocks and some old TVs. I would like to smash them but I don't. When Chuck Rollins is on a mission he doesn't have time for games so neither do I.

The woods appear. They are the type of thing old people tell stories about to scare kids. Things like *There is a man in the woods with no legs with hooks for arms who swings from tree to tree and chases after little booger-eaters.* I don't eat boogers but I think I hear chains clanking. It's okay though. The bug spray and compass are still in my pocket. Also in there is the puker's handkerchief. It's crusty with our vomit and smells like a teenager's socks.

On the other side of the trees I see a graveyard of rusted old cars stretching forever until they meet the sun. They're facing the road like they're about to go to war. Some look like they hit trees or mailboxes or people or each other and were dragged here to die. Some are all nice like they were just parked and forgotten.

Despite the sunlight all over the place I walk up and down the rows. I feel up some hood ornaments and handles. Chrome flakes off in my hands. A '56 Oldsmobile calls my name so I get in. Springs push through the seat. My heels settle in the divots on the floor. Maybe this belonged to Great Big Man, my grandfather. I wonder if he was a winner and a doer. I wonder if he took Grandma Ninny on dates in cars like this. Or maybe he got drunk and took long drives at night and ran over baby skunks for fun. I wonder—

Something in the mirror. No, gone. Now it's there again.

"Hey!" someone yells. "Come on out."

I don't move. A guy comes closer and stands in front of my door. He looks like the mooses but is not as big. His skin is dark with a tan like he's not afraid of the sun. His shirt looks like it was sucked through a lawnmower. A ferocious medieval wolf stands drooling beside him. I can't open the door or I'll whack the guy's knees so I roll down the window. It bottoms out in the door frame with a *thunk*.

"Just *luh luh* looking."

"This isn't a dime store."

I look up at the man like I'm at the drive-thru. Fries with that? "I *kuh kuh* can *luh luh* leave."

"You gonna fix that window?"

I try to roll it up but the handle just spins. "*Suh* seems to be a *puh puh* problem. *Huh huh* how much?"

"Come on out of there. But don't try and run or I'll send my dog after you."

The guy leans over to see better through the window. I slide my hand into my pocket but when I find the bug spray I accidentally shoot it into my hand. It's colder than I expected and I squeak a little.

"Murray?" he says.

I freeze. "*Yuh yuh* you—"

I can see the guy better now. He's carrying a shovel and a bucket and has long loose hair and rings in his ears and scars on his face and blotchy tattoos that might have been made while driving a boat or running a chainsaw. He looks familiar in a weird way. He steps back and I get out.

"You found me, bro!" The guy drops the shovel and wraps his arms around my shoulders. The wolf which is not a wolf but a mutt with pointy ears and a bent tail nuzzles my knee which I find funny but not in a ha-ha way.

"*Wuh wuh* what?"

He lets go of me. I see it then. Something in his face. An ugliness that women find irresistible. Not a quality I possess but something Tucker has. My ugliness is resistible.

"I've been waiting years for this."

"*Yuh yuh* years?"

He nods and it's not unlike my nod. Meanwhile the mutt moves his nose toward my crotch. To stop him I scratch behind his ears.

"This is Matón. It means 'thug' in Spanish. Our mother— me and the boys—" he sweeps his arms back toward the building where he lives though we can't see it from here. "Our mom is Mexican. Our dad—well, you must have figured that out."

"*Fuh fuh fuh* figure out *wuh wuh wuh* what?"

Salvatore's face flattens. "We should go inside and talk. Just one more swat." He raises the shovel. Its shadow falls over me. I block my face but it just swishes through the air.

Plonk.

The bucket contains tennis balls. He is using the shovel to hit the balls so that Matón can chase them.

"I need to tire him out or he paces and barks and keeps me up all night."

I should get a shovel for Bugle even though he doesn't fetch anything but snacks.

Salvatore's apartment is hipper than my place but still the type of place you'd expect a half-moose like him to live in. Clothes and books and papers sit on shelves. He has three stereos. A small TV. A view out into the hills where clouds are snapping apart. I can smell the napalm baking next door. He gets us beers from the fridge. They are sweaty and look colder than the backside of Pluto. Which isn't even a planet anymore. Or is it. I can't remember. Fuck Pluto. From there the sun is a speck.

"Just need a can opener. Aha, you fucker."

I don't think beer is good for me when I am confused but it is cold and probably refreshing and confusion is nothing new for me so I take it. Salvatore uncaps it, hands it off. Next thing I know my throat is being coated with the stuff. It's fancy and delicious in a beery way.

"Big Man is my father too. He had an affair with my mom, Sofia. This was years ago. For a while he maintained two families. We didn't know about you either until he disappeared. Have you seen him or heard from him?"

Shake.

"Us either."

We sip. His apartment is quiet save for the napalm neighbor singing to himself.

"I always wanted to, you know, talk to you. I've seen a, uh, picture of you. I know you're down in North Gaslin but I figured it was best to leave you in peace."

"*Arr arr* are those *muh* mooses my *bruh* brothers too?"

"Mooses?" He looks at me like everyone else does when they find out how my brain works. I puff myself up so that it seems like I have muscles. He laughs, says, "Nah, those guys are my half-brothers and I'm your half-brother so you don't share any blood with them. But my blood is enough. Once I tell them the truth they'll act as if they're your brothers too."

My head hurts. I look around. Salvatore seems more like Big Man than I am. He is into tough stuff that you do in the woods or in water. He probably has guns. Then I spot something interesting on the kitchen table. I go over and pick it up. It looks like a staple gun but with a small plunger attached to it. I bring it close to my face but Salvatore leaps up and grabs it.

"Careful. It's got more kick than it seems."

I don't get it.

"It's for turning off the lights when I'm too lazy to get up. Watch." He aims at the far wall and squeezes. The plunger flies through the air and sticks to the clock with a *ga-thunk*.

"You *muh* made it?"

He looks away, embarrassed. "It's stupid. I just tinker."

"*Nuh nuh* no. *Aww aww* awesome."

He returns to his chair. "You think so?"

I nod and move to the fridge. There's a picture of a pretty woman who is small but tough-looking. Salvatore and the moose brothers surround her.

"That's Ma. She's down south now. Too cold for her here."

I continue my tour. I don't see a TV. I want to know if he likes *You'll Eat It And You'll Like It!* but am afraid to ask. Instead I ask if he has met Tucker.

He takes a gulp of beer, says, "Tucker is the one who found us. He came up here and we got into a fight but not before showing me some pictures of you guys while saying, 'This is Big Man's family, his real family, fuck you, et cetera.'"

This makes sense.

"He was angry like we did something wrong." Salvatore leans forward, the chair creaking. "Look, we thought *we* were Big Man's family. We thought you were the other one, the side hustle. The truth is, yeah, you guys came first. He never even married our mom. Still that's not our fault." He sits back. "Tucker didn't tell you?"

Shake. I close my eyes. With the beer in my veins and the new information in my brain I feel the hell of a thousand suns surging through me, like some sort of Deluxe Retrieval. I want to fight Tucker and Salvatore at the same time but I would need to be armed with more than shovels and bug spray and a compass. Maybe Godkiller a.k.a. Charles Phelps could fight in my place.

"You're angry."

I shrug. Then I nod.

"Give it time to sink in."

"*Hoo hoo* who did he *luh* love?"

Salvatore finishes his beer and stares down its neck. I know for a fact there are no answers in there. I have looked many times. "Does it matter? He left all of us. I assume he was torn up by it all, managing two families, two lives, a thousand lies."

We hang out in silence for a long time. Then I nod. I keep nodding until I'm at the door.

"Process this, bro. Then come back so we can talk more. We should get to know one another."

I reach for the knob but I see something wedged between the floorboards beneath my feet. A nail. It looks like any other nail except it's extra shiny and has a blob of glue on the head. I stoop over and tug it out and hold it up to the light.

"*Wuh wuh* what the—?"

There's another door in this place. It hosts a rack holding dog leashes and jackets and hats and such. I know it's rude but I go and open it. It reveals a small room with a workbench and bins full of all sorts of junk and parts and craft supplies. Including beads.

Salvatore was the guy I saw in the craft store that night. But that's not all.

The walls are lined with pegboard and hanging from its hooks are all the masks Joe Purple has worn over the years. The paper bag mask. The papier-mâché mask painted to look like

Carl Jake. The robot head made from hammered tin. There's even a new one of Astro Fire Cop with his spacefireman helmet and everything. Which is so amazing my throat clenches with tears. My half-brother Salvatore sits here and makes masks so he can come to Heli-Non and spy on me.

"I know what you're thinking. But it was to protect you. Before he disappeared Big Man said he was worried about you and that he had been a terrible father to you and that you needed someone to watch over you. He said Tucker would never do it and that maybe I could but from afar. This was the only way I could think of doing it. And, well, I only came once a month because it's so hard getting there. And because it's such a weird thing, Murray. Your group. Your phobia."

I nod and back out. I stand there listening to my heart which speaks in drums not words. I shut the door to the room. I open the front door. I step outside. I shut the door. I leave.

The door opens behind me. Matón and Salvatore follow me to my truck. By the time I am sitting there trying to get it started the other mooses have joined their brother and stand watching me turn the key so many times that it feels like it is going to bend in my fingers. Finally at long last when I cannot be sweating any harder or swearing any dirtier the engine catches. I do a nine-point turn and roll down the driveway.

Up ahead a large tree looms. I don't know why but my brain freezes up like I just sucked down an entire Slushie without pausing once. Which I did once on a dare. I can't stop. I can't turn. I drive right into the tree.

It's My Birthday and Almost Tucker's
so the Party is at His House and Oh Yeah
Annabelle Comes too and all My Friends

I am driving my sweet new used Plymouth Voyager which replaced the truck that is dead forever. It has a sliding door and extra seats and all its tires and parts. Like a real car. Tucker helped me get it. He has been nice lately. It's a strange feeling after years of just being related. All we had to do to become friends was burn down our old house and put our mother in a special home and sit down over fancy coffee to talk about Salvatore a.k.a. Joe Purple and our missing father and his secret family and the Nevada lady and the time I got my balls fondled and all the spankings and beatings I received etc.

Today is my birthday and the party is at his house. His birthday is soon too so he's piggybacking mine and making it a double party.

"Hi, hon'," Roxanne says when she opens the door. I wave but she leans in and kisses me on the cheek. I get a mini-boner.

Her hair is bright blond now and she's wearing a business-type suit.

"What'd you bring?"

I hand over a bag of CornPows.

"Mmm. Looks delicious."

I shut the door. Then I remember that Annabelle and Bugle came with me. I open the door. Bugle sprints off to sniff. Annabelle gives me a look and I shrug.

"Tucker's friends are out back," Roxanne says from the kitchen, "along with Honey and Thin Man. Are any of your other people coming?"

I smile to myself.

A minute later there's a knock on the door. Salvatore steps in with a girl so beautiful she makes Annabelle look like a herpes scab. Her name is Mila. Salvatore gives me a bro-hug and hands me a present wrapped in leaf skin or something. Roxanne gives him a dirty eye but a polite smile and hands them beers which they carry out to the porch.

Roxanne brings me and Annabelle gourmet root beers. I haven't had real beer in a month.

"Thanks," I say.

She looks at me funny with one eyebrow arched.

I shrug.

Annabelle grabs my arm and leans against me.

The doorbell rings.

"Well, hello!" Martin says and waddles in. He's dressed in a sweater and exercise pants that go *zhip zhip* each time he takes a breath. With him is Marlene. She's wearing a cardigan that reaches to her knees and underneath that a T-shirt and jeans with paint spatters. Martin hands me a present. "This is from You Know Who."

I don't know who but I nod.

I'm about to close the door when I see Liza and FX coming up the walk. We hug in the doorway. FX gives me a CD of his songs and has one for each of my brothers too. Liza gives me a platter of baked goods. They also get drinks and go to the back porch where Tucker has kindly set up a canvas covering to shield my people from the sun. In time I will have to tell my friends who Salvatore really is. That he's not just Joe Purple but my half-brother.

"What a bunch of freakazoids," Tucker says when he comes back in to get chips and snacks. "At least you didn't invite gayboy."

The doorbell rings.

Tucker looks at me.

I smile again.

Mikey enters with Godkiller a.k.a. Charles Phelps. Charles Phelps looks different during the day and when wearing normal clothes but he still has to duck to get inside. Tucker swallows hard and nods to Charles Phelps.

"Heyyyy," Mikey says and charges Tucker to give him a hug. Tucker slaps Mikey's back but doesn't take his eyes off Charles Phelps.

Roxanne distributes more drinks. "Let's all move outside, Murray," she says.

"*Sss* soon."

"Okay, hon'."

Annabelle goes too, gives me space.

The kitchen radio's on. It's going *Here comes the pitch. Swing and a miss! Rumor has it that he's going to eat a fancy four hundred squalid roadblock erratic schism triangle...* I stand alone at the sink and look out the window. Tucker and his friends are tossing lawn darts and sipping beer or wine. His man-friends are all wearing tan shorts and collared colored shirts and the ladies are in dresses with flowers on them. They cast frequent glances at my people who are large and weird and dressed like members of a homeless jug band except for Mikey and Godkiller who look like professional football players who escaped prison after doing too many muscle drugs and are now at a coach's picnic. Then there is Honey Mom on a lawn chair wrapped in blankets like an Egyptian skeleton with Bugle in her lap. She seems to be singing the birthday song to him over and over. Thin Man is snoozing beside her. My half-brother Salvatore is talking to FX and Mila is pouring wine into Liza's glass.

It's nice inside the house. Cool. Still. Lemonade and snacks occupy the counter. Uncut cake waits for me and Tucker. I unbutton my longcoat. Underneath it I'm wearing a crisp shirt with a collar just like the ones Tucker and his friends are wearing. I had one as a kid. I remember that now. I remember my birthday party at that strange woman's house with all the kids who hated me. She eventually married Carl Jake of all people. I don't want to think about that so I sip the root beer which tastes nice. I feel funny inside. I guess people would call it happiness. Not in general but just this moment.

Soon we will open presents. Tucker's will be shiny or wooden or both and will sit on a shelf along with other things that are shiny or wooden or both. Mine will be silly and jokey or clothing-related like new undies or socks. The other presents make me curious though. I go and open the one from Salvatore whom I met just one month ago. Inside is a weird contraption made from springs and car parts and metal and rubber. He's made an instruction guide too. The pictures say you slide it over your wrist and hand and put a tennis ball in the mouth and aim upward and press the button and it shoots the ball real far for Bugle. Bugle will have to learn ballchasing I guess. It's pretty much the best thing I've ever owned in my life. Even better than the Galaxy Voyager.

Still curious I pick up the one from You Know Who. I open it. Inside is a special edition *CHUCK ROLLINS GOES TO H.E.L.L.!* graphic novel.

It's from Carl Jake.

I don't want it. I toss it aside.

Then I pick it up. What I'm interested in now are the pictures. More specifically the men in the background, men whose skulls Chuck Rollins crushes while raiding the nation of H.E.L.L. They are goons, bruisers, thugs, dumb guys who get in the way of the hero while trying to protect the villain. Stooges with a gun or a bat or a taser who don't know how to use a gun or a bat or a taser.

They are Murray Sandmans. Middling Scufflers. Mediocre Scrappers.

Later that night Salvatore and I head out into the country in his black van. He tells me what's up and then we don't talk. The radio is playing a song called "Beaverbasher" by a sludgy metal band called Ancestral Schlong. I bang my head to the beat until he turns it off.

Salvatore kills the lights and we veer onto a dirt road. We bounce along for about ten years. Finally a large house appears.

It's like a barn but one people live in or animals live in or maybe all of them together. Salvatore steers behind some trees and turns off the engine. He takes out a flask and offers it to me. I take a tiny sip. The liquor sizzles in the hole where a tooth is missing.

He looks at me, nods.

We climb out and close our doors so quietly even mice don't wake up. It's chillier out in the country. As we inch closer to the farmbarnhouse I peer up into the windows but from this angle I can't see anything because the back half of the farmbarnhouse is built into the earth. Behind us the meadow stretches forever toward the horizon. We crouch. Under the porch there's a rickety door covered in vines and slimy gunk.

"Clear that off," Salvatore says. "Slide it open slow as a tugboat."

I tug and tug until it comes loose.

Salvatore shines a flashlight into a cluttered basement with all sorts of dusty rakes and shovels and stacks of newspapers and such. On the far side is another door. It's covered with spiderwebs which is gross but nothing like sunlight so I scrape it off and pull it open. Salvatore shines the light inside and we see piles of ancient potatoes magazines tools junk shit crap but I guess some of it's valuable to Salvatore and his half-brothers. More specifically the car parts.

Max Codpoodle called me recently and left a message saying that I was right about the guns not working in cold temperatures and that my intel was a big help. Mazzie avoided lawsuits and product recalls. But because I lost the guns and had to get the cops to return them covered in mud and lied and didn't do the report I couldn't be hired again. Max gave me a little money anyway which I used to buy Bugle a new collar and Mikey some sneakers. Before hanging up Max said I should study comput-ers and barcode scanners because everything is about to change. Soon no one will need pricing guns except yokels running food-marts out in the country.

I believe him but I'm not interested. I'm with Salvatore and his brothers now. Three days a week I drive to Spry Poi. I always bring Bugle and he and Maton play and chase vultures but I have to keep Bugle on a long rope or he'll vanish into yonder which is what Salvatore's neighbor calls the grass and woods around the property. Every now and then the brothers sell a car and I get a small cut. People need them as movie props or for photo shoots or to get hold of a sliver of their youth or to just feel cool. Some-times they just need a part or a hubcap. I don't know anything about cars so I shine the metal and vacuum the insides and make sandwiches and fetch beer. It's better than fixing pricing guns. Almost as good as making comic books.

In the farmhouse Salvatore fill our arms with hubcaps and license plates. He stuffs our pockets with hood ornaments and handles and random car bits. This place is a gold mine but one where the gold is junky old metal. I swore not to get back into crime but this is my brother. We share blood. Probably more than Tucker and I. This is who I am.

Salvatore grabs my shoulder. "*Shhh.*"

Someone is awake upstairs.

"Crap. We gotta scram."

We back out of the little room and are about to sprint to the van when a light comes on upstairs. "You little sheepfuckers," a raspy old voice says as a lady steps onto the deck. When I glance up I see something long and cold in her hands.

"Run like the wind, bro!"

I run like a lump of wet socks. Salvatore pulls ahead. Then I hear *fwipp!* and something stings me in the neck. I slap my skin and drop a hubcap. When I turn to grab it I hear *fwipp!* again and something bites me in the forehead. Then the tip of my ear. The pain is extraordinary. I think a piece of flesh is missing. I'm bleeding.

I smile.

Epic Log: A New Day and a New Group Led by a Guy in Loafers and Something Else Happens at the End

The schoolhouse looks different in the daylight. Like a photo of an old dream. Even the wheelchair ramp's boards feel different. Dry and cracked from years of sun.

Zig. Zag.

On the door is a sign with a drawing of a guy whose face is all twisted like he's got a brontosaurus tongue instead of his own. I knock. It opens. "Welcome to Stutter and Stammer Stoppers," some guy says. "I'm Ron but you can call me Ronaldo." He laughs. I don't. He offers me his hand. We slap our palms together, mix our sweat, slide our palms apart. His hair is blond and he's wearing a buttoned shirt and some soft brown shoes that you might want when you get up to pee in the middle of the night.

The other people look normal, worried but not scared. Then there's me in my floppy hat and longcoat. It's a hot day, sunny.

I sit. I get out a notepad just in case. On the notepad is a price tag. *$3.79.* Judging by the slightly beveled corners it's a Mazzie tag.

First we listen to Ron tell us about life. It's dull. After that we have to loosen up by talking real loud all at the same time. Kind of like Heli-Non sessions only faster. We say anything just to keep our mouths moving while not caring what words and swears come out. Peter poaches perfect fucking pickles and things like that.

Now that we're warm and loosey-goosey we introduce ourselves. Only one guy doesn't stutter. Years of work, his big moment. We clap for him. Then Ron takes Polaroids so we can see what we look like when we talk. In mine I look like a drunken glasseater who just grabbed a live wire.

We're a minute into something called Predictive Visualiz-ing when there's a knock on the door. Everyone stops working. Ron opens the door, letting in sunlight that makes us all cover our eyes. I try to keep my shit together as Ron steps back and motions for the person to step inside. I am aware there are two open seats in the room. One up front and one beside me.

"Here for Stutter and Stammer Stoppers?"

He grunts and takes the seat up front. The door shuts and we can see again. I exhale.

Ron has us put on blindfolds for a silly game. We walk around the room trying not to grab each other's boobs and such while telling people who we can't see that we're there. "I'm *heh heh* here. *Heh* here." Still we laugh and grab each other's boobs.

At breaktime we drink bug juice and eat crackers. I notice that on the chalkboard is the faint outline of a cyborg I drew a long time ago. I would like to add an antenna and a better nose but that feels wrong now. Plus I need to go to the bathroom.

I head to the hallway but stop at the top of the stairs with my hand on the cold banister. I hear the *Rays of Hope* audiobook in my head going *Your brain is like an overheated attic, your heart like a dark basement. Do you really want to go there alone?*

I can hold it.

Stepping back into the room I come face to face with the new guy. His eyes land on mine but he still doesn't say anything, just smiles. A smile that stretches back years. Farther than the sun can reach. It's Wiley Horowitz. Jet's father. As scummy as the scummiest scummy North Gaslin has to offer. He snorts then turns and picks up two glasses of bug juice. He hands one to me and downs the other then says, "Hi Murray. Fuck you."

*   *   *

Acknowledgements

First and foremost, thank you to my partner, Raisa Kettunen, and to my parents, Joyce and Tom Dresser and Bill and Barbara Jones, for their support throughout the many years of writing and revising this work.

A *massivethankyou* to MacKenzie Dietz for multiple readings of the book, for your editing prowess, for your encouragement and support, and for laughing at all the right spots.

Thanks as well to Ania Vesenny for reviewing early drafts and for pushing me through the doldrums.

Thank you, Adam Thomas, for hosting writing retreats and for the endless support.

Thank you to Laird Hunt and Matthew Kirkpatrick for your kind words and encouragement.

Thanks to Charlie and everyone at Montag Press for bringing me into the fold and getting this book out into the world. Thanks as well to Scott Navicky and brother Jefferson for the introduction.

Author Bio

Originally from the island of Martha's Vineyard, Christopher X. Ryan now lives in Helsinki, Finland, with his wife Raisa and their Serbian rescue mutt, Oscar. He works as a writer, ghostwriter, and editor, and his stories have been published widely. This is his first novel. Find him at www.christopherxryan.com.

Milton Keynes UK
Ingram Content Group UK Ltd.
UKHW041456190923
428972UK00004B/262

9 781957 010236